Based on
the Movie

Based on the Movie

A Novel

Billy Taylor

ATRIA BOOKS

New York   London   Toronto   Sydney

ATRIA BOOKS

A Division of Simon & Schuster, Inc.
1230 Avenue of the Americas
New York, NY 10020

This book is a work of fiction. Names, characters, places, and incidents either are products of the author's imagination or are used fictitiously. Any resemblance to actual events or locales or persons, living or dead, is entirely coincidental.

First Atria Books hardcover edition August 2008

ATRIA BOOKS and colophon are trademarks of Simon & Schuster, Inc.

For information about special discounts for bulk purchases,
please contact Simon & Schuster Special Sales at
1-800-456-6798 or business@simonandschuster.com.

Designed by Davina Mock-Maniscalco

Manufactured in the United States of America

1   3   5   7   9   10   8   6   4   2

Library of Congress Cataloging-in-Publication Data
Taylor, Billy.
Based on the movie : a novel / Billy Taylor.
p. cm.
1. Motion picture industry—Fiction. 2. Cinematography—Fiction.
3. Separated people—Fiction. I. Title.
PS3620.A935B37   2008
813'.6—dc22   2008015498

ISBN-13: 978-1-4165-4877-5
ISBN-10:   1-4165-4877-7

To Anne,
for everything

Based on
the Movie

Chapter 1

Dolly Grip

Q: Why were dollies invented?
A: So grips could learn to walk on their hind legs.

WE WERE STANDING under the Brooklyn Bridge when a production assistant ran over to tell us the actors were on their way. There was no time to rehearse the last scene, and if we didn't nail it before sunset, everything we'd shot with Julia Roberts would be worthless. Worse, Julia Roberts had to catch a plane that night for Prague, where she was shooting a costume drama with Brad Pitt. Since our half week in New York with Julia Roberts was the only reason the studio was making this movie in the first place, there was a strong chance that if we blew the last scene, they'd pull the plug and we'd never go to Texas and finish the movie. There was only enough light to do it once, and the only person who could screw it up besides the actors was me. The dolly grip.

"Do you need anything?" the production assistant asked, staring at me like I had a bull's-eye stapled to my forehead.

"Would a blow job be out of the question?"

"I'll take that as a no," he said and stomped off.

"Thanks for the understanding, fella," I shouted and trudged back to the eighty feet of dolly track I had set up two hours earlier. There was nothing to do, but I unlocked the brake on the dolly anyway and pushed the five hundred pounds of metal, rubber, and hydraulic fluid to the end of the track and back. On a movie set it's always good form to make it look like you're busy. My cell phone rang, and before I could pull it from my cargo shorts the production assistant was back in my face.

"Make sure that's off when Julia arrives."

"Absolutely." I felt like pushing him in the East River, but after twenty years in the film business, I'd learned that sometimes even the lowliest gofers grew up to be producers.

"You near a computer?" my friend Hank Sullivan asked when I answered the call.

"No. Why?"

"I just gave dickhead's movie the green light. It was supposed to be announced in tomorrow's *Hollywood Reporter*, but *Variety* posted it on their Web site an hour ago."

"You're kidding me."

"Nope, there's even a picture."

"Does it mention Natalie?" I asked.

"A least a half-dozen times."

"Damn it."

"Sorry, pal, but I had to do it. There's a management change at the studio, and I need to have my third movie in production before they start firing people."

"No biggie," I said. "I wish you all the best."

"That was an excellent line reading. For a second I almost believed you."

The production assistant was back. "The actors are here," he shouted. "Cell phones off."

"I gotta go," I said.

"Hang in there, Bobby. When we get to Texas I'll buy you a drink."

"Right. See you in Texas."

Before I could begin to feel sorry for myself the big guns arrived and panic hour began. Production assistants ran in circles while the crew set up equipment they would never use but had to have standing by.

"Why did the scene in the taxicab take so long?" I asked Troy, the camera operator.

"Fucking first-time director. He wanted every take to be perfect. Even for shots where Julia Roberts was off camera. You want to go out for beers after this?"

"No, thanks. I have to pack for Texas."

"You sure you're okay?"

"The shot's just a walk-and-talk." Then I understood what Troy really meant and said, "You heard about the article in *Variety*, huh?"

"The sound guy had it on his laptop. You need somebody else to push dolly on this one?"

I shook my head. "I can handle it."

"It's your call."

"Oh, Troy, darling," said a singsongy voice with a thick Polish accent. We turned and saw Andrzej, the director of photography, strolling onto the set. He held a light meter in one hand and an ice-cream cone in the other.

"Go see what Andrzej wants," I said. "I'm okay. Really."

Troy slapped me on the back and dashed off.

More and more people arrived: camera, sound, video, script, makeup, hair, and wardrobe joined the gaggle of grips and electrics already working. The air filled with shouts and bursts of walkie-talkie static as Brooklyn-bound traffic clogged the streets of Manhattan. Car horns blared. Cabdrivers cursed. Sirens wailed.

"Why do they always have to schedule rush hour and sunset at the same time?" I whined.

"Run-through with second team!" the first assistant director yelled into his bullhorn.

"Run-through with second team!" the second assistant director screamed.

"Run-through with second team!" a half-dozen production assistants shouted in unison.

Troy climbed onto the dolly and said, "Keep an eye on my right hand. I'll signal you if the actors get too close or too far away."

"Here we go," the first AD shouted. "Action!"

The stand-ins for Julia Roberts and Ryan James Donahue, our male lead, walked toward us, and I eased the dolly into motion. My job was to keep the camera exactly six feet two inches from Julia Roberts at all times. If she slowed down, I slowed down. If she walked faster, I walked faster. If she grew a foot, I raised the camera.

Forty feet into the shot, Troy took his eye from the camera and said, "You think I should sleep with Julia's stand-in?"

"You haven't yet?"

"My ex-wife was in town."

"Courtney?"

"No, the first one."

We reached the end of the track, and I slowed the dolly to a stop.

"Cut!" the first AD shouted. "Everybody back to one."

As I pushed the dolly to the first camera position, I noticed the soundman glancing back and forth between me and his laptop.

"You set?" I asked Troy.

"Like a jelly."

"Then I'll be right back." I locked the brake on the dolly and ran to the sound cart.

"Okay," I said. "Let's see it."

The soundman turned the laptop around, and there he was:

Elias Simm—Harvard dropout, Kennedy cousin, and the man who stole my wife.

I scanned the article. It said that Hank Sullivan was pleased to announce preliminary financing for *The Ant Eater Goes Down,* the third movie in his three-picture deal at Columbus Pictures. *Ant Eater* (as *Variety* called it) was the heartwarming tale of the favorite nephew of an assassinated American president who grew up in splendor, flunked out of Harvard, and overcame drug addiction to fuck my wife.

Okay, so that last part wasn't in the article, but I knew the script and didn't need to read the synopsis. I skipped down to the third paragraph, where it mentioned Natalie:

> Producing chores for *Ant Eater* will be handled by Natalie Miguel, veteran of a dozen features including Wit Carson's *Empire, The Somnambulists* and the Beverly Brothers' *Au Bar Bouncer Blues.* Miguel has shepherded *Ant Eater* through every stage of development and has partnered with Simm to form Miguel-Simm Productions. Simm and Miguel have opened offices on the studio lot and are looking forward to a spring start date.

As I tried to decide whether to vomit or send a congratulatory telegram, I felt someone tap my shoulder. I turned to see the production assistant hovering over me and was about to smack him with his walkie-talkie when I saw the fear in his eyes.

"What's wrong?" I asked.

"Look," he said and pointed toward the camera.

"Shit," I said when I saw Andrzej holding the viewfinder to his eye. "They can't change the shot now. We don't have time."

I raced to the dolly. There would be plenty of opportunities to feel lousy later. I grabbed my tape measure and a piece of chalk and ran to where Andrzej stood with the director.

"Oh, there you are, Bobby, darling. It seems our director wants to change the shot." Andrzej put the viewfinder to his eye and said, "This is two."

I ran my tape measure from the viewfinder to the ground and measured the exact height and position where Andrzej expected to find the camera after I tore up an hour's worth of work and re-assembled it in the few minutes left before sunset.

"Got it," I said and marked the position on the ground.

"And this . . ." Andrzej said, taking twenty loping steps forward and fine-tuning the viewfinder, "is one."

"Got it."

Andrzej grabbed a fistful of my hair and smiled. "You're going to earn your money today, Bobby."

"Every day, Andrzej."

Andrzej clapped his hands and shouted, "Fellow filmmakers, we are losing the light. We must hurry."

I spun around and almost collided with Julia Roberts. Time stopped. The sun wasn't setting, and my wife wasn't sleeping with Elias Simm. I was inches away from one of the most famous movie stars in the world, and for one brief and surreal moment our eyes locked.

"Pardon me," I said.

"No, I'm sorry. I wasn't paying attention."

I squinted at her and said, "Wow, with your hair like that you look just like Ingrid Bergman in *Spellbound*."

"The Alfred Hitchcock movie?"

"Yeah, have you seen it?"

"No, but I've always wanted to."

"You'll love it. It's got this totally surreal dream sequence designed by Salvador Dalí, and Ingrid Bergman says the sexiest word in all of cinema."

"Really? What word is that?"

I took a deep breath and, doing my best Ingrid Bergman, whispered, "Liverwurst."

"Liverwurst?" Julia Roberts giggled. "That doesn't sound very sexy."

"It does when Ingrid Bergman says it."

I stepped out of her way and descended into hell. I ran to the dolly, and before I could unlock the brake, the first AD was all over me.

"This is a fucking disaster," he said. "How much time you need?"

"Not much, just keep everybody out of my way."

"Gotcha." He put his bullhorn to his lips and said, "Everyone please step back and let the grips do their jobs."

We moved the track to the new camera position, and I dove onto the ground to level the rails. I was almost finished when I looked up and saw the entire crew staring down at me with anxiety on their faces: sixty nervous people with families, mortgages, and assorted substance abuse problems who were screwed if I messed up and the studio shut down the picture. Luckily, the ground wasn't bumpy, and we were good to go in less than two minutes.

"Lock it up," the first AD yelled through his bullhorn. "This is for picture."

"Lock it up," the second AD and production assistants echoed.

"And how does this new camera position differ from the last one?" I whispered in Troy's ear.

"Not one fucking bit. And this guy's supposed to be an actor's director."

"Roll sound!" the first AD screamed.

"We have a plane," the soundman said.

The first AD turned to Andrzej, and Andrzej shook his head.

"Roll sound!" the first AD shouted.

"But we have a plane!"

"I don't care. Roll sound!"

In the cinematic equivalent of rock, paper, scissors, camera beats sound every time.

"Speed," the soundman said.

"Rolling!" production assistants everywhere shouted.

The first AD turned to the collection of video monitors, director's chairs, and VIPs known as Video Village and waited.

And waited.

"Oh, action," said the director from behind his monitor.

"Action!" the first AD repeated.

I glanced down to make sure I had unlocked the brake on the dolly and watched Julia Roberts and Ryan Donahue walk toward me. Their concentration was amazing. Less than a minute earlier, hair, makeup, and wardrobe people had been swarming over them like a cloud of gnats, and now Julia Roberts was telling Ryan Donahue she was leaving him. I believed every word she said and had to force myself to pay attention to my job and not her performance. When the actors reached six feet two inches, I began walking backward between the rails. Troy's hand flew off the camera and signaled for me to move faster.

"I can't go on like this," Julia Roberts said with tears in her eyes. "I need a husband who will treat me like a human being, not like a character in a story. I'm Anne O'Hara, damn it. Not Anna Kournikova."

Everyone froze.

"Shit!" Julia Roberts said, breaking character. "I meant Anna Karenina."

"Keep rolling," Andrzej and the first AD yelled.

"Okay, okay," she replied. Julia Roberts shook her head, took a deep breath, and returned to the scene with the blink of an eye.

"I can't go on like this, Robert. I need someone who'll treat me like a person, not like a character in a story. I'm Anne O'Hara, damn it. Not Anna Karenina."

"Cut," the director called.

"I'm so sorry," Julia said.

"That take was no good for sound," the soundman announced.

"That's a cut," the production assistants echoed. "Release the lockup."

Andrzej, Troy, and the director huddled around the monitor to watch the playback. You could tell from their expressions they were not happy. The video ended, and they wasted a precious minute of daylight arguing.

"But I want to do it in one take, Andrzej," the director whined.

"C'mon, c'mon, c'mon," the first AD shouted at the crew. "Everybody back to one."

"This fucking sucks," Troy said, hopping back on the dolly.

"What the hell are we doing?" I asked. "We can't shoot. There's no light."

"The director wants to wait until the sun sets and then bash a light into the actors' faces. Maybe we'll get it before the background turns to mud, and maybe we won't."

"But that'll look like shit."

"Hey, I'm only the operator," Troy said in disgust. Then he smiled and slapped me on the back. "You did great on that last take, by the way."

The grips and electrics rigged a soft light on the dolly, and I added a seat for Andrzej to ride. Andrzej and the new equipment brought the total weight of the dolly to a thousand pounds. I weighed in at a svelte one-fifty.

We started shooting the moment the sun went down and banged out three quick takes before we lost the light. Andrzej and the director huddled around the monitor to watch the playback, but everyone knew there was a fifty-fifty chance we'd blown it. Either way, the scene was going to look terrible. Nothing's worse than busting your ass for thirteen hours and knowing your work sucked. No, that's not true. Nothing's worse than busting your ass for thirteen hours, reading an article about your soon-to-be-ex-wife in *Variety*, and knowing your life sucked.

"Fucking British asshole director," Andrzej muttered as he stomped off set.

"That's one pissed-off Polack," I said.

"He's got every right to be," Troy said. "Making the most beautiful woman in the world look like a pile of dog crap could destroy his career."

"You think?"

"They have to blame somebody. If you hadn't moved that track in record time, it would have been your ass instead of Andrzej's."

He was right. And all because of some inexperienced clown who didn't know which end of a viewfinder to look through. "The hell with it," I said.

"The hell with what?"

"This business."

I pulled out my cell phone and called Hank Sullivan. "I'm sorry, Hank," I said when I got him on the line. "But I can't do this anymore. I quit."

"What the hell happened? I just got off the phone with the head of production, and he said you guys blew the Julia Roberts scene."

"That's what I'm talking about. I can't stand around anymore while some idiot director who knows one-tenth of what I do gets to call the shots. I can't do it. I just can't."

"Calm down. You can't quit this movie, Bobby. I need you there, man."

"Come off it, Hank. I'm a piece of lint on this job. If I got hit by a bus no one would remember me this time next week."

"Stop being pathetic and listen. If this job doesn't come in on time and on budget, the studio will pull the plug on my third picture."

"And wouldn't that suck for Elias?"

"And for me. And for you."

"Why for me?"

"Name one other person besides me who would help you make your own movie if you ever got off of your ass and wrote a screenplay."

"Natalie Miguel."

"Not anymore, pal."

He was right. "What do you want me to do?" I sighed.

"Anything you can to light a fire under the crew and help us get through this movie alive."

"I'm not sure how much help I'll be. I barely have the strength to crawl home to Brooklyn and pull the covers over my head."

"Stop being so dramatic. We only have one day left in New York. After that, we're in Texas for three months. And trust me, once we get to Texas everything's gonna be great."

Q: How can you tell when a producer's
   lying to you?
A: His lips are moving.

Chapter 2

The Phases and Stages
of Cinematic Adultery

QUICK, WHAT DO Jack Nicholson, Humphrey Bogart, and Burt Lancaster have in common? Yes, each won an Academy Award and has a star on Hollywood Boulevard, but what else? Give up? They all played The Cad, that two-fisted, hard-drinking son-of-a-bitch who shows the Jessica Langes and Deborah Kerrs of the world just what they've been missing. Audiences never grow tired of this character and reward the actors who play him with riches and fame. Fair enough. But what about The Faithful Husband, that poor schnook back at the ranch who thinks that twinkle in his wife's eye is there especially for him? Who plays that guy? Only hard-core film nerds remember Jerome Cowan, who played Miles Archer in *The Maltese Falcon,* or John Colicos, who played Nick the Greek in the Jack Nicholson version of *The Postman Always Rings Twice.*

In movies, as in life, casting is everything. It was bad enough that my wife dumped me for another man, but the thought that in the movie version of my life I'd be portrayed by some obscure character actor while the part of Elias Simm went to Jude Law

... well, that was more than I could take. But it was my own damn fault. I'd been in the movie business long enough to recognize the phases and stages of Cinematic Adultery. I just refused to see them until it was too late.

STAGE 1: Flirtation

Most men are too self-involved to notice the early warning signs of their wives' affairs. The flirtation stage is a critical juncture in every relationship, when a simple bouquet of flowers or a piece of jewelry from Target can make the difference between years of marital bliss or your wife playing a skin flute sonata on some dude from her office. Unfortunately, this can be a tricky stage to identify because some women flirt all the time. Certainly all men do, as do most blondes born in states that lost the Civil War. The key is to pay attention to your wife's appearance and question every change the moment you spot it. Husbands tend to think that every tight skirt or trashy piece of underwear from Victoria's Secret is purchased with their filthy needs in mind—if they notice it at all. My advice is to make sure that it is. Say one day your wife comes home with a brand-new look and a couple hundred bucks' worth of cosmetics from Elizabeth Arden. This is the perfect time to ask such time-tested questions as "How was your day, darling?"

Be warned, you may be forced to listen to a blow-by-blow account of your wife's latest phone call with her mother in which they discussed the old gal's recent colonoscopy. But your wife may also mention how she ran into an old college chum named Steve whom she hadn't seen in ages and whom she used to have the *biggest* crush on. Ding ding ding! It's time to make reservations for a romantic weekend at that bed-and-breakfast she's been talking about for the last few years. Don't worry—you can always cancel them later. The important thing here is to get rid of this Steve character, and fast. Otherwise, you may find yourself blowing the money you've been squirreling away to lease that Lexus on something stupid like alimony.

I committed two major blunders during this stage. First, I introduced Natalie to Elias Simm. Second, I encouraged them to work together. Oops.

I met Elias Simm at Movie Night. Movie Night was a weekly get-together with my old film school pals where we watched old movies, drank beer, and hit the East Village for pierogis and borscht. The main attraction of Movie Night, besides the movies and borscht, was Hank Sullivan. Hank was our friend from film school who had Made It. His first feature—shot in twelve days for no money—was a hit at the festivals and was bought by an up-and-coming distributor named Miramax. By the time he was thirty, Hank had produced a dozen movies and had become one of the founding fathers of independent film before anybody realized it was a movement.

As Hank became successful, he made many new and far more fabulous friends than the knuckleheads he went to film school with and who wound up carrying film equipment up and down the streets of New York for a living. But Hank knew who his real friends were, and spent at least one night a week hanging out with the help. Every so often he'd bring one of his new and fabulous friends to Movie Night, and one of those friends turned out to be a chap named Elias Simm.

By this point, Elias had abandoned the Ivy League, taken the obligatory expat trip to Europe, and spent two years working on the first chapter of a novel. He couldn't sing, paint, or sail, so the only career option left for someone with his unique pedigree was film director. Hank met Elias at one of those fabulous places in

Manhattan where fabulous people did fabulous things, and the two were soon best friends.

I can say a lot of negative things about Elias Simm (and I probably will), but he is the most charming person I have ever met and has excellent table manners. I mean perfect table manners. That man holds a knife and fork with the same elegance that Tiger Woods holds a four-iron. Furthermore, not once in the six months before he began sleeping with Natalie did Elias ever forget to excuse himself when he rose from the table or say "Thank you" when I refilled his wineglass. And when Elias spoke to you, he looked you straight in the eye and made you feel like you were the only other human being on the planet.

I talked to Elias for more than an hour on the night we met. He was so handsome and self-assured I felt flattered he'd even introduced himself. When I got home to my apartment in Brooklyn that night I couldn't wait to tell Natalie all about him. I must have rambled on about the guy for ten minutes when Natalie asked me what we talked about.

I opened my mouth to tell her, but nothing came out. What the hell did we talk about? I remembered everything I said, but the strange part was I couldn't remember anything Elias said. And then it hit me: Elias didn't "say" anything—what he did was take my words and repeat them back to me in the most charming, polite, and self-effacing manner possible. The more I thought about it, the creepier it made me feel. I've often wondered if Elias used this conversational parlor trick for insidious reasons or from a genuine desire to please people. I do know he used it to his advantage on a daily basis. It was amazing what Elias could talk people into—like getting me to give his script to Natalie, for instance. Or getting me to invite him to spend a couple of weeks at my weekend place in Sag Harbor where he and my wife could fine-tune his screenplay, draw up a budget, and play hide the salami while I stayed in town and worked on a lucrative series of peanut butter commercials.

But hey, I'm getting ahead of myself here. Let's just say that knowing what a smoothie Elias was, I should have kept my eyes open for all the Stage 1 warning signs—like the thousands of dollars' worth of clothes Natalie bought at Barneys, or the weekly trips to Bliss Spa to get waxed. But like most self-centered chumps, I thought that cute little Mohawk she got downstairs was for my benefit. Wrong again.

STAGE 2: Distraction

After flirtation comes distraction. Magazines pile up unread, shirts and dresses are left at the dry cleaner's for weeks, and important details like birthdays and theater tickets are forgotten. You may find your wife staring off into space for long periods of time. Dinner conversations may become very one-sided. Your side.

This is because your wife is deciding whether or not to cheat on you. You may be a good guy, or you may be a snake. Either way, your wife said that stuff at the altar and she meant it. Now she's wondering if she should throw caution to the wind and go for it with the guy she's been flirting with for x number of days, weeks, or months.

An important note: If you ever catch your wife masturbating and it's been more than forty-eight hours since she's seen a George Clooney movie, there's a strong chance that she's in Stage 2. Proceed with caution. Most American males, when confronted with their wife in this embarrassing position, find it a major league turn-on and want to join in the festivities.

Don't.

Why? Because if your wife is flying solo, chances are she's not contemplating your fat, beer-bellied ass. Think about it, Einstein. Why would she waste all that time and energy when all she has to do is slip into something black and silky, and you'll do the heavy lifting for her? No, my friend, if you stumble upon your dearly beloved with her finger on the magic button, her mind is probably filled with images of some Nautilus jockey from her health club and not you.

What to do? If there was ever a time you needed to become Mr. Sensitivity, that fictional character they prattle on about in women's magazines, now is the time. In Stage 2, you have to hit the gym. Your wife is not going to toss her life into the shitter for some skanky piece of man meat who is fatter and uglier than you are (unless he has a lot of money, in which case—sorry, pal—you're screwed). Who she really wants is you, ten years and twenty thousand Egg McMuffins ago. Gentlemen, start your crunches.

In the distraction stage, a cheesy necklace or a $4.99 bouquet of convenience-store posies won't cut it. You need to break out your wallet and spend a little cash. Thinking about cheaping out? Don't. If you still don't understand the extreme importance of what I'm telling you, call a few divorce attorneys and ask about their hourly rates. Compared to those piranhas, a diamond tennis bracelet is a bargain.

Like most guys, I never thought my wife would have an affair. Natalie and I were in love, right? We were mature, successful, and sane individuals who happened to work in a crazy business. Yes, Natalie saw a shrink once a week, but we lived in New York and that's what people did there. It was almost the same as my mother seeing her hairdresser every Thursday for her wash and set. Natalie had a hairdresser too, of course. As well as a manicurist, a masseuse, an acupuncturist, a dental hygienist, an ob-gyn, a personal shopper, a diet doctor, and an aesthetician. (That's the technical name for someone who gives facials. How many of you straight guys knew that one?) The monthly nut for this maintenance was huge, but Natalie and I didn't have kids, and pissing away every dime we made wasn't a problem. My point is, I thought we had it together. Sure, our nights weren't as passion-packed as they had been when we first hooked up, but after ten years of relative harmony, it seemed like the melodrama was behind us.

The film business tends to be feast—fourteen-hour days, six days a week—or famine—no work, no phone calls, no nothing. Natalie lived for the feast and was great at her job. She could assemble a hundred-person film crew in an afternoon, negotiate a union contract while getting a pedicure, or shut down Fifth Avenue with a couple of phone calls. But when famine time rolled around, Natalie would develop a nasty case of the I'm Never Going to Work Again Blues. The real problem was that Natalie had no interests besides shopping, movies, and beauty appointments. It wasn't like she didn't try. Our garage in Sag Harbor was filled with some of the most expensive leisure paraphernalia imaginable. We had it all: a photo lab's worth of darkroom equipment, a rowing machine, a pottery wheel like Demi Moore had so much fun with in *Ghost,* a NordicTrack, and my personal favorite, a custom-made torture device for Pilates called—I shit you not—a Reformer. But none of these gadgets held Natalie's attention for long, and after a few weeks of arts and crafts or personal-trainer-assisted exercise she'd slip into depressions so deep that days would pass when she didn't get out of bed.

This was where that great humanitarian, Elias Simm, came to the rescue. I believe it was D. W. Griffith who once said that there are only two types of people in the world: those who have written a screenplay and those who are working on one. Natalie was constantly barraged by people of both types, and all of them wanted her to produce Their Movie. Thus, our apartment became a depository for some of the worst screenplays ever written.

Natalie read these scripts out of loyalty to her friends and coworkers. She was happy to offer whatever advice or criticism she could, but that was as far as she went. If one of these fledgling

Quentin Tarantinos wanted more than a lunchtime's worth of chit-chat, he had to pay Natalie to do a budget, which is the next step on that impossible journey from page to screen. Budgets provided a nice side income for us, but more than that, budgets got those people with just a screenplay and a dream off our backs. If some-one was serious enough to pay Natalie for a budget, she'd give him as much of her time as the project required. After that, it was the screenwriter's job to go out and raise the money for his movie. And that was usually the end of it. Occasionally, some rich or well-connected smarty would come back with one-tenth of the money and a desperate scheme to shoot the movie in sixteen-millimeter or digital video, but Natalie didn't work cheap. She'd pawn off these characters on one of the many ambitious assistants who had worked for her over the years, and then that was the end of it.

Until Elias Simm slunk into our lives.

Not only was Elias able to talk Natalie into doing her first complimentary budget, but after three months of the most skillful seduction this side of Sharon Stone in *Basic Instinct,* he got her to sleep with him *and* produce his movie. I've never asked Natalie if she slept with Elias before or after she agreed to produce his movie, but knowing how skilled Elias was at such things, my guess is that it was simultaneous.

STAGE 3: New Best Friend

Once your wife decides to cheat on you, the hard part is over and the rest is just scheduling. Zipping across town for a nooner is now just another line in her Filofax penciled in beside appointments with her nutritionist and lunch with the girls. This is where cellular phones, the quintessential tool for keeping hubbies in the dark during Stages 1 and 2, can present a major problem. Even during football season, or the NCAA Final Four, there are only so many times a wife can "forget" to turn on her cell phone before even the most hard-core *Sports Center* junkie starts to wonder why he can never get the little woman on the phone to ask her to pick up a fresh bag of Cool Ranch Doritos and a suitcase of Bud Light on her way back to the house.

Enter the New Best Friend. This person can be either real or imaginary depending upon how suspicious you are. The perfect NBF is either an old sorority sister or a gal-pal who has moved to the suburbs. The NBF will be someone your wife has seen only sporadically over the last few years and a person you may have met just once or twice. Oh yeah, and the NBF will not be a hottie.

Here's the scenario: One day the NBF calls out of the blue and needs to see your wife right away. Your wife will return from this encounter reeking of red wine and reciting the tragic tale of NBF and her recent medical and/or marital difficulties. Overnight, your wife becomes this poor soul's closest friend, sole confidante, and constant lunchtime companion.

And the person your wife happens to be with every time *you call her cell phone.* Get it? And how could you be angry with your wife for not taking your call when you phoned right in the middle of NBF's heartbreaking tale of the doctor discovering her tumor/lump/growth on/under/in her breast/uterus/colon. Either that or your wife and NBF were at a movie and "you know how you always make me turn off my cell phone in the movies, honey."

Foolproof, huh?

Besides his good looks and charm, how did Elias Simm get Natalie to produce his movie for him? It's complicated. During our decade of marriage a seismic shift occurred in the film business. While Natalie spent her downtime in bed banging out budgets and worrying she'd never work again, the legion of ambitious young assistants she'd trained hooked up with guys like Hank Sullivan and invented independent film. I can say from experience that it's a major kick in the balls to read the name of someone you gave his first job to in letters five feet tall on the silver screen. Especially when your name is exiled to the fine print at the end of the movie and seen only by slow-moving seniors and slackers sweeping up the theater.

And that's exactly what happened to Natalie and me.

For the first few years we reminded ourselves how those crazy kids worked for bupkes and lived in East Village shitboxes, while we rented a fabulous apartment in Brooklyn Heights and owned a weekend house in Sag Harbor. Living well was the best revenge, right? At least it was until those snot-nosed brats started selling movies at Sundance and buying brownstones in the West Village. But the straw that broke the producer's back was when Natalie's ex-assistants began competing with her for jobs. And getting them.

Not only did this piss her off, but losing jobs to her ex-assistants made Natalie feel *old*. And no matter how much money she spent on wrinkle cream, twenty years of ninety-hour weeks had taken their toll. Natalie wore every one of her forty-seven years on her face for the world to see and pass judgment upon. High-end clothing and expensive beauty treatments slowed the march of time, but all the Wolford control-top panty hose in Bergdorf's could not prevent Natalie from becoming middle-aged.

So I guess it wasn't my most brilliant move, at a time when Natalie was feeling elderly and vulnerable, to pull into our driveway in Sag Harbor with a hot red Porsche named Elias Simm. But that's what I did, and it wasn't long before Natalie's friend Becky (whom I despised and never wanted to hang out with) developed breast cancer, and Natalie cast herself as Florence Nightingale. Natalie valiantly held Becky's hand through round after round of chemo (no cell phones in the hospital), helped her shop for wigs ("God, it was heartbreaking. We were both in tears. Sorry I couldn't take your call"), and escorted her NBF to the kind of movies she never would have seen in a million years.

The Princess Diaries 2? What the hell was she thinking?

STAGE 4: Schizoid Behavior

Just when NBF is well on her way to recovery and your wife is beginning to act like her old self again, things take a hard turn for the weird. Maybe you come home one night to find the old gal passed out on the couch next to a full ashtray and an empty bottle of cabernet. Or perhaps she starts seeing her shrink more times a week than you floss. You know something is wrong, but your wife is so touchy, you hate to bring it up out of fear that she'll bite your head off. Out of desperation, you ask one of her friends if she knows what's going on, and the friend replies, "It's probably just a phase."

The friend is correct. Your wife has entered Stage 4, the phase of schizoid behavior.

This stage is brought on by guilt—either your wife's or that of the stud muffin she's sleeping with. What has really happened is that the thrill is gone. The happy couple hasn't been caught, and the lovin' is starting to get a little, well, regular. So one of them decides to call it quits, and the other goes out of his or her mind. "Last dates" are planned and canceled, cell phones chatter like pigeons, and the dumpee starts staking out the dumper's office or apartment.

Do the words *Fatal Attraction* mean anything to you?

Natalie flew to LA twice a year for meet-and-greets. She made the rounds of the studios, took meetings with production executives, and had lunch with old friends. Movies can be shot in Kansas or

Kathmandu, but unless the money's coming from a Texas oilman whose trophy wife has caught the movie bug, all roads lead to La La Land. On the trip in question Natalie brought Elias along to drum up interest in *Ant Eater*. They took up residence at the Mondrian on Sunset and had a grand old time ordering his and her acupressure treatments and cocktails from the Sky Bar. I know this because I happened to come across the four-page itemized hotel bill, and believe me, there are few things more humiliating than finding out your wife dropped twenty-six bucks for a room-service bottle of Astroglide at 12:42 on a Tuesday night.

Natalie rarely came back from LA with a job in hand. The purpose of her trips was to remind the studios that she was still alive, and to keep her in mind for future projects. This time, however, one of the studios was so close to pulling the trigger on a movie that they asked Natalie to do a budget for them. She couldn't have been happier. It was the first time a trip to LA had paid for itself on the spot.

But when Elias found out about it, he went ballistic.

"What about my movie?" he demanded.

"What about it?"

"The guy at Larkwood Pictures said he wanted to make it."

"I know, and that's great."

"But now you're taking this other job."

"Honey [Honey was technically my name, but as we all learned in college, it's best to call everyone you're sleeping with the same thing], you can't get your hopes up when you talk to these people. They all say stuff they don't mean."

"Then how do you know when they're telling the truth?"

"When they spend money," she replied. "Until then, it's all bullshit."

A month later, the studio green-lit the movie Natalie had done the budget for and offered her the job as line producer. The guy at Larkwood Pictures swore on the lives of his children that he was going to make *Ant Eater,* but failed to send the money for a revised budget even after Natalie had dropped her fee to a paltry three thousand dollars. When another month went by and Mr. Larkwood Pictures still hadn't sent a check, Natalie took the studio gig.

That's when Elias broke up with her and my wife lost her mind.

As usual, I was the last to know. We had reservations at a hot new restaurant, and I showed up my usual fifteen minutes early. Each time a cab arrived, I glanced up from my paperback to see somebody who wasn't Natalie climb out. I didn't care because I was used to it—Natalie was born late and never caught up—but the hostess kept giving me the fish-eye and that made me nervous. I dialed Natalie's cell, and she answered on the first ring.

"Don't you *dare* hang up on me again, you fucking asshole!"

"Uh . . . Natalie?" I said.

The phone went dead, and when I hit the redial button it just rang and rang. I double-checked to make sure I'd dialed the correct number, and I had. Strange. I suffered the hostess's wrath for another fifteen minutes and gave up the table in defeat. Natalie slunk home three hours later a complete wreck. No amount of makeup or breath mints could hide her puffy eyes or the half dozen Ketel One martinis on her breath. She gave me some bullshit excuse about getting raked over the coals by the Studio Executive from Hell and NBF's cancer relapsing, but her story was so full of holes I just shook my head and went to bed.

The next month was such an emotional roller coaster that if the studio hadn't abandoned the picture when their star backed out, Natalie would have been fired. She shut down the production office, shipped the paperwork to LA, and did the Larkwood Pictures budget for free. As if by magic, life was once again lovey-dovey between my wife and her manipulative lover. I still refused to see what was going on, and even if I had, the previous month had been so insane *even I* would have been relieved to hear that Natalie and Elias had worked out their differences.

I guess you could say I was in the total denial stage.

STAGE 5: Same Ole, Same Ole

After the unrelenting stress fest of Stage 4, Stage 5 should feel like a cool island breeze and everyone from your doorman to your cat will notice the improvement. Now that your wife is cheating on you full-time (and has that human-excuse-machine otherwise known as her NBF at her disposal), her affair can motor on unimpeded and it will almost be like she has two husbands. During this stage, life will return to something resembling normal. Your wife's monthly maintenance bill will drop below four figures, her drawerful of fancy undies will grow old and frayed, and that cute little Mohawk will morph back into the furry friend you've known for years. She'll be less distracted, more fun at parties, and may even toss you the occasional quickie to show she still cares.

The biggest danger during Stage 5 is complacency. After months of getting away with it the happy couple will grow sloppy, reckless, or just plain stupid. Hotel credit card receipts, smooching in broad daylight, or getting caught playing Naughty Night Nurse and Paralyzed NASCAR Driver are examples of behavior so blatant that a guy's gotta wonder if his wife isn't *trying* to get nailed.

And so it went with Natalie, Elias, and me. They had our place in Sag Harbor to run off to in case they needed to "work on Elias's script," and Natalie invented a cash-only personal trainer named Rashid to explain the multiple withdrawals from our checking account.

To keep myself out of their hair, I took a job on an Adam Sandler movie, injured my back, and got hooked on painkillers. As everyone but Elias expected, the deal at Larkwood Pictures dried up and blew away. Natalie and her partner spent the rest of the fall pitching *Ant Eater* to New York producers with more dreams than capital. They weren't expecting to get a deal, but they wanted to fine-tune their act for their second assault on LA after the holidays.

Natalie loved everything about Christmas. We were flying to St. Bart's on the morning of the twenty-fifth, but that didn't stop Natalie from throwing her annual tree-trimming party on Christmas Eve. Elias was spending the holidays in Aspen, but, ever the gentleman, offered to help me schlep the tree back to our apartment before he hopped on a plane. Buying a tree two days before Christmas took longer than we expected, and Elias had to leave as soon as we screwed the tannenbaum into the stand. Natalie helped him carry his bags to the corner to catch a cab, while I checked the mail and gave the super his Christmas tip.

Our mailbox was jammed with season's greetings from crew people across the country. Natalie usually opened the cards, but the return address on one of them struck me as a little . . . strange. Lo and behold, it was from Becky, Natalie's NBF, telling us she had moved to Pittsburgh in August. *August?* That didn't make sense. That would mean. That would mean . . . Oh shit!

I ran outside and slipped on a patch ice. My legs flew out from underneath me and as I sailed through the air I saw Elias climb into a cab and Natalie lean in and kiss him. Hard. On the mouth. I crashed onto the sidewalk and scrambled to my feet. My only thought was to rip out Elias's eyeballs and stomp on them like a couple of cocktail olives. But I was too late. The cab pulled away, and I locked eyes with Elias through the back window. He knew that I knew, and I knew that he knew it. Polite to the end, Elias waved good-bye.

Merry Christmas to all, and to all a good night.

Chapter 3

Moose on the Loose

"Yo, Bobby," Moose McMahon shouted as I rolled the dolly off the grip truck. "It's Dollar Day. You in?"

"Sure," I said, pulling a dollar out of my pocket and writing my name across it. I stuffed the bill into the manila envelope in Moose's hands and asked, "Who's picking the winner?"

"I don't give a shit. How about the director? He seems like an honest little squish."

"Sounds good to me. As long as it's not a Teamster."

"What's the matter with a Teamster picking it?"

" 'Cause you guys always win."

"That's because we put more money in than all you cheap fucks combined. It's called improving the odds."

"It's called the house always wins."

"Oh yeah? How about a little side bet? I'll bet you fifty bucks that a Teamster doesn't win."

"I don't have fifty on me."

"You can owe it to me."

"Moose, you're the last person on earth I'd want to owe money to."

He wrapped an arm around me and smiled. "You're a smart kid, Bobby."

Making movies in New York is impossible. From the moment we arrive, it's like we're picking a fight with the city. Our trucks take up all the parking, the crew screams and shouts into the night, and production assistants won't let people pass when we're rolling. New Yorkers hate being inconvenienced, and everyone from Wall Street executives down to the nut job on the corner has a problem with us. The police department assigns a couple of cops to every production, but the people who really protect us are the Teamsters.

Shooting a movie without Teamsters is like trying to swim in sand. You can't do it. A few clueless producers have tried, and by strange coincidence their trucks have vanished from bonded and well-lighted parking lots and reappeared days later stripped and burned to a crisp. I'm not saying Teamsters had anything to do with it, I'm just saying it's a good idea to have Teamsters drive your trucks.

I looked around to make sure no one was listening and asked Moose, "You hear anything about them shutting down the movie?"

Moose's eyes bulged. "They're shutting down the movie?"

"I was just wondering if you heard anything. You know, after the whole Julia Roberts fuckup last night."

Moose shook his head, but I could see his mind working. "Naw, I haven't heard anything. But me and Packy and Pete are supposed to drive the grip and prop trucks to Texas tomorrow. If they're gonna pull the plug on this thing, I gotta know now. Fuck, I got shit to do."

"Like I said, I was just wondering if you heard anything."

"I'll ask around. Thanks for the heads-up, Bobby."

"No problem."

Moose stomped off clutching his envelope full of cash. If Hank wanted me to light a fire under the crew, telling Moose that the studio was going to shut down the movie was an excellent beginning. But only so many people would listen to a sweaty, two-hundred-and-twenty-pound truck driver who smelled like Bushmills and Budweiser at seven in the morning. With that in mind, I pushed my dolly onto the set.

Think of a film set as a dartboard. The outer ring is populated by trucks and Teamsters, the inner ring by equipment and technicians, and the bull's-eye is the camera. Moose was the perfect person to light the outer ring on fire, but for the inner ring I needed someone a little more refined. Gossip is the lifeblood of movies, and the hair, makeup, and wardrobe departments—known collectively as the vanity crafts—run the blood bank. If you ever want to whip a film set into a frenzy of anxiety, there's no better place to start than with the women who wield the combs, powder puffs, and safety pins.

"Hi, Georgette," I said, stepping into the Hair & Makeup trailer. "Looking forward to Texas?"

"Am I ever," replied the sixty-two-year-old woman dressed in hot pants and a tank top. "I can't wait to round up some dumb cowboy who falls asleep thirty seconds after he shoots his wad. This guy I'm dating now? He wants to talk all night. Like I really give a shit about his feelings? After I come, all I want to do is watch HBO."

Georgette planted a coffee-smelling kiss on my cheek and inspected my face like a piece of salmon at Zabar's. "When we get to Texas have that craft service gal give you a B-twelve shot. It'll clean up those bags right away."

"Does that stuff really work?"

"Are you kidding? B-twelve shots are *fabulous*. When I was on the road with Aerosmith, we gave them to each other all the time. They're ten times better than Botox. I'd get one every week, but after I OD'd I swore I'd never touch another needle for the rest of my life. I don't know what'll happen if I get diabetes."

"You talk to Moose this morning?"

"Why would I talk to him? I don't need anybody whacked."

"He thinks the studio's gonna pull the plug on the movie."

"I knew it!"

"Knew what?" came a scratchy voice from behind us.

I turned and saw what appeared to be a bag lady entering the trailer, but it was only Medea, the hairstylist.

"Moose thinks they're shutting down the movie."

"Oh gawd," Medea moaned. She collapsed in a barber's chair and put her forehead on the counter. "I just canceled three months' worth of appointments with my psychic."

"Fuck that," Georgette said. "If they cancel this movie, I gotta come up with another way of paying Johnny's tuition next semester."

"Is this one mine?" Medea asked, staring at the Styrofoam coffee cup six inches from her nose.

"Yeah," Georgette said, dialing her cell phone.

"Thanks, doll. What else did Moose say, Bobby?"

"That's it. Just that after last night's debacle, the studio's gonna shut down the picture."

"What? So Moose is running things now?"

"Hey, Cassandra," Georgette shouted into her phone. "It's me. Don't turn down that Sam Jackson movie yet. I may not be going to Texas, and I need a Plan B. Call me as soon as you get this."

"Wait a minute," Medea said. "When did Paula say she was leaving for Prague?"

"I don't know. Noon?" Georgette said.

"Call her, and see how pissed off Julia was when she left last night. For some reason, Julia thinks that little Limey director of ours is a genius."

"Who's Paula?" I asked.

"Julia's personal. She goes everywhere with her. As if Julia Roberts actually needs a personal makeup artist making eighty-five hundred a week. My dog could do her and she'd look breathtaking."

The trailer door opened and Ryan Donahue, the star of our little photoplay, walked in. This movie was a big break for him, and if he found out the studio was shutting it down, it would have ruined his performance for the day.

"I better get going," I said. "Keep me posted if you hear anything."

"Sure thing, Bobby."

"Great work yesterday," I said to Ryan. "You better start working on your Academy Award speech."

"Yeah, right," he said with a yawn.

I pushed my dolly into the bull's-eye. The camera is the geographic and psychological center of set and the spot where the three most important players on a movie—the director, the director of photography, and the first assistant director—spend their day. The director is the person responsible for everything you see on-screen, from the leading man's performance to the color of the villain's getaway car. It's an insane amount of responsibility, and of the ten thousand skills needed to direct a movie, the most important is the ability to make quick decisions. Unfortunately, when the studio handed Sir Richard Davis, our neophyte snob of a director, the controls to the most expensive train set in the world, they forgot to include an owner's manual. A celebrated theater director in England, Sir Richard knew less than nothing about the fine art of filmmaking and relied on his director of photography to determine everything from the shots to the locations to what he should eat for lunch. Every day began with Sir Richard asking Andrzej tons of questions, Andrzej offering a variety of solutions, and Reg, the first AD, failing to get them to commit to anything.

Andrzej Koscielny, our director of photography, was a big deal in Poland, where he shot movies for Miloš Forman and Krzysztof

Kieślowski. He fled communism in the early seventies and landed in Hollywood, where he became a bigger deal by at least sixty pounds. Andrzej was the most gifted cameraman I'd ever worked with, and his skill as a director of photography was rivaled only by his talents as a glutton and gourmand. On a typical day, Andrzej would dedicate more time to making dinner reservations or grilling cow cheeks on his hibachi than lighting the set, and he'd still do a better job than ninety-nine percent of the other cameramen out there.

It looked like we were doomed to another endless morning of Filmmaking 101 when a production assistant ran up to Reg and whispered something in his ear. Reg's eyes grew wide with panic, and I knew my rumor had hit its mark. The first assistant director is the person responsible for keeping the set moving and the movie on schedule. A shut-down movie has the same effect on an AD's career as a sexual harassment charge does on a girls' school principal's—it *eviscerates* it. Reg wasn't a bad AD, but he was no match for Sir Richard's inexperience and Andrzej's bluster, and his fear of a career meltdown drove him to make a tactical error. Instead of sending the production assistant back into the field to substantiate my rumor, he went straight to Sir Richard and Andrzej.

"What?" Sir Richard screamed.

I checked my watch. It had taken just eighteen minutes for my rumor to travel from the lowliest truck driver to the three most important people on the movie.

And they say one man can't make a difference.

When I cooked up my little scheme, I had forgotten that the film business operated on Pacific Time. Because of the time difference between New York and LA, there was no one for Reg or Sir Richard to scream at. The West Coast was fast asleep, and the East Coast was still on its way to work. Sir Richard debated giving his agent a wake-up call, but decided against it until his agent had somebody to yell at. To further complicate matters, the movie's producers were on planes to LA and Texas. With nothing better to do, Sir Richard, Andrzej, and Reg went back to work. Resigned to losing his first directing assignment, Sir Richard stopped asking mindless questions and let Andrzej set up the shots.

My plan was a success. By ten minutes to twelve we were ahead of schedule for the first time ever. Not one to rest on his laurels, Sir Richard broke early for lunch to polish his cell phone and get ready for when the studios opened at nine, LA time.

"That's lunch, one half hour," Reg called into his bullhorn.

"Wait! Wait! Wait!" came a voice from behind us.

The crowd parted, and Moose barreled toward the camera. "It's Dollar Day. How could you guys forget it was Dollar Day?" He handed the manila envelope to Sir Richard and said, "Here."

"Is this for me?" Sir Richard asked.

"No. You reach inside, pick out a dollar, and announce whose name is on it."

"Oh, I see," Sir Richard said. "It's like a raffle."

"There you go, chief."

Sir Richard pulled out a bill and announced, "Packy Finley."

The crew let out a collective moan.

Sir Richard looked around, wondering if he had done something wrong. "What's the matter?" he asked.

"Nothing, they're just pissed that a Teamster won."

"Is that bad?"

"I don't think so," Moose said as Packy Finley burst through the crowd.

"Are you Packy?" Sir Richard asked.

"That would be me."

"Congratulations."

"Thanks," Packy said as he took the envelope and peered inside. "Holy shit," he yelled. "There must be a hundred and fifty bucks in here."

I held my head high as we walked toward the church basement where lunch was being served. It had been a productive morning for everyone, and I felt proud of what I had accomplished. Someone tapped my shoulder, and I turned to see Moose with a big grin on his face.

"You should have taken that bet, Bobby. You'd be fifty bucks richer as we speak."

"That's okay, Moose. I didn't want to take your money."

"Better you than my ex-wife. At least you're fucking Irish."

Chapter 4

Grips and Agents

Q: What's the difference between a grip
   and a bucket of cold steel nails?
A: The bucket.

GRIPS ARE THE Marines of the crew, the hardest-working, toughest-drinking mofos on the movie. We're the guys who storm the beach at dawn, rescue babies from flaming buildings, and dive through skylights to capture the bad guys. While those petite flowers in the camera and electric departments sit around all day eating bonbons and reading French novels, grips build the scaffolding for their lights and the cranes for their cameras. We pound stakes into hard earth with sledgehammers, hump metal from one end of set to the other, and toss sandbags back and forth like Frisbees. Need a light rigged eighty feet in the air? No problem. Want a camera strapped to the side of a Lamborghini going a hundred miles an hour? Make it two. Require someone to chug a bottle of mescal without gagging on the worm? Bring it on.

The key grip is the head of the department and the guy responsible for all rigging, camera movement, and light control. The key takes orders from the director of photography and is never far from camera. His second-in-command is called—drumroll, please—a best boy. Best boys are responsible for ordering equipment, booking day players (additional crew), and keeping track of a thousand other details the key can't be bothered with because he's too busy keeping the DP happy. The rest of the crew, the guys responsible for doing the brunt of the work, are called grips, hammers, or thirds. It doesn't matter how many thirds are on the movie, they're all called thirds. That's because grips can't count higher than three.

The dolly grip is the double agent of the crew—half grip and half member of the camera department—and is responsible for mounting the camera whenever it's not on a tripod. This includes everything from teeny-tiny dollies made from skateboard wheels all the way up to big honking Titan cranes mounted on the back of a Mack truck. How can you tell a good dolly grip from a bad one? It's just like making love to a beautiful woman—the proof is in the pushing.

Grips work side by side with electricians, and the departments share a truck on smaller jobs. It's easy to confuse the two, and the rule of thumb is that if a piece of equipment has a plug on the end, the person carrying it is an electrician. The head electrician is called a gaffer because in the old days gaffers carried a long pole, or gaff, to adjust the lights. Now gaffers carry walkie-talkies and make their crew do the fine-tuning. The gaffer's second banana is also called a best boy and the rest of his crew are called electrics, juicers, or thirds.

Another rule of thumb is, "The gaffer sets the lights and the grips make 'em right." This is the light-control part of the job. Picture a room lit by a bare window or a naked lightbulb. Pretty ugly, right? But put a shade over that bulb or some curtains on the window, and things start looking good fast. That's what grips do. We *sculpt* light. We cut it, diffuse it, bounce it, and bend it to our will. Our tools are flags and nets, silks and cards, muslin and foam core. Grips turn day into night, and night into day. Inside or out, it doesn't matter. Given enough time and beer, grips can do *anything.*

We got back from lunch and three men in expensive suits were standing around Video Village and talking on cell phones.

"Who the hell are those guys?" Troy asked.

"Agents," I said.

"What are they doing here? It's daylight. Shouldn't they still be in their coffins?"

"They must be junior agents," I replied.

Which wasn't far from the truth. The men who represented Ryan, Andrzej, and Sir Richard were, in fact, still in LA, where they lived, worked, and paid tribute to their Dark Lord Satan with the rest of the big-time movie honchos. The suits near Video Village were low-level flunkies from the New York offices. Their job was to provide a Presence, and their arrival en masse was typical Hollywood overkill. In any other business, the people in charge would have quashed my rumor with a couple of quick phone calls and something tasteful from the local florist. But movies aren't like any other business, and the next time I glanced at Video Village, there were five men in suits talking on cell phones. Ten minutes later there were seven.

"What the hell's going on?" I asked Reg.

"Word hit the street that there's a problem on the movie. Those other guys are from competing agencies that want to steal Ryan and Sir Richard. We're not going to get shit done this afternoon."

My plan had backfired big time. "Why would anyone want to steal Sir Richard?" I asked. "The guy can't direct his way out of a bag of fish and chips."

"Shh. Here he comes."

"Oh, Reggie," Sir Richard called. "Do you remember which one of those nice boys is from my agency?"

An hour later there were enough agents hanging around to field a pickup basketball game, and we were once again behind schedule. Whenever we needed Andrzej, Ryan, or Sir Richard they were off getting blown by some agent. It was ridiculous. The high point—or low point, depending upon how you looked at it—of the day came when one of the agents slithered up to the dolly.

"Excuse me, are you Bobby Conlon?"

"I sure am," I said, holding out my hand. "And you are?"

"John Scholes." He looked down at my hand before shaking it, and I immediately hated his guts. I *knew* that look. It was the same one I gave homeless people who wanted to shake my hand after I tossed them a quarter. What was this guy expecting to see? Boils? Open sores?

"You're married to Natalie Miguel, right?"

"We're getting divorced, actually."

"Sorry to hear that. But you still talk, right?"

"On occasion."

"Outstanding." He handed me a business card. "Do you know if she's happy with her current representation?"

"I have no idea."

"Rising Artists is always interested in representing up-and-coming young producers like Natalie."

Young? I thought. *Up and coming? She was working on movies before you made your bar mitzvah.*

"That's wonderful," I said.

"Could you do me a favor? Next time you speak, could you ask her to give me a call?"

"Uh, sure."

"Great." He pulled some kind of handheld computer from his pocket. "And when do you think that will be?"

"I don't know," I sighed. "How about a week from Tuesday?"

"Outstanding," he said as he slithered away.

"Here, Bobby. Sign these."

I turned and saw Mitch Markham, the key grip.

"What are they?" I asked.

"The contracts for Gerti."

"What contracts for Gerti?"

"Troy said last night you told him you were quitting the business. I figured this meant you would finally sell me your truck."

"I say that every night."

"Don't mess around. I just paid an associate at my father's law firm three hundred bucks to draw these up."

"What's the hurry?" I asked as he handed me the contracts. The figure $150,000 jumped off the page.

"I want to take advantage of you while you're still upset about Natalie."

"Thanks for the compassion, asshole."

This was Mitch's first job as a key grip. He had been my best boy for years, and helped me maintain the forty-foot grip truck I had named Gerti. Andrzej originally asked me to key grip this job, but I turned him down. I was way too fucked up from Natalie and painkillers to handle the pressure. It was Hank Sullivan's idea to bump up Mitch to key grip and for me to push dolly. That I could do: back and forth, back and forth, smile, smile. I had no doubts that Mitch could key the movie, and all Hank asked was for me to keep an eye on him. Hank and I shook on it, pretending we were giving Mitch his big break. Of course, the real reason Hank wanted Mitch on the job was to keep an eye on me.

I stared at the paperwork in my hands. Was my truck and equipment really worth one hundred and fifty thousand dollars? That was what the studio had insured it for, but I never thought anyone would actually pay that much for it. The idea of so much money dropping into my lap was intoxicating. With a hundred and fifty grand I could take a killer vacation, lease a Porsche 911, or invest in something sensible like a chinchilla farm. As appealing as these options were, I knew what I was going to do with the money before my eyes left the page.

I was going to direct a movie.

I had no choice. That money was my dowry from the grip department, and as much as I would have enjoyed watching those chinchillas go at it, I would have regretted not making a movie for the rest of my life. The budget would be tight and no one would get paid, but it was the only way I could redeem myself from the endless series of wrong turns, procrastinations, and mistakes I had made since graduating from film school. After twenty years of watching losers get to call "Action" for a living, my time had arrived.

I flipped through the contract and saw the name Wesley Markham listed in a dozen places. Wesley was Mitch's father, a big-shot attorney who hated the idea of his only son carrying heavy equipment for a living. I had only met the guy a few times, but got the impression that he blamed me for keeping his little Mitchy out of law school.

"But this is a contract between me and your dad," I said.

"Where do you think I'm getting the hundred and fifty large?"

"Hundred and fifty large? Who are you supposed to be? Robert De Niro?"

"John Travolta. Donna and I caught the last half of *Get Shorty* on cable last night."

"Small, medium, or supersized, I'm not sure I want to go into business with your father."

"You're not going into business with him. I am. Once you cash the check you'll never have to deal with him again."

I acted like I was thinking it over, but I had already made up my mind. Nobody else was offering me that kind of money for my forty-foot box of wood, metal, and cloth. Besides, Mitch loved

Gerti almost as much as I did. I grabbed a Sharpie off the dolly and signed the contract.

"When do I get my money?" I asked.

"I'll bring the check to Texas tomorrow afternoon."

"I thought you were taking the morning flight with me."

"I switched to a later flight. I have to deal with this legal stuff in the morning."

"Speaking of legal stuff, there's no time to change the registration on the truck, but you better call Elvira at the production office and have her transfer the insurance over to your dad."

"You want to go out for beers after this and celebrate?"

"I'd love to, but I still have to clean up my apartment and pack."

Mitch laughed. "You haven't thrown away that tree yet, have you?"

I yanked the contract out of Mitch's hands. "You mention my tree again and I'm tearing this up right now."

"Jesus, Bobby, you're the most pathetic human being I've ever met. You better go back to that shrink of yours before it's too late."

"I'd rather have Sir Richard Davis remove my spleen with an oyster fork."

"Oh, Mitch, darling," came a voice from Video Village. "Could you come here for a moment?"

"Sure thing, Andrzej." Mitch eased the papers out of my hands. "Gotta go."

"Right. It was a pleasure doing business with you."

"Likewise. I'll bring you a copy of the contract after my father signs it. And good luck with that tree."

I lunged for the papers, but Mitch was gone.

Chapter 5

Oh, Tannenbaum

THE PARTICULARS OF my pending divorce were that Natalie got the house in Sag Harbor and I got Gerti. I also got to keep our apartment in Brooklyn Heights, which seemed like a major score until I started paying for it myself. Together, Natalie and I pulled down a quarter million dollars a year. On my own I made as much as a bus driver. I soon realized I couldn't afford the apartment and would have to give it up when my lease expired in January. Rent wasn't the only problem. Every floorboard, doorknob, and electrical outlet in the place reminded me of Natalie.

It was during this nosedive into financial humility and despair that my shrink introduced me to the wonderful world of Xanax. I hated needing an antianxiety drug to get through the day, but without Natalie's financial assistance I could no longer afford Vicodin. And that really gave me anxiety. I know it looks like I traded one drug for another, but that's not the case. I took Vicodin for Real Physical Pain, man. Just like firefighters and athletes. Antianxiety drugs are for guys who can't handle the pressure of simple day-to-day activities like their wife leaving them for a younger dude with a full head of hair. Not only did taking Xanax make me feel like a stone-cold pussy, it turned me into my therapist's punk-ass bitch. This was never more apparent than two months into treatment when I got pissed at one of Dr. Koch's more ridiculous pronouncements and stormed out of his office vowing never to see him again.

A week later, and out of Xanax, I got the brilliant idea to visit Natalie's new apartment. She was in Sag Harbor for the weekend, and I let myself in with the key I sort of accidentally copied on the day she moved out. I have no idea what I was looking for—maybe the answer to why our marriage went sour, or perhaps some sign that she still loved me. I don't know, I was out of drugs. I raided her medicine cabinet, read her college diaries, and worked my way through her vast supply of skin care solutions. I came to my senses two hours later with my face covered in Clinique Dramatically Different Moisturizing Lotion and sobbing out the words to "It's Too Late, Baby" as Natalie's high school copy of *Tapestry* spun around and around on a shiny new turntable. Delirious as I was, I knew that if I didn't get out of there fast, I was in danger of turning into a middle-aged woman. I erased all evidence of my intrusion, dropped the key down the sewer, and sulked back to Dr. Koch feeling pathetic and weak. A week later I was back to medicated normalcy.

My second attempt at kicking Xanax came courtesy of the International Alliance of Movie Technicians. Unlike Natalie's union, which had excellent benefits and would have paid for heroin as long as I mailed in a receipt, my union's second-rate health-care plan selected Atavan as their antianxiety drug of choice. I carried a prescription for the Big A in my wallet, but before I could start enjoying the pleasure of its company, I had to let the Xanax leach from my system. Dr. Koch was supposed to supervise this happy-pill handoff, but he and I had parted company once more. Why? Because he began each session with the same words:

"Did you throw it out, Bobby?"

The "it" in question was the Christmas tree that Elias and I had dragged back to my apartment on the day I found out about his affair with Natalie. And my answer to Dr. Koch's question was always "No."

Okay, maybe it was a little strange, nine months after the holidays, to have a dead Christmas tree sitting in the middle of my living room, but that was my problem and not Dr. Koch's. Some people have cats. Some people have dogs. I had a tree. Big fucking deal. I'd removed the lights, so it wasn't a fire hazard, and when I stood next to it I could almost smell Christmas.

And what little boy doesn't enjoy that?

To be honest, if Natalie's cousin Roger and his horse-faced wife, Bess, weren't coming from London to spend the fall in my apartment, I would have kept the tree up until the following Christmas. I was, after all, trying to conserve money, and what better way to save a few bucks than to use the same tree two years in a row? That's what my parents did, and they put three kids through college on a telephone worker's salary. Granted, my parents' tree was made of plastic and spent ninety percent of the year in the basement, but I was much more into holidays than they were. Thus, at Casa de Bobby, every day was Christmas. So what if Natalie took all the decorations with her when she waltzed off with Elias. Grips are nothing if not resourceful, and I overcame this depressing lack of ornamentation by decorating the tree with empty Xanax and Vicodin bottles. It looked a little bare at first, but by summertime the little fella had filled out just fine.

I didn't plan on the tree turning into such a big deal and probably would have thrown it out in January if Dr. Koch wasn't such a jerk about it. But the guy was unrelenting. No matter what *I* wanted to talk about, he always steered the conversation back to the tree. Was I still watering it? Did it bother me that Natalie took the ornaments with her? What did I think the tree meant?

"Jesus fucking Christmas!" I screamed in desperation. "Can't a tree be just a tree?"

"Although I appreciate your wit," Dr. Koch said without cracking a smile, "paraphrasing Freud won't solve your problems."

Oh, sweet cinematic Jesus, how I wanted to strangle that man. Except without him, there was no one to keep my veins coursing with the drug that tamped down the terror of my lower back exploding and rockets of pain shooting up my spine. Yes, I know I could have jumped ship to any of the ten thousand other shrinks who populated the Upper West Side of Manhattan, but I'd cast my lot with Dr. Koch, and I was bound to either kill him, conquer him, or quit. The day I took the job in Texas was the day I sent him packing. I had to endure a twenty-minute soliloquy explaining why giving him six hundred bucks a month was "really the best thing" for me, but after that I was rid of the man forever.

Getting rid of the tree, however, turned out to be even harder. I had visualized the process for weeks and pictured myself laying a large piece of plastic on the floor, tipping the tree over, and rolling it up like a giant Christmas enchilada. I would drag it to the service elevator, deposit it in the trash room, and ride the elevator back to my apartment in triumph. After that, a little zip zap zip with the vacuum and the tree would be historic. I had walked the route a half-dozen times, reviewed the elevator inspection certificate thoroughly, and had bought a new HEPA filter for my vacuum.

Unfortunately, I had forgotten to visualize the damn Xanax and Vicodin bottles. There must have been five hundred of the little bastards hanging from the branches, along with dozens of those mini Ziploc bags I got from dealers when I could no longer find a doctor willing to write me a prescription. Worse, every Xanax bottle bore the name of the evil Dr. Koch. If I closed my eyes I could almost hear them whispering, *Did you throw out the tree, Bobby? Did you? Did you?* I thought I was being the ultimate Mr. Smarty Pants when I had hung them there, but now each bottle was like one of Dr. Koch's dead gray eyes staring me down with that smug, $145-an-hour gaze of his.

I felt overwhelmed and desperate, but I could not let that sanctimonious son-of-a-bitch beat me. I cranked up the air-conditioning to cool things down from the late-summer heat and checked my watch. The movie had booked a car to take me to the airport in five hours, and I still hadn't eaten, showered, or packed. My apartment looked like a depressed grip had been living in it for nine endless months, and the tree was growing into a bigger obstacle by the second. I had to pull myself together.

If there was one thing I'd learned in my twenty years of working in a business that required me to accomplish the impossible on a daily basis, the best way to tackle an impossible task is to break it down into small, manageable steps. I approached the tree and yanked off a needle with a quick flick of the wrist. Success! I snapped the needle in two and dropped it in the trash. It was time to up the ante. I spotted a lone Xanax bottle hanging from a saggy branch. It was exactly the kind of low-hanging fruit I was looking for. I reached out to grab it and noticed Dr. Koch's name on the label.

"Did you throw it out, Bobby?"

I jumped back as if the tree were possessed by demons. Removing the bottles was going to be a lot harder than I had anticipated. I grabbed a beer and scoured the apartment looking for some kind of tool or appliance to help me with my troublesome tannenbaum. In the hall closet I found a cache of old wedding presents that Natalie considered too tacky to take to her new apartment. There was a Crock-Pot, an electric carving knife, a fondue set, and snow globe containing a bride and groom holding hands. Our wedding date was printed beneath the happy couple along with the words *Till death do us part.* I shook the globe and watched as plastic snow drifted down upon us.

"Rosebud," I whispered under my breath. "Rosebud."

I was tempted to let the globe fall from my fingers to more fully re-create Orson Welles's death scene in *Citizen Kane*, but the way my luck was going, I would probably slip on snow-globe juice and cut my throat on a shard of glass. Then what? If I died right then and there would anyone even remember me? What if the person who found my body didn't know anything about movies and missed the reference to *Citizen Kane*? Talk about dying in vain. And what was Natalie doing at that moment? Was she spooned against Elias and purring like a kitten? We were still legally married, so the Crock-Pot and fondue set would go to her as part of my estate. Would she think of me whenever she made fondue? Would her tears mingle with the Gruyère and Swiss? Would she remember the good times we had? The fun? The laughs?

That was when I realized I was going through Xanax withdrawal. Embarrassed, I put the snow globe back in the closet and popped one of my last pills. Then it hit me: the electric carving knife! I yanked open the closet and pulled the eight-inch Toastmaster 6104 off the shelf. It wasn't a chain saw, but it would have to do. I plugged it in, wrapped my fingers around the comfort grip, and squeezed the trigger. Party time.

The Toastmaster slid through the first branch like a Butterball on Thanksgiving afternoon, and a bottle fell to the floor in a shower of pine needles. I tapped it with my sneaker. Nothing. No movement. No obnoxious questions from Dr. Koch. It was dead, Jim. I picked up the bottle and held it high in the air like a grouse or rabbit I'd bagged. My heart pounded from the thrill of the kill, and my brain bubbled with the desire to share my triumph with someone who would really appreciate it. I grabbed the phone and dialed a number I knew by heart.

This is Dr. Laurence Koch. I'm not available to take your call, but I do want to speak with you. Please leave a message along with your name and number, and I'll get back to you as soon as I can. If this is an emergency, please call 212-555-1232. Peace. BEEP.

"One," I said and hung up.

I dropped the bottle in the trash, jammed the branch down the garbage disposal, and flipped the switch. GRRRRR. The smell of Christmas filled the air, and I strolled back to the living room with a swagger in my step. My next victim dangled from a branch near the top of the tree. I fired up the Toastmaster and attacked my quarry with a vengeance born out of nine months of humiliation and despair. The bottle flew across the room and hit a bare spot on the wall where a Warhol silkscreen once hung. I checked to make sure there were no Xanax inside, pushed the redial button on the phone, and waited for the beep.

"Two," I said and hung up.

Two down, four hundred and ninety-eight to go.

Chapter 6

Roadkill

Crew members traveling to Texas by air should refrain from packing contraband in their bags. Drugs, moonshine, and light sabers are just a few of the items that will get you in hot water with the Transportation Safety Agency. Production has authorized Travis County bail bondsman Sandoval Ramirez to post bonds of up to $1,000 for all employees of the film. His number is on the contact list and should be committed to memory. FYI, Texas prisons are not air-conditioned.

—From Elvira's Texas travel memo

I ARRIVED IN TEXAS determined to put the last nine months behind me. Shooting started in three days, and that gave me seventy-two hours to get clean. I wasn't worried. I had barbecue to eat, music to enjoy, and shit to kick. Yee-haw! Austin was one of my favorite places in the country, the city that Natalie and I had fantasized moving to when we got fed up with New York and wanted to settle down in a town with big-box retail and decent parking. We were going to restore a 1920s bungalow, drive big old American cars, and hang out with Willie Nelson and Lance Armstrong. It was a beautiful dream.

Okay, I'll admit it. The main reason I took this job was to get back at Natalie. In my own petty, living-well-is-the-best-revenge kind of way, I wanted to hurt her. I wanted her to sigh when she told people I was working in Austin. I wanted her to sniff back a tear when she saw the letters *TX* on the envelope containing our divorce papers. I wanted her eyes to drift to the center of the country every time she watched the Weather Channel.

"I'm Bobby Conlon," I said to the skinny kid manning the front desk of the production office. He was reading a book on the director Douglas Sirk and had "recent film school grad" tattooed all over him.

"And?"

"I'm the dolly grip."

"Here's your welcome packet." He handed me a thick manila envelope and said, "The hotel's two blocks away. Ask for Emilio at the front desk, and he'll lend you a luggage cart to bring your stuff in."

"Great."

The kid went back to his book as if I were no longer there. I wasn't expecting them to roll out the red carpet for me, but I was hoping for something a little more welcoming than a wet-nosed brat with more attitude than a producer after a boffo opening weekend. I couldn't wait for the day the kid showed up on set so I could make him do something pointless and degrading.

As I leaned down to jam the welcome packet into my shoulder bag, the front door opened and I heard someone say, "Does that ass belong to Bobby Conlon?"

"That depends who's asking," I said, looking up to see Elvira, the production office coordinator. She dropped her lunch in the film school brat's lap and wrapped her arms around me.

"You look great," she said. "When'd you get here?"

"Just now."

Elvira was a local gal with dyed black hair and a fireplug figure that didn't stop her from wearing clothes that were two sizes too small. We'd worked together on my last job in Austin and were buds. "Hey, Spielberg," she screamed at the film school brat. "Did you offer to bring Bobby's luggage to the Omni for him?"

"No, I—"

"Then get humping, kiddo."

"I thought I was supposed to watch the front door."

"The door will get along fine without you. Now *vámonos*!"

Elvira dragged me into the production office. "Listen up," she shouted at the dozen exhausted crew members sitting at folding tables and talking on telephones. "For those of you who haven't had the pleasure, this is Bobby Conlon. He's the dolly grip on this show, and he's just back on the market. So, if anybody sleeps with him before I do, you're toast."

"Does that include me?"

We turned and saw Carni Bettencourt, the movie's line producer and our boss.

"I can't fire your ass, Missie Thing," Elvira said, "but I can certainly kick it."

"Bobby, I need to talk to you."

"Okay." I turned back to Elvira. "Will you be here for a while?"

"Only till midnight."

Nobody called Carni "Carni" to her face. Her real name was Katherine, but in one of those transformations that kept the gossip wheels of the film business working overtime, the 230-pound Wharton Business School grad I'd met sixteen years earlier was now a 105-pound wastrel with a serious Prada dependency. Rumor had it she'd gotten her stomach stapled shut like Carnie Wilson, the fat girl in the nineties pop group Wilson Phillips. Thus the nickname. Unfortunately for our Carni, her sagging flesh made her look more like a cancer survivor than a pop star.

"I know it's your travel day, but I need you to start work right now," Carni said as we entered her office.

"No problem. What's up?"

"Moose rolled the grip truck on the Pennsylvania Turnpike this morning. He's okay, but the truck is trashed. I got hold of Tom D. at Showbiz Rental in Dallas, and they're pulling a new package for us as we speak. It's your job to handle Showbiz Rental while Mitch deals with the wreckage in Pennsylvania."

"Sure . . . Shit, what happened?"

"I haven't seen a police report, but Packy was caravanning behind Moose, and said it looked like Moose fell asleep behind the wheel. I sure hope he wasn't drunk."

Was Moose ever not drunk? "What do you need me to do?"

"I faxed your inventory to Tom D. He said he had most of the equipment in Dallas and could drop-ship everything else from LA. Just make sure we have enough equipment to shoot on Monday."

"No problem."

"Oh, and just so you know, Andrzej is making noises about firing Mitch and making you key grip."

"Why?"

"Andrzej hates Sir Richard. The studio won't let him quit, and he's taking it out on everyone. You don't even want to hear the shit he's pulled on the art department. They've already had to paint some sets three and four times."

"Andrzej never should have taken this job."

"Hank told him that he could direct the third picture in his deal if he shot this one for him."

No wonder Andrzej was so pissed off. "What's the movie?"

"Some action thing in Vancouver. Didn't you read about it in *Variety*?"

"I've been avoiding the trades since Natalie's name began appearing in boldface type. Who was supposed to be in it?"

"A rapper and some Korean guy the kids on the Internet are calling the next Jackie Chan. Personally, I never cared for the last one."

"*Drunken Master II* is one of the greatest action movies ever made."

"Whatever. Hopefully Sir Richard will start letting Andrzej do his job and this whole Mitch thing will blow over. Otherwise . . ."

Otherwise I'd have to key-grip the movie, which was impossible. I could barely throw out a Christmas tree. Taking over for Mitch would kill me.

"Sorry," I said. "But I gave up being a key grip for Lent."

"I'm just telling you what Andrzej said."

I walked out of Carni's office and tossed back a Xanax without water. I couldn't believe it. Gerti was gone.

Life on the road gets so lonely that film crews spend a ridiculous amount of time decorating their vehicles and making them feel like home. I had put more thought and energy into customizing Gerti than my house and apartment combined. There were shower curtains above every door, a rolltop desk in the bulkhead, and three bullet holes in the left side from when I bet a Vietnam vet with a fake leg that if he beat me in a foot race, he could shoot my truck. (I lost.) The walls were plastered with Polaroids of grips in every imaginable situation, and above the lift gate, in big black letters, somebody had painted the words PAIN IS BEER LEAVING THE BODY. The entire truck was wired with Dolby 5.1 surround sound, and I had bolted a dance-club-quality subwoofer to the undercarriage. When you cranked up the volume, the equipment rattled so bad it felt like you were getting your teeth drilled. That truck *rocked*.

And now it was gone.

"I take it Katherine told you about Moose's little wreckie?"

I blinked and saw that I was standing in front of Elvira's desk.

"Here," she said. "Have a medicinal french fry. They're from Huts."

"Just out of curiosity, did you switch the insurance over to Mitch's father yesterday?"

"Of course. I never mess around when it comes to the insurance company."

"Outstanding."

Elvira handed me a flyer.

"What's this?"

"Your invitation to the Sex Rodeo."

"Sex Rodeo? What's that?"

"Our kickoff party at Don's Depot."

"I'm not really up for a party, sex, or a rodeo."

"Too bad, cowboy. You're going."

"You can't make me," I said, folding my arms over my chest.

"No, but Troy can. And I'm sending him to your room tomorrow at six. So giddyup."

I found an empty desk in the corner of the office and dialed Mitch's cell phone.

"Yeah?" he answered.

"I'm calling from Amalgamated Insurance Company. We never received your last premium and canceled the policy on your truck at twelve-oh-one this morning."

"Don't even joke about that."

"You in Pennsylvania?"

"Yep."

"How's Gerti doing?"

"I'm sitting shivah for her right now."

"That bad?"

"She's fucking toast, man. It looks like a rental house exploded on the highway. And the salvage crew the state troopers sent down from Philly are ridiculous. It's a total mob deal, and they won't even let me near the equipment."

"I'm sorry, buddy. I really am. Don't worry about things on this end. I'll deal with Showbiz Rental."

"Thanks."

"Oh, and Mitch, I know this sucks, but you know you still have to pay me for the truck. The insurance is in your father's name."

"We'll talk about it when I get there."

"What's that supposed to mean?"

"It means that I'm not having this conversation on the side of the Pennsylvania Turnpike with tractor-trailers rushing by me at seventy miles an hour. Jesus, Bobby."

"You're right. I'll see you in the morning, okay?"

"Sure. See you in the morning."

"And don't forget that check."

Chapter 7

Holiday Greetings

NATALIE AND I named our house in Sag Harbor Casa de Gaffer's Tape because that's what paid for it. Dollar for dollar, I made more money selling gaffer's tape (a kinder and gentler form of duct tape) than I did renting my entire truck of grip equipment. Tape, rope, visqueen, clothespins, baby powder, Lemon Pledge, screws, nails, plywood, Masonite, wood, chalk, and chain were just some of the expendables I pawned off on movies, commercials, and TV shows. Selling gaffer's tape is one of the last great scams left. Once somebody tears the first strip off a roll, it's almost impossible to tell how much is left, and as long as you make sure to collect the tape at the end of the job, you can keep selling the same partial roll over and over. I've never kept track of it, but I'm sure I've sold some rolls of tape at least a half-dozen times. Combine that with all the other goodies I sold, and within a few years I had enough cash to make a nice down payment on a place in the Hamptons.

Which was where I went when I found out about Natalie and Elias. I thought I was fleeing to a safe harbor, but as soon as I walked through the front door, I realized that everything had changed. Casa de Gaffer's Tape was no longer my weekend refuge from the oppressive forces of the New York film industry. It was ground zero for Natalie's infidelity. I stared at the furniture I'd spent months refinishing and the hundred-year-old walls I'd sanded down to present-day perfection and felt like burning the place to the ground. After everything I had done for that house, I couldn't believe it just stood there while Elias stuck it to my wife.

"I thought you were my friend," I screamed as I yanked open the liquor cabinet. I grabbed a bottle of Maker's Mark—Elias's drink—and tore off the cute little red cap. After hours of fighting back tears and anger and images of Natalie and Elias woven together like snakes, I threw back the bourbon and let nightmares wash over me.

By the next afternoon, the Maker's Mark was gone, and I was deep into a bottle of Absolut Citron. It was Christmas Eve, and I had hoped to greet the day with something festive like a Cosmopolitan. Unfortunately, there was no cranberry juice in the pantry, and I couldn't remember if the other ingredient was Triple Sec, Grand Marnier, or Adolph's meat tenderizer. My head felt like someone had dropped a dozen sandbags on it, and when I caught sight of myself in the stainless steel cocktail shaker, I realized that I wasn't dressed well enough for such a sophisticated beverage. Not wanting to lose the holiday spirit, I ground up two Vicodin with the bottom of my cocktail shaker and snorted them off the kitchen counter.

Meanwhile, back in Brooklyn, the guests were arriving for Natalie's tree-trimming extravaganza. I felt incredibly left out and contemplated sending a stripper in my place. The back pages of *The Village Voice* were filled with options, and my heart bubbled over with glee at the thought of the lovely Miss Chocolate Cannonball crashing Natalie's soiree. With the possible exception of chestnuts roasting on an open fire, there's nothing better than a 250-pound Haitian transvestite with Christmas ornaments dangling from his nipples to get folks in the holiday spirit. Ultimately,

I decided against it. The way my luck was going, Ms. Cannonball would have ended up marrying my wife.

Along with the tears, curses, and transvestite delivery schemes came moments of surprising lucidity. I knew Natalie's affair was a life-altering experience, and the frustrated writer/director/narcissist in me felt the urge to record my thoughts for posterity. *Who knows?* I thought as I fired up the computer. *Maybe I can put this in a movie someday.* But after a few lame attempts at describing my shattered mental condition, I understood that I had neither the talent, the guts, nor the objectivity to play war correspondent with my soul. Instead, I put on a Lucinda Williams CD and stared at the carpet until the postman jammed a large green envelope through the mail slot. Inside were a pair of socks and a holiday form letter from my great-aunt Clare. As I reviewed the highlights of another action-packed year at the Shady Oaks Retirement Community, a new strain of mischief popped into my booze-addled brain. Holiday form letters were the sole aspect of Christmas that Natalie despised. What better way to get back at her for turning my life into a greasy pile of owl shit than by banging out a little holiday greeting of my own?

I filled my glass with straight Absolut and, using Great-Aunt Clare's letter as a guide, set to work:

Dear Family & Friends,

I hope this letter finds you in the best of health. I'd love to send each and every one of you a handwritten note, but time and poor penmanship prevent me from doing so. Please be assured I am thinking of you.

It's been such an exciting year that I don't know where to begin. I guess I'll start with my wife, Natalie, fucking another guy. How exciting! How sordid! Yes, indeed, it's all that and so much more. It seems that last August, while I was slaving away on a series of lucrative peanut butter

commercials—the ones with the monkey and the organ
grinder, I'm *sure* you saw them—my dear wife of ten years
got hot pants for a young directorial stud named Elias
Simm.

Elias, as many of you know, is a real bucket of pond
scum who uses his distant relationship to the Kennedys
(third cousin once removed, or some such nonsense) to get
decent and hardworking folks with less-distinguished family
foliage to give him stuff for free. I discovered Natalie and
Elias's six-month-long fling yesterday when I caught them
red-handed (but not bare-assed, thank God) swapping spit
seconds before Elias jetted off to the slopes of Aspen for the
holidays. Swoosh, Elias!

With no place to hide, my lovely Natalie came clean—
or as clean as someone who's been sleeping with another
man can come. Now she says she's confused, and who can
blame her after receiving such a deluxe schtupping from
Elias?

And you know what? I'm confused too.

In closing, my dear friends and family, please keep me
in mind this holiday season as you carve your Christmas
turkeys and guzzle your holiday cheer. Remember what a
whoring bitch Natalie Miguel truly is, and what a chump
I was for believing her during her six-month blitz of
fornication and lies.

Happy Holidays One and All!

Bobby Conlon
Cuckold Extraordinaire

My original intention was to send the letter to Natalie and Natalie
alone. But as I reached the bottom of my bottle of Citron, I felt
an overpowering desire to share my joy with others. By this point,
typing twenty separate e-mail addresses into AOL seemed like far

too much work and I selected them all. By *all* I mean every friend, business acquaintance, and studio executive Natalie and I had ever met. Maybe this wasn't the smartest move, but I was so damn proud of my letter I couldn't help myself.

So I pressed SEND and destroyed any chance of saving my marriage.

The week between Christmas and New Year's is a dead time in the industry. Everyone's on vacation, and Sundance is weeks away. Into this void dropped my e-mail, which was forwarded between New York and LA so many times the FBI thought it was a computer virus. I don't know what I was expecting when I pushed that SEND button, but it backfired big time. The president getting caught in a three-way with Prince Charles and Madonna wouldn't have generated as much publicity as my 318 words of drunken idiocy. By January 2, every development person on both coasts wanted to read *The Ant Eater Goes Down,* and Natalie and Elias were hotter than the winners of a TV reality show. The phone rang nonstop, the fax machine purred like a kitten, and my landlord threatened to charge the FedEx man rent for all the time he spent in our hallway. Meanwhile, Hank got his three-picture deal and, on what I thought was a visit to New York to see how I was bearing up under Natalie's infidelity, signed Natalie and Elias to a development deal at Columbus Pictures. For Natalie, who usually spent the month of January in her pajamas, it was heaven on earth.

And did she thank me? Did she find the time to enter couples counseling? Did she even consider dropping out of the project out of deference to my feelings?

Hell, no! *Ant Eater* was hot, and that's all that mattered.

Natalie was gone by the end of the month.

Chapter 8

A Having

MITCH ARRIVED IN Texas with a stick so far up his butt you could have turned him upside down and spun him around like a top. What he did not bring was my check for one hundred and fifty thousand dollars. I felt bad for the guy, dropping so much money on a pile of roadkill, but a deal was a deal, and I wasn't going to let him slide because fate had dealt him a crappy hand.

"I'm sorry I don't have your money," Mitch began. "But we have a problem here. A real situation."

"No, we don't. Your father bought my truck, and now he has to pay me for it."

"Of course he's going to pay you for it. It's just a matter of figuring out the money."

"That's easy. It's a hundred fifty grand, and I accept cash, checks, and all major credit cards."

"C'mon, Bobby. This isn't easy for me."

"What isn't easy? Fucking me over? It's not supposed to be, you douche bag. That's why God invented guilt." I stared Mitch in the eye, and he turned away. Not a good sign. Two decades of getting jerked around by fast-talking producers had taught me how to spot a liar. This made me feel awful in a dozen ways. I had trusted Mitch with everything from my apartment keys to my bank card, and not once in ten years had he borrowed so much as a roll of gaffer's tape without first asking. I know it sounds corny, but the guy was like a brother to me.

"I'm not going to fuck you over," Mitch said.

"That's right, you're going to have your father do it for you, you spineless sack of shit. C'mon, Mitch, grow yourself a pair of balls and screw me like a real man."

"Will you please stop saying that?"

"Then give me one good reason not to." I held out my hand. "Put a check or a signed contract in my palm right now."

"Oh yeah, about the contract . . . there's a problem."

"Do tell."

"It blew out the cab window on my way home Thursday."

"It what?" His words stopped me cold, and that's when I remembered something Natalie told me years earlier when Hank asked us to invest in one of his movies: "Money separates friends. Big money separates families." The Markhams were circling the wagons, and if I wanted to walk away from Gerti with anything more than a few scratched Polaroids, I had better play nice.

"Look," I finally said. "We only have a few hours to get this truck ready for Monday. Let's deal with this money business later."

"Good idea," said Mitch.

The rest of the day was all about playing catch-up, repacking the truck and figuring out what equipment we did and did not have. Mitch's best boy, Steveo, had flown to Dallas for the load-out, but he only had a few hours to supervise Showbiz Rental's shop rats before the truck pulled out for Austin. Steveo had done the best he could, but Tom D. had misrepresented the amount of equipment he had on hand. Most of Showbiz Rental's gear was rented out on two other big shows, and we got the dregs of their inventory.

"How's it going?" I asked Steveo as he unlocked the truck. He'd spent half the night on the road from Dallas, and his stringy black hair was dripping wet from a quick shower at the hotel.

"We're being *had*, babe," Steveo said as he unlocked the truck. "This job is turning into more of a having by the minute." Steveo warned us that the equipment was in bad shape, but it was worse than he had described—the stands were ancient, with stripped-out risers and bent knuckles, the apple boxes were scraped and splintered, and the sandbags leaked everywhere. The job is hard enough with good equipment; shit equipment makes it impossible. The next week was going to be drop-ship hell as we airfreighted a decent package from LA. The paperwork alone would be eight inches thick.

Mitch freaked out. He climbed into the truck and tore a crate of hardware off a shelf. "Fucking Showbiz Rental," he screamed. "This equipment sucks!"

Steveo turned to me and shrugged. "I had a similar reaction when I saw it."

"Welcome to Texas," I said.

Our thirds were a couple of local grips Mitch had hired over the phone. They weren't used to seeing their boss throwing equipment around like a wild animal, and I watched as they gave each other a what-the-hell-did-we-get-ourselves-into look. They immediately volunteered to fetch breakfast and disappeared for the next hour and a half—probably to make calls looking for other jobs. When they got back, they kept loading and unloading the same twenty sandbags just to stay out of Mitch's way. Nothing was getting done, and when we broke for lunch the truck was in no better shape than when we started. I could see my chances for keying the movie increase with each passing moment, and knew I had to do something fast. If Mitch got fired, his father would never pay me my money. I had to keep him on the job no matter what.

"Look at me," I said, pulling him aside.

"What!"

"Calm down."

"I am calm."

"No, you're not. You're running around like a crazy person. Now chill the fuck out for a second and listen to me. I know this sucks, but it's not as bad as it looks. The next three days are daylight exteriors. That gives Steveo three days to get the package in shape and for you to gain Andrzej's confidence."

"I don't need to gain Andrzej's confidence. He loves me."

"No, he doesn't. He wants to fire you and have me key the movie."

Mitch deflated in an instant. "Andrzej really said that?"

I nodded.

"How come? I did a good job in New York."

"You did a great job in New York. But Andrzej's pissed at Sir Richard, and he's looking for somebody to take it out on. If you're not careful, that somebody could be you."

Mitch's eyes narrowed. "This is because of the truck, isn't it?"

"No, Mitch. I'm the guy trying to quit the business, remember? If I still wanted to be a key grip, you'd still be a best boy and that would have been my equipment spread across the Pennsylvania Turnpike."

"What should I do?"

"Keep your nose planted firmly up Andrzej's ass. Say yes to anything he asks for, no matter how stupid or difficult. And pray that he starts hating the prop guy."

"I can't lose this job, Bobby. Donna wants to send Simon to the Montessori school, and it costs a fortune."

"I'm sorry I brought it up. Just concentrate on keeping Andrzej happy, okay? And stop thinking like a best boy. It's Steveo's job to worry about the equipment, not yours."

"You're right. It's just that this Gerti thing has me really fucked up."

"Tell me about it."

Out of the corner of my eye I noticed a gangly woman in a flowered dress standing near the back of the truck. She appeared to be either lost or retarded.

"Can I help you?"

"Are you the grips?" she asked in a thick country accent.

"That depends on who's asking."

"Excuse me?"

"Yeah, we're the grips," Mitch said. "What's up?"

"The girl in the office said I should ask if y'all need an intern."

"Steveo!" Mitch screamed at the top of his lungs.

"Stop yelling at me," Steveo said, appearing at the back of the truck with a screw gun in one hand and a twenty-ounce bottle of Mountain Dew in the other.

"Say hello to your new intern."

Steveo stared at the woman. When no one broke out laughing, he realized it wasn't a joke.

"This is such a having," he said and gestured for the woman to follow him into the truck. "C'mon, toots, we only got about five million things to do before Miller Time."

"What's your name?" I asked as she climbed onto the lift gate.

"Sara Lee."

"Sara Lee what?"

"Just Sara Lee. You know, like the cake."

Mitch and I watched as she disappeared into the truck.

"Ten bucks says she doesn't last an hour," Mitch said.

"I give her until the end of the day."

"You're on."

"Sucker."

Four hours later, Sara Lee was still there, and I was ten dollars richer. Her dress was torn and filthy, but she didn't seem to care.

She thanked everyone for a great day and promised she'd be on set Monday morning for call.

"What was it like working with her?" I asked Steveo as we grabbed a beer in the Omni bar.

"It was freaky. She kept thanking me for showing her things and having faith in her. And I busted her ass. She was *had*."

"What's your take on Mitch?"

"He's tweaked. He's super-tweaked. He's super-tweaky."

"He's got to chill out."

"At least he's not in jail."

"What are you talking about?"

"We had a half pound of weed stashed in the truck."

"You guys used Gerti as a mule?"

"We had to, man. After 9/11 there's no way you can sneak dope on a plane. Thank God Moose tossed it in the river before the state troopers showed up."

"You potheads are fucking amazing." I looked around to make sure no one was listening and asked, "Have you found a new connection?"

"I asked the local boys, but they acted like they never heard of marijuana before."

"They just don't trust you yet. Talk to Gus on the pre-rig crew. He'll set you up."

"Cool."

"And don't let Mitch get high during lunch. If he shows up on set smelling like a bong, Andrzej will fire his ass for sure."

"Troy pounds beers during lunch."

"Troy's not on probation. Do us all a favor and keep Mitch away from the ganja until you guys are back at the hotel. Otherwise I'm going to be keying this movie from the dolly, and that's the last thing I want to do."

Chapter 9

Sex Rodeo

IF YOU THINK a film shoot is a bad place to kick Xanax, it's an even worse place to earn your celibacy merit badge. Out-of-town jobs are like college except with more spending money and relaxed-fit jeans. The crew fucks like bunnies, and even the most happily married men find themselves in situations they'd rather not think about again. Some folks pair off and form shoot-length locationships, while guys like Troy grind their way through the crew list one department at a time.

"Get this," Troy said as we drove to the kickoff party. "I spoke to the bell captain, and he said *Disney on Ice* is staying at our hotel next month."

"Darn, I forgot to bring my ice skates."

"Laugh all you want, but I've had a serious woody for Snow White since I was like four years old."

"You live in LA. Why don't you just go to Disneyland?"

"I tried that once, and the gal playing Snow White had really fat calves. But Snow White on ice? Those calves should be exceptional." He looked at me and said, "Hey! That was supposed to be funny."

"Sorry, man. This thing with my truck has me totally bent. Maybe you should just drive me back to the hotel."

"No way. It's times like this when you have to force yourself to go out and score some companionship."

"For you, maybe."

"For everybody. Did I ever tell you about the time I worked on this *60 Minutes* piece about Henry Miller? You know, the guy who wrote all those sex books."

"I know who Henry Miller is."

"We shot at his place in Big Sur, and the dude was just amazing. He was like eighty years old and had this hotsy-totsy girlfriend who was young enough to be his granddaughter. He and I got to be pretty good friends after he saw me hitting on the production babes. I guess he figured we were kindred spirits.

"Anyway, at the end of the first day I asked his girlfriend to show me a place where I could plug in the camera batteries to charge overnight. While I was talking to her, Henry walked by and gave me this *look*. And I thought, *Oh shit, Henry thinks I'm hitting on his old lady.*

"The next time I saw him I said, 'Look, Henry, it's not what you think.' And he broke into this huge grin and said his girlfriend was her own person and could do whatever the hell she wanted. But I got really upset and said, 'No, Henry, I wasn't hitting on her. Really.' Then he wrapped his arm around me and said, 'Troy, you gotta plow through a lot of cunt in this life before you can stand on your own two feet as a man.' Honest to God, Henry Miller said that to *me*. So my advice to you, Bobby Conlon, is to go out there and start plowing."

Troy and I entered Don's Depot and bellied up to the bar. We ordered beers, and I watched the master go to work. He scanned the room with more concentration than he ever used on set, and his face lit up when he saw someone he either knew or wanted to know better.

"I'll be right back," Troy said, walking away.

"Right. I'll see you Monday."

I drank my beer and watched as the women on the crew arrived in pairs and by department. They were freshly bathed, shaved, and moisturized and looking for men to buy them drinks, dazzle them with bullshit, and treat them like ladies instead of co-workers. And if that didn't work, there was always meaningless sex.

Full disclosure: Natalie and I hooked up on an out-of-town job. Actually, it was more like an out-of-town nightmare. *Vampire Serenade* was the worst pig fuck in the history of a business that prides itself on leaving no pig unfucked. The director was a fire-breathing coke fiend who inhaled blow by the Baggieful and thought nothing of dragging the rest of us through the gutter on his insane death-spiral of a movie. This was before America learned to Just Say No, and by the second week the entire crew was snorting their paychecks just to stay awake. The days were twenty hours long with ten hours off to sleep, drink, or score more drugs. Night and day lost all meaning. Grown men whimpered like schoolgirls. Schoolgirls took their toys and ran home to Mommy.

Natalie was the only sane and sober adult on the movie and tried everything to keep it from flying off the rails. She might have succeeded too, but got caught in a downpour and developed a horrible case of bronchitis. Even sick, I found her ravishing—especially when she'd light up a Marlboro in the middle of a coughing jag. One night I saw her hack up something green and ugly and suggested that she spend some time in the hotel's hot tub.

"Great idea," Natalie replied. "Wanna join me?"

Ten hours later I had a brand-new girlfriend and my own case of bronchitis. And the next morning when Natalie's phone rang and she put a finger to her lips as she answered it, I realized I was sleeping with another man's woman.

"Ooh," Dr. Koch said when he heard this juicy tidbit of information. "You never told me Natalie had a history of infidelity."

"I wouldn't exactly call it a history."

"Then why do you find it so shocking that she was unfaithful to you?"

"Jesus, Larry, that was fourteen years ago. Even cancer patients get a clean bill of health after four or five years."

"Cancer isn't an addiction. And as I've told you before, please refer to me as either Doctor or Laurence."

"Whatever."

Endless hours, coked-up co-workers, and a badass lung infection are not a winning combination on a movie. I quit *Vampire Serenade* the night I slipped off the back of the truck and cracked my skull on a hamperful of dolly parts. I felt terrible leaving the other grips in the lurch, but most of them were too fucked up to care. I wrapped a bandanna around my bleeding forehead and called Natalie at the production office to tell her I was leaving.

"You can't do that," she said. "You're the only thing keeping me on this piece-of-shit movie."

"Sorry," I said. "I'll finish the day, but that's it. Book me on the next plane, train, or rickshaw out of this cesspool."

Thirty minutes later Natalie appeared with a suitcase in each hand.

"Grab your stuff," she said. "We're out of here."

"You mean you're quitting too?"

"Yep."

"Can you do that?"

"Fuck it," she said. "We can do whatever we want."

Fuck it, we can do whatever we want. Those were the hottest words I'd ever heard in my life. And as I climbed into the van back to New York, I felt like a red-hot amalgamation of Elvis, Hercules, and Dennis Quaid in *The Big Easy*. But little did I realize—according to Dr. Koch, anyway—that I was just another stop on Natalie's lifelong package tour of infidelities. All aboard! Next stop, Elias Simm.

Knowing my previous locationship lasted fourteen years, I was wary of getting involved with anyone in Texas. I was still legally married, and for some dumb reason—what the hell, let's call it pride—I wanted to maintain my faithful husband status until I signed my divorce papers. Unfortunately, watching the Sex Rodeo without Natalie there to provide color commentary was a lot more depressing than I'd imagined. It's a lot easier to make fun of other people's loneliness when you have a little bit of Old Regular back at the ranch. As I stood there with the sweat from my beer bottle dribbling down my leg and no one to bounce witticisms off of, I felt more like the pimply-faced dork I was in high school than the world-weary New Yorker I fancied myself to be.

"Hey, you!" someone behind me shouted.

I turned and it was Elvira. She was decked out in full cowpunk regalia, with tight jeans, a black tank top, and boots so pointy you could use them to pick brisket from your teeth.

"Howdy, cowgirl."

"Need another beer? The bartender's a pal of mine, and she's slipping me freebies."

"Sure."

"Sorry to hear about you and the missus," Elvira said as we headed toward the bar. "But I did enjoy that e-mail you sent out."

"Not one of my finer moments."

"What are you talking about? You're a role model for burned spouses everywhere."

"That's not the kind of notoriety I want out of life."

"Stop being so F-ing picky. You know what they say—there's no such thing as bad publicity."

"I'll have to remember that when my next wife has an affair."

Friendships in the film business are unique. Lifelong bonds are forged in seconds as the crew is jammed into the tight, hot corners of set. Secrets are revealed, back rubs applied, and dreams spun. Then the movie's over and the crew is torn apart just as fast. Everyone promises to keep in touch, but they never do as they're sucked into the insanity of their lives and careers. Years pass. Christmas cards keep you up to speed on births and address changes, but that's about it. Then the phone rings with a job in Texas or North Carolina. The FedEx Pak arrives with your airline ticket and script, and when you scan the crew list you spot the name of an old friend you haven't seen in a long time. And just like that, the prospect of three months in a strange city without your family or stuff seems bearable. You arrive on location and everyone's a little older and a few pounds heavier, but the smiles are exactly the same. Cheeks are kissed, backs slapped, and conversations get picked up right where they were left off.

"I never would have taken Nat for such a *puta*," Elvira said, handing me a beer. "I always thought she had more class than that."

"Well, Elias is a classy guy."

"That's his name? How could she sleep with somebody named E-li-ass?"

"The same way she slept with somebody named Bobby." I took a pull from my beer. "How's Desmond doing?" Desmond was Elvira's husband, an excellent bass player who had been in a dozen bands, none of which had taken off. On our last job in Texas Natalie and I double-dated with them.

"Desmond's great. He's on tour with Rosanne Cash right now, but he finally got it together to record a CD of his own material. Want to hear it? I got a copy in my truck."

"Sure."

We slipped out the back door to where Elvira's F-150 Super-Crew was parked. Why a five-foot-two-inch movie secretary needed such a big-ass pickup was beyond me, but I had learned never to question Texans about their trucks. Or their guns. Still, I couldn't help but get a dig in.

"You got a tissue?" I asked, climbing into the cab. "The altitude is giving me a nosebleed."

"Save it, Yankee." She slipped a CD in the stereo and fired up a roach from the pile in the ashtray. "You want a hit of this?"

"No, thanks."

We listened to the music, and I sipped on my beer. The CD was well produced, but there was nothing special about it. Nothing at all.

"What do you think?" she asked.

"It's tight."

Elvira sighed. "I know what you mean. For years I told myself that Desmond was this amazing singer-songwriter, and that once he recorded an album of his own stuff the world would see what I did. It turned out to be exactly the opposite. Now I see what everybody else does. That my husband is solid bass player, but that's about it."

"That's nothing to be ashamed of."

"I guess. I was just hoping for something a little better." Elvira turned to me. "You wanna fuck? You know, this being a Sex Rodeo and all."

"C'mon, Elvira, Desmond's my friend."

"That's okay. He's fucked most of my girlfriends one time or another." She leaned in to kiss me, and I pulled away.

"You don't get it, do you? After what Natalie did to me, I—" The words stuck in my throat, and I flailed for the door handle.

"Don't be that way, Bobby."

"Tell Desmond I said hello."

I was hoping to make a dramatic exit, but I forgot how tall Elvira's truck was and fell to the ground like a rodeo clown. Gravel cut into my palms and ruined the one good pair of pants I'd brought to Texas. I didn't know if what Elvira had said about Desmond sleeping with her girlfriends was true, but I knew what it felt like to learn your wife was sleeping with another man, and I was not going to spread that pain around like a virus. Not for Elvira. Not for Henry Miller. Not for anyone.

Everybody knows the story of the woman who confronts her husband with proof of his infidelity, and he replies, "But honey, it didn't *mean* anything to me." There's a variation on this theme unique to the film business that goes, "But honey, it was *out of town*." The logic here being that as long as the affair ends when the movie does, it's okay because it doesn't mean anything. To adulterers, then, affairs are only bad when they mean something. So, how does an affair acquire meaning? When you think about it.

Does this mean that as long as adulterers don't think about what they're doing, it's okay? Bullshit! Everybody knows when they're crossing the line. They just choose to ignore it. The most painful revelation about Natalie's waltz through the sewer with Elias Simm was that she didn't fall into his arms right away. Oh no, they talked about it for an entire month before they got down to business. They thought about it. They weighed the options. They measured the ramifications. And then they fucked. And then they fucked some more.

When I think about the chain of events that destroyed my marriage, it's this month that causes me the most anguish. Why? Because maybe I could have done something to stop it. Maybe I could have been a better husband. Or a more attentive lover. Or I don't know. I *do* know that I wasn't given a fair shot. If I had known that any word, mood, or action might have made the difference between my marriage failing or succeeding, I would have tried harder. I would have brought my A game.

Chapter 10

Sayles Girl

I WOKE UP SUNDAY morning and poured water into the complimentary coffeemaker in the bathroom. Natalie and I had stayed at the Omni on our last job in Austin, and out of perversity I chose our old room. Room 619 was as generic as could be, yet for some weird reason it felt like home. I dug out my Xanax bottle and tossed back the last couple of pills. I had been saving them for a special occasion, but the Sex Rodeo had left me sad and lonesome. Plus, I felt crappy about what had happened with Elvira and stupid for wasting half the night walking back to the Omni. My reentry into the dating game was going to be much harder than I had thought, and I could feel the world turning blue.

If there was one thing I had learned in the months since Natalie dumped me, it was that the best way to fight depression was to keep moving. I poured my complimentary coffee down the drain and left room 619 behind. The elevator stopped on the fourth floor, and the door opened to reveal Carni. She was dressed in black workout clothes and carrying a water bottle.

"Going up?" she asked.

"Down. You going to the gym?"

"That obvious, huh? I didn't see you at the kickoff party last night."

"I left early."

"Where are you off to now?"

"The Starbucks on South Congress to get a Sunday *New York Times*."

"Ooh, can you pick me up one?"

"Sure."

"I wouldn't ask, but they run out early."

"It's not a problem, really."

"Thanks. Just leave it at the front desk for me, or . . . What are you doing this afternoon?

Besides quitting Xanax? "Nothing."

"I'm going to the mall. Want to join me?"

"Why not?"

"Great. Meet me in the lobby at noon."

The elevator closed, and I felt a tingle of guilt in my belly. I agreed to go to the mall because I had nothing better to do, but Carni also happened to be the one person on the movie who could intervene with the insurance company if Mitch's father decided to screw me. Even better, Natalie absolutely despised her. And in the imaginary battle I was waging against the female partner in Miguel-Simm Productions, spending quality time with Carni Bettencourt was a major score. Yes, I know I was acting like a third-grader, but my victories over Natalie were so meager, hard-won, and pathetic that I took everything I could get. And if that meant spending Sunday afternoon in a shopping mall, so be it.

Natalie's hatred for Carni was irrational and intense and could be boiled down to the fact that Carni had a better career. This was almost forgivable, but then Carni went out and lost all that weight. *This* was pure heresy. It didn't matter that Carni looked like she'd just finished chemo. She could now squeeze into a size two—something Natalie hadn't been able to do since she'd quit smoking years earlier. If Carni lobbed a flaming sack of dog shit into our living room while Natalie hosted a fantasy dinner party for Audrey Hepburn, Mick Jagger, and Gandhi, she could not have pissed her off more.

My history with Carni went back more than a decade before her trip under the knife. I knew her as one of the original Sayles Girls, a group of five women who had broken into the business working for independent filmmaker John Sayles and whose cult-like devotion to him approached the perverse. The Sayles Girls were a tight-knit, bitchy, and arrogant bunch who looked down on anyone who didn't work for "real filmmakers like John." Naturally, this included everybody but them. Except the Sayles Girls harbored a dirty little secret. Despite the award-winning films on their résumés, they didn't know shit about making movies for anyone other than John Sayles.

I met Carni on a tomato sauce commercial that was her first job without the rest of her coven. The shoot was a disaster, and after fifteen grueling hours Carni was forced to negotiate an overtime deal with the crew to keep us from walking off the job. It had never occurred to her to put overtime in the budget. There was never overtime on a John Sayles film because everyone "did it for John." The bad news for Carni was that everyone did commercials for the money. The guys representing the crew were brutal and called her names that would make a Teamster blush.

I found Carni outside the soundstage with tears streaming down her face. I put an arm around her shoulders, walked her around the block, and tried my best to explain the importance of not giving a shit. There was nothing sexual about this, by the way. Back then Carni was as arousing as a bag of grass clippings. I thought I was doing the right thing, but in retrospect, this act of kindness turned out to be a mistake. I'd seen Carni in a moment of weakness that she preferred not to remember. She'd had plenty of opportunities to hire me after that tomato sauce fiasco, but never did. This job was the first time we'd worked together in six-teen years.

I was making a rough estimate of the money I'd lost by being nice to Carni when she failed to show up at noon. I waited an-other fifteen minutes, grabbed her *New York Times,* and took the elevator to her room. Carni greeted me at the door wearing a matching bathrobe and phone. She mouthed the words *I'm sorry* and gestured for me to come inside. I placed the newspaper on her bed and wandered into the adjoining room, which was set up like a mini production office.

I heard Carni say, "Well, Ryan likes him, and if nobody has the balls to call Julia in Prague, then I vote to wait and see what hap-pens when Ryan's movie opens next weekend."

It sounded like our director's head really was on the chopping block.

Carni was making the right move by putting off the decision to fire Sir Richard. The longer we shot, the more money we spent. The more money we spent, the less likely the studio was to pull the plug—especially if, as Carni pointed out, nobody had the balls to call Julia Roberts and ask her opinion.

"I'm not sticking up for him," Carni said. "But I am the person down here in cow-cow land actually making this movie. If you're not going to support the man you hired, then fire him already and send me down someone who can shoot a call sheet in less than fourteen hours."

There was an old copy of *The Austin Chronicle* lying on a table and I picked it up to see that both Megadeth and Harry Connick, Jr., had played in town the week before. They didn't call Austin the Live Music Capital of the World for nothing.

"Sorry about being late," Carni said from the doorway.

"That's okay, I'm in no hurry."

"How much of that conversation did you hear?" she asked when I joined her in the next room.

"Enough to know that I'm glad I don't have your job."

Carni sighed. "Can I ask you a favor and—"

I held up my hand. "Don't worry, Katherine, I've been hearing conversations like that for years. Your secret's safe with me."

"I forgot about that. Was it ever a problem with Natalie?"

"Being in bed with production? No, it's like anything else. You learn what you can say and what you can't."

"Like to Moose?"

Shit, busted.

"What do you mean?" I sputtered.

"C'mon, Bobby. One minute you say I can trust you, and the next minute you lie to me. What's it gonna be?"

"Was I right? Were they gonna shut down the movie?"

"No, but only because advance word on *Trail of Broken Hearts* is so good. If it's a hit, we all look like geniuses for hiring Ryan Donahue for scale plus ten."

"What happens if it's dead on arrival?"

"I don't know. I just want to make it through the next week alive." Carni craned her neck and said, "Have you ever been to a chiropractor?"

"I'm a grip. What do you think?"

"You know how they crack your back between your shoulder blades? Could you do that to me?"

"I don't want to hurt you, Carn—Katherine."

"Don't worry. You couldn't make it worse than it already is." She climbed onto the bed and said, "Why'd you do it, anyway?"

"Do what?"

"Start that rumor."

"Take a deep breath and exhale slowly."

I placed my hands between Carni's shoulders and pressed. Even through her robe, I could feel how loose the skin was over her bones. It grossed me out, but I kept pressing until a few vertebrae cracked.

"How was that?"

She rotated her shoulder. "You got some, but not all of them."

"The bed's too soft. Those tables in chiropractors' offices are a lot more firm."

"Try it on the floor."

We got down on the carpet, and I leaned over her.

"Take a deep breath and exhale slowly," I said, pushing down. Her vertebrae popped like bubble wrap.

"Oh God, that was it," she said. "So why'd you do it?"

"Talk about wham, bam, crack you, ma'am. I feel so cheap."

"You gonna tell me or not?"

I couldn't say that Hank wanted me to set a fire under the crew because that would have sounded like he was going behind her back. Instead, I said, "I'm hooked on Xanax, and I couldn't quit in New York with all the ghosts of my marriage floating around. If the studio shut down the movie I was hosed."

Carni snorted. "That's the first time I've heard that one."

"Thanks for the compassion."

"Too bad. I should fire your ass for all the trouble you caused."

"Sorry."

"Is it true what they say about Xanax?"

"What do you mean?"

"You know. That it, uh, affects your performance."

"That's Prozac. Xanax doesn't work that way."

"I was hoping you'd say that," Carni said with a smile.

There was a crackle of static electricity, and Carni pulled open her robe to offer herself to me. I'm no lingerie fiend, but I've spent enough time with the Victoria's Secret catalogue to know that what Carni wore beneath her robe was utterly unique. It was a combination full-body stocking and girdle with woven elastic panels over the belly, adjustable Velcro straps on the sides, and a three-foot zipper up the middle. Despite the ornate lace trim, the thing looked more like a piece of grip equipment than an article of clothing. And it was not a turn-on.

"I'm sorry, Katherine. I can't."

There was another burst of static, and Carni pulled the robe tight to her neck. For a moment I thought she was going to cry.

"It's not that I don't want to," I said, hoping to rescue whatever chance I had of her helping me with the insurance company. "But . . . and I know this may sound like the dumbest thing in the world, but I swore on the day I married Natalie that I'd remain faithful to her, and until I sign my divorce papers that's exactly what I plan on doing."

Carni looked deep into my eyes and the smile returned to her lips. "When's that?" she asked.

"Her attorney said something about the end of the month."

"I've waited sixteen years for you, Bobby. I guess I can wait a little longer."

The worst thing about film school is that it gives you a taste of what it's like to direct. And oh, what a sweet and addictive flavor that is. There's no greater rush on this planet than leaning forward and saying "Action." It's honey, sex, and heroin combined. The cameras roll and the outside world fades away. The characters rise from the page and become human and magnificent right there in front of you. They have memories that go back for decades and lives that stretch on forever. You see dreams in their eyes and want to protect them like children. I wasn't proud of lying to Carni, but I had no choice. The last year of my life had busted me up inside. Without Natalie or my truck to hold me together, I was in danger of falling apart completely. That's why making a movie was so important to me. Directing was the only thing I cared enough about to pull myself together for.

I've waited sixteen years for you, Bobby. I guess I can wait a little longer.

Damn, was that terrific dialogue, or what? And somebody said it to me. Beaten-down, screwed-over, tossed-aside me. Talk about an ego enhancer. There's nothing like a woman confessing to sixteen years of unrequited passion to make you feel like you belong on the cover of a romance novel.

That said, I absolutely had to get the money for my truck before my divorce papers came through, because there was no way in hell I was sleeping with Carni Bettencourt. And it wasn't for the obvious reasons. Like most successful people in the film business, Carni had a presence and allure that went way beyond her appearance. She was classy and bright and exactly the kind of woman I would have hooked up with if I hadn't hooked up with someone just like her fourteen years earlier. We have a little saying around the grip truck: Hit yourself in the face with a hammer and you're an idiot. Hit yourself in the face with a hammer a second time and you're a fucking idiot.

Chapter 11

Frick and Frack

Q: How many producers does it take to
   screw in a lightbulb?
A: Producers don't screw in lightbulbs.
   Producers screw in hot tubs.

FRICK AND FRACK were the two knuckleheads producing our movie, and if they weren't the root of all evil, they were definitely the trunk and leaves. Frick's real name was Joe Testa and Frack's real name was Jeff DeBlasio. Or vice versa. It didn't matter because Frick and Frack did everything together. People said this was because Frick and Frack didn't trust each other, and Joe was worried that Jeff was going to stab him in the back the moment he turned around. Or vice versa.

Of all the jobs on a movie, the producer's is the most spongy. It used to be the producer was the guy responsible for developing the project and securing the financing. Nowadays, people are so hot to see their names on the silver screen it's not uncommon to see three, five, or ten producers weighing down the opening credits of a movie. What do they all do? The hell if I know. On our job, Frick and Frack were the producers, Hank the executive producer, and Carni the line producer. What that really meant was that

Hank put the project together, Carni handled day-to-day operations, and Frick and Frack played golf with the suits who ran the studio.

Frick and Frack spent their first hours in Texas buying boots, jeans, and Stetsons and arrived on set looking like a couple of rejects from the West Village rodeo. The moment Frack (or was it Frick?) climbed out of their longhorn Mercedes he marched straight up to the publicity photographer and yelled, "Hey, stills, are there any cows or horses around here? I need you to take some pictures of us with lots of Texas shit in the background. My guy at *The Hollywood Reporter* wants to do a feature."

We were in downtown Austin at the time.

Frick and Frack had cell phones glued to their ears every waking moment of the day and carried extra phone batteries the way diabetics carried insulin. It was never hard to know what they were thinking or who they were talking to, because Frick and Frack did everything at maximum volume: "Marty, baby! It's me, Joe. You'll never guess where I am. No, not the Ivy. I'm in Texas. What you think I'm doing here, drilling for gold? I'm making a picture. Yeah, that's right, the Julia Roberts thing. The story? It's kind of like *Bridges of Madison County*, only without all those fucking bridges. Wait, I got a call on the other line. What? Who's this? Robert, baby! How the hell are you? You'll never guess where I am. No, not the Ivy. I'm in fucking Texas . . ."

And on it went. Frick and Frack blew three takes within twenty minutes of arriving and Reg banned all cell phones from set. This didn't stop Joe and Jeff from spending the rest of the day crammed inside their Mercedeses with the air conditioner blasting. For as much attention as they paid the movie, they could have been in LA. Of course, then they'd have had nothing to talk about on their cell phones: "Morris, baby! It's me, Jeff. You'll never guess where I am . . . Yeah, right, the Ivy. How'd ya know?"

Nobody appeared more relieved to see Frick and Frack disappear than Carni. It was embarrassing enough to be listed next to them on the crew list, but when Carni had to sit beside them in Video Village she looked as happy as a recovering alcoholic at a wine-tasting. With Frick and Frack out of the way she could return to what she'd been doing all morning, which was making goo-goo eyes at me.

The attention was flattering, but I was torn. I thought I'd have no problem stringing Carni along until I got my money, but I could feel the guilt monster eating away at my insides. Combine that with the Xanax monkey hanging from my back, and the memory of Carni's freaky girdle contraption bouncing around in my brain, and I was a wreck. I had to do something to distract myself, and pulled out my cell phone to call Roz Chaffman, Natalie's divorce attorney.

"Where are you, lovey?" Roz asked when I got her on the line.

"Texas."

"Texas? What are you doing in Texas? Don't you need to get shots to go there?"

"I'm working on a movie."

"Oh, fabulous! Did I tell you my daughter Beverly's father-in-law was in the business?"

"I think so."

"He's general council for one of the big cable networks. I don't remember which one. Personally, I don't approve of a lot of what they show on cable. I watched that *Sex and the City* once, and I couldn't believe what came out of their mouths. Absolutely disgusting. But the body on that Sarah Jessica Parker—my God. Even after she had the baby. For a body like that, even I would go to the gym. So what can I do for you, lovey?"

"I was wondering when the divorce papers are going to be ready."

"Sandra's out this week getting her wisdom teeth removed, but I'm sure they'll be done by the time you get back."

"I'm not getting back until the holidays."

"Yom Kippur or Rosh Hashanah?"

"Christmas, Roz."

"Oh, they'll be done by then. Give us two weeks."

"There's no rush."

"Don't forget, you still have to get them notarized."

"They have notary publics in Texas."

"Not ones licensed by the state of New York, they don't."

"You mean I gotta fly back to New York to sign the papers?"

"Either that or I can fly one out to you."

"You're kidding me."

"Of all the things in the world, why would I kid about that?"

I said good-bye to Roz and walked to craft service for a Diet Coke. With me in Texas and Natalie in LA, it would be months before we signed the divorce papers. It would be tricky breaking the news to Carni, but it looked like I could get out of Texas without having a close encounter of the flabby kind. Excellent.

"You want a B-twelve shot, Bobby?" Meg, the craft service gal, asked.

"Why? Do I look tired?"

"You're working on a movie. What do you think?"

"Sure. Why not?"

I rolled up my sleeve, and Meg rubbed an alcohol swab on my arm. As she took out her syringe I looked down at the spread laid out before me: doughnuts, granola, chips, Twizzlers, energy bars, soup, vitamins, Advil, Tums, Band-Aids, Sea Breeze, and a dozen types of beverages both hot and cold. No wonder everyone but Carni was ten pounds overweight.

"Les, baby!" Frick (or maybe it was Frack) said as he approached the table. "It's Jeff. You'll never guess where I am. No, not the Ivy. I'm in Texas. Yeah, the Julia Roberts thing, that's right. Naw, she's already wrapped and in Prague. Huh? It's kind of like

A River Runs Through It only without all those fucking rivers. Wait a second . . . Hey, doll, what's in the needle?"

"B-twelve."

"Izat legal?"

"Sure. When I'm not working on movies I work for EMS."

"No shit." Frack turned to look for Frick. "Hey, Joe! Get your ass over here and get a shot with me."

"What kind of shot?"

"B-twelve. C'mon, it's good for you."

"Izat legal?"

"Yeah, this girl's a PMS."

I waltzed back to camera on a B_{12} high and met Carni along the way.

"Hey, boss," I said.

"Don't call me that."

"Oh, sorry."

"It's Miss Boss to you." Carni smiled.

"Yes, Miss Boss."

Back at the craft service table Frick and Frack were arguing over who would get the first shot.

Carni shook her head. "Look at those two."

"How'd they ever make it in Hollywood?"

"They are Hollywood." Carni touched my cheek. "God, I miss New York."

"Why don't you move back?"

"I'm in LA now."

"But if you miss New York . . ."

"Once you've had a kitchen bigger than a phone booth it's kind of hard to go back."

"What about all the great museums and stuff?"

"When was the last time you went to a museum?"

"I don't know. A couple years ago."

"Both cities have their trade-offs. New York has culture, but it's hard to live there. LA is easy, but it's a cultural vacuum."

"What about Philly?"

"No, thanks. I served my time in Philadelphia."

As we got closer to set I saw Troy pulling a small case off the camera cart.

"Here comes the viewfinder," I said. "Gotta go."

"See you."

"Yes, Miss Boss."

"Bobby," Carni whispered as I walked away.

"Yeah?"

"Sit next to me tonight at dailies."

I arrived at camera as Troy placed the viewfinder in Andrzej's hand. Andrzej brought it to his eye, leaned down six inches, and said, "Here."

I marked the position as Andrzej walked backward and crew members jumped out of his way. He stopped, fine-tuned his shot, and said, "So tell me, Bobby, darling. Have you started fucking our little line producer yet?"

Shit! How did he know? "I have no idea what you're talking about, Andrzej."

"Don't lie to me, Bobby, darling. Otherwise I'll do terrible things to you."

I took the measurement and said, "Not yet. Soon, maybe."

"Not soon. Tonight. Her little pussy is wet for you."

"Not until I sign my divorce papers."

Andrzej stared at me, and when he saw I wasn't joking grabbed my shoulder and dug his fingers under my collarbone. "Why are you playing games with her?"

"Sorry, I didn't know you liked her."

"I don't. But I want her to produce my movie." He dug his fingers in deeper. "This better not have anything to do with your wife and that boyfriend of hers. I don't care what it says in *Vari-*

ety, I'm the one who's going to be directing that third movie for Hank Sullivan. And if you get in my way I'll pop your head like a pimple."

Andrzej let go.

"Jesus," I said, rubbing my shoulder. "Can't a guy just be true to his marriage vows anymore?"

Andrzej shook his head and said, "Not in this business."

Chapter 12

Dailies

Harrison Ford dies and goes to Heaven. He arrives at the pearly gates, and Saint Peter tells him there's a short wait and to take a seat in the waiting room.

"Don't you know who I am?" he asks. "I'm Harrison Ford. I was in *Star Wars*! I played Indiana Jones!"

"Of course we know you, Mr. Ford, and we're all big fans. But this is Heaven and people are admitted on a first come, first served basis."

Peeved, but seeing no alternative, Harrison Ford takes a seat and picks up a copy of *People*. He's halfway through an article on Jennifer Aniston when he glances up and spies a man with a long white beard and flowing robes holding a viewfinder to his eye and telling a group of angels where to lay some dolly track.

Harrison Ford can't believe his eyes. He

jumps out of his chair and runs straight to Saint Peter.

"I can't believe this place!" Harrison Ford screams. "You let a cameraman into Heaven before me!"

"What are you talking about?" Saint Peter asks.

"I just saw a guy with a long white beard telling some angels where to lay dolly track."

"That's not a cameraman," Saint Peter says with a laugh. "That's just God. He only *thinks* he's a cameraman."

DAILIES ARE A screening of the previous day's work. Every shot, angle, and acceptable frame is strung together and shown unedited, one after another. Andrzej was one of the last cameramen who screened dailies on film instead of DVD, and he required the camera crew, gaffer, and dolly grip to attend. This sucked in New York, where all I wanted to do at the end of a hard day was go home and collapse, but it was great on location. While the rest of the crew got stuck wrapping the truck, I parked the dolly by the lift gate and hopped in the first van out of there.

Food was important at dailies, or at least it was to Andrzej. He spent most of the day discussing and debating dinner options until he arrived at precisely what he wanted to nosh on that evening. Beer and wine were served, and if the food was late or the beer less than icy cold, the appropriate parties were flogged. If someone fell asleep during dailies, he got a slap upside the head or a beer dumped in his lap. Of course, when Andrzej fell asleep you had to be extra quiet or he'd wake up in a foul mood and throw a beer bottle at you.

I scored a couple of excellent seats for dailies, but Carni was late and I had to give them up. It hurt to part with such good real estate, but I didn't want to make it look like I was saving her a seat. As more crew members arrived, I had to move farther and farther back in the room. It was Frick and Frack's first time at dailies, and we quickly learned that the brains behind such masterpieces of modern cinema as *Toboggan Bunnies* and *Scooter and Timmy's Acapulco Vacation* watched dailies like a couple of fourteen-year-olds in their parents' basement.

"Holy shit, Jeff. Didja see that fucking shot?"

"What? You think I'm blind? Of course I saw that fucking shot."

"Just making sure you're still awake. Jesus, these cowboy boots are killing me. Maybe I should take 'em back for a bigger size."

"You can't take 'em back. You've been wearing 'em all day."

"Big deal. My wife buys shit at Fred Segal and wears it for weeks before she takes it back. Half the clothes in her closet have price tags on them."

"You can do that?"

"Fuckin' A. As long as you don't have stuff altered they'll take back anything."

"No shit."

As luck would have it, the first scene up was the Julia Roberts debacle, and we watched in embarrassed silence as the sights and sounds of failure filled the screen. The mood in the room grew uglier with each take, and I kept expecting Andrzej to pummel Sir Richard with a wine bottle.

"Jesus fucking Christ, Andrzej," Frack said. "This scene looks like shit. The way you lit it I can't tell if that person on the screen is Julia Roberts or Robert De Niro."

"Hell," Frick joined in, "I can't tell if it's Julia Roberts or Julia Child."

"Or Raul Julia."

"Or Julia Louis-Dreyfus."

"Or Julia Boyle?"

"Who's that?"

"Some chick I nailed in high school."

"You didn't nail any chicks in high school, you lying sack of shit. You were jacking it the whole time just like I was."

"*Enough!*" Sir Richard Davis screamed. "The scene is fine. Joe and Jeff, please either shut up or leave. Thank you."

"Uh, sorry," Frick muttered.

"Don't you apologize to that Queen Anne faggot," Frack hissed in Frick's ear. "He works for you and me just like the rest of 'em."

"Yeah, but he was right."

"Like I care? Nobody disses us in front of the crew."

Carni sat beside me.

"What's going on?" she whispered.

"Sir Richard just got into it with Joe and Jeff. Jesus, watching dailies with these guys is a nightmare."

"You should try going to casting sessions with them. I kept expecting them to ask the actresses to take their shirts off." Carni eased her knee next to mine, and I could feel the static electricity pulling the hairs on my leg toward her. It tickled, and I was surprised by how sexy it felt. She placed a hand on my leg, and I had no choice but to place my hand over hers. In the dark I could almost pretend it was Natalie.

"Hey, Andrzej," Frack shouted. "Am I going nuts or is the camera moving in?"

"Yes, it's a Mickey Rooney."

"Mickey Rooney? What the hell's a Mickey Rooney?"

"A little creep!" the entire crew shouted in unison.

"A little creep? That's a good one. Hey, dolly guy, you here?"

"Yeah."

"Good Mickey Rooney, man."

"Thanks."

The roll ended and the lights came up as the projectionist changed reels. Carni's hand retreated to her lap, as did mine. Andrzej stood up to stretch and spied Carni sitting next to me.

"Katherine, darling, you certainly look lovely this evening."

"Thank you, Andrzej."

"What about you, Bobby? Don't you think Katherine looks lovely?"

Fucking Andrzej. "Absolutely."

"What the hell was that about?" Carni whispered as soon as the lights went down.

"Andrzej knows about us."

"How? Did you tell him?"

"Of course not. He saw us making eyes at each other and put two and two together. The guy doesn't miss a thing."

"Hmm," Carni said, erecting a wall of ice between us. I kept waiting for her to put her hand back on my leg, and when she didn't, I felt surprisingly disappointed. *Oh, what the hell?* I thought and put a finger on her leg. She placed her hand over mine and for the rest of dailies all was right with the world.

"Do you want to grab a quick drink after I check my voice mail?" Carni asked when the lights came up. "I have to meet with Joe and Jeff at ten, but that gives us forty minutes."

"Sure."

Carni dashed off to her office, and I munched on some cold moo shu pork left over from dinner. When that got sickening, I stopped by the crew mailboxes and read a lengthy but exquisitely written memo from Elvira on laundry procedures. *Yet another college degree gone to waste,* I thought, and sighed. I heard the pitter-patter of Gucci mules and looked up to see Carni walking toward me. Our eyes met, and I was about to say something witty and suave when Andrzej's voice boomed across the room.

"Those divorce papers arrive yet, Bobby, darling?"

The smile fell from Carni's face, and she stomped past me. I couldn't decide whether to run after her or hit Andrzej with a chair. I chose Option C: crunched up my laundry memo and threw it at Andrzej. It hit him in the back of the head, and he spun around to face me.

"You better get some sleep tonight, Bobby, darling, because tomorrow morning you're slime."

"I'm already slime, Andrzej."

"What? From little Carni running away like that? That's *nothing*. Go fuck her, and she'll forget everything."

I ran to the hotel, but Carni wasn't at the bar. I called her room, but there was no answer. With no other place to go, I took the elevator to the sixth floor and found her sitting outside my door.

"Katherine," I said as soon as I saw her.

"I thought you said you didn't tell him anything."

"You don't understand. Andrzej's like Hannibal Lecter. He gets people to do things they don't want to."

"It's not funny, Bobby. I'm not going to turn into some kind of grip truck joke."

"You're not. Look, I can't control what other people do."

"That's right, you can't even control yourself. I can't believe you told him about your divorce papers."

"It slipped out. He threatened me with bodily harm."

"What? He said he'd hit you?"

"Worse. He threatened to work me to death."

"If you're not going to be serious—"

"I am serious. On the first job I did with Andrzej the AD screwed up the schedule and called us in three hours early. Andrzej had nothing to do, and just to fuck with me, he set up a dolly shot that ended two feet into the side of a mountain. I spent three hours in ninety-degree heat hacking away at solid rock with a shovel. By the time I was finished, my hands were bloody with blisters and I could barely raise my arms. And then the asshole cut the shot."

"What did you do?"

"Nothing. He was my boss. I took a handful of Advil and went back to work."

"Really?"

"Sure, and he's going to do the same thing to me tomorrow."

"Why?"

" 'Cause I beaned him with Elvira's laundry memo."

"That was stupid."

"Fuck him, he shouldn't have embarrassed you like that."

Wham! Carni was all over me. She threw her arms around my neck, and I barely had time to catch a breath before she jammed her tongue down my throat. I returned the kiss. It was undeniably pleasant until I wrapped my arms around her waist and felt the skin slosh back and forth under her Jil Sander blouse. *There is no way I'm having sex with this woman,* I told myself. But Carni had me up against the door to my room, and it wasn't like I could run away. Not to mention that there were a hundred and fifty thousand dollars and my future as a film director on the line. I felt tawdry and cheap.

The elevator rang, and I heard footsteps approaching.

"Somebody's coming," I said, breaking free.

"I don't care."

"Well, I do."

Carni stared at me. From her expression I could tell that she thought I was embarrassed to be seen with her. She was right, of course, but I didn't want her to know that. "You know how people talk in this business," I whispered. "I don't want them thinking this is some kind of one-night thing."

"You're right," she whispered back.

I was hoping she'd take this as a cue to hightail it down the hallway, but she didn't move, and I was forced to dig into my cargo shorts for my key card. I was still searching when Medea and Georgette appeared.

"And what do we have here?" Georgette asked.

"Hey, guys," I said, trying to act like Carni and I weren't totally busted. "Did either of you save this morning's *USA Today*? I was telling Katherine about this article in the Life section, but I think the maid threw out my copy."

"Which article was that, Bobby? The one on premarital sex?"

"Oh gawd."

"I have no idea what you're talking about, Georgette."

"Hmm . . . Sorry, but I left mine in the van on the way to set."

"Darn," Carni said.

"You ladies have a nice night," I said, finding my key card and slipping it in the door.

"You two do the same," Georgette replied.

Then we were in my room, and Carni was all over me again. On any other night, I could have come up with a plausible excuse to get rid of her, but my brain was trashed from Xanax withdrawal. *Maybe I can fake an epileptic seizure?* I thought as Carni reached between my legs and found an erection that had appeared out of nowhere. So much for excuses.

"And what do we have here?"

"Damned if I know."

"I guess we'll just have to see, then," she said as she unsnapped my cargo shorts.

It had been centuries since a woman had gone down on me, and if it was anyone else but Carni Bettencourt, I would have been thrilled. But I couldn't get the snap, crackle, and pop of her orthopedic undies out of my mind, and the thought of what lurked underneath them was terrifying. Besides, in the eyes of God, man, and the Empire State I was still legally married.

"C-Carn, Kate, Katherine, hold on a second. Stop."

"What?" she said, looking up.

"I—I spoke to Natalie's divorce attorney today. She said that the papers will be here in a couple of weeks, but I won't be able to sign them until I get back home."

"Why?"

"They have to be notarized by somebody licensed in New York."

"You're kidding me."

"I wish I was."

"Then today's your lucky day. *I'm* a New York State notary public."

"What?"

"I haven't used it for years, but it came in handy when I worked for John Sayles."

"Well, I'll be fucked," I said.

"Not for two weeks," Carni replied, taking me in her hand. "But this ought to hold you until then."

Erect, defeated, and out of excuses, I closed my eyes and let Carni have her way with me.

Chapter 13

■■■■■■■

Slime

Q: What's the difference between a PA and
   a roll of gaffer's tape?
A: You can't make a roll of gaffer's tape
   cry.

Slime was Andrzej's favorite expression for that infamous entry-level position known as production assistant or intern. Such is the power and allure of cinema that it doesn't matter where you work, there is always an endless supply of fresh meat lined up and begging to be ground into breakfast sausage. And lucky for them, the film business is filled with people who love to crank that grinder. Though it's not like we don't warn them. I always tell potential slime that they'll be called upon to do lots of really difficult things. But it doesn't matter what you say, their response is always the same:

"That's okay. I'll do anything. I'll even get coffee."

Even get coffee? Wow, I never realized that running to Starbucks for a Grande no-fat latte was such a challenging assignment. So please, allow me to spell it out for you, pencil dick. In a business where cruelty is looked upon as the highest form of human expression, somebody asking you to fetch him coffee is the real-world equivalent of a slap on the back or a hundred-dollar tip. I've seen slime forced to do everything from scrubbing the crew's underwear with a toothbrush to scoring drugs, to sleeping in line for playoff tickets, to getting beer, to picking up sales brochures for all-inclusive sex tours of Southeast Asia, to eating fire ants, to massaging every piece of equipment on the grip truck with baby oil (guilty!), to getting beer, to identifying a dead body, to buying chocolate-flavored condoms and teenage midget transvestite porn, to getting beer, to simonizing a '67 El Camino, to getting beer, to walking down Seventh Avenue holding a male love doll with a hard-on the size of a forty-ounce malt liquor bottle.

Oh, and did I mention getting beer?

Slime, slave, minion, gofer, lackey, junior assistant toilet bowl cleaner—call them what you want. The important thing is to treat them like dirt. Why? Because you can. And because it's fun. And because somebody did it to you five, ten, or twenty years ago. It's a rite of passage like the bar exam, circumcision, or taking a shower in sixth-grade gym class. Somebody has to show the little fucks that working on movies is a divine privilege and not to be taken for granted. Constant and never-ending abuse keeps the slime on their toes and teaches them to remain calm in the face of impossible pressure. Besides, misery loves company, and picking on those beneath you is the best way there is to pass along that load of shit your boss just dumped in your lap. 'Cause here's another little secret about the film biz: it doesn't matter who you are, or how many movies you've worked on, sooner or later you're gonna be somebody's slime.

Andrzej's revenge was swift and merciless. At exactly one second after seven he fired Mitch, marked off a one-hundred-and-eighty-foot dolly shot, and demanded two eighteen-foot towers of scaffolding. The fat son-of-a-bitch wanted to break me, and if I weren't so determined to get my money and make my movie, he would have succeeded. I'd had so little sleep and had so much to do in such a short period of time that there was no room for panic or anger. Worse, the rest of the grips were so freaked out by Andrzej's antics that they were less than useless. The final straw came when one of the local grips accidentally smashed me in the forehead with a crate of wedges.

"You guys suck!" I screamed. "Get the hell out of here and send me Sara Lee." I rubbed my forehead and saw blood on my fingertips. "Fuck!"

"Are you incapable of performing the minor but necessary tasks I need of you this morning, Bobby, darling?"

I turned to face the personification of all things evil and Polish. Andrzej was perched in his director's chair and staring at me through a rolled-up copy of *The Hollywood Reporter*.

"I'm cool, Andrzej. Can I get you anything from craft service?"

"No, thank you. I'll just sit here and enjoy the lovely view."

"You wanted to see me, Bobby?" came a voice from behind me.

I spun around and Sara Lee was standing there. It was her first time on set and she looked so happy I thought she was going to dance a jig.

"I need a hand laying some track."

"You're bleeding."

"I know." I pulled a bandanna from my back pocket and tied it around my head. "So what has Steveo taught you so far?"

"I know the names for most of the equipment, and I can tie a bowline, a square knot, and a clove hitch."

"How are you at carrying dolly track?"

"Okay, I guess."

"You got the job. Let's go."

Working with Sara Lee was easier than I expected. She did ex-

actly what I asked and was surprisingly well coordinated for someone so gangly. The hardest part was having to deal with the other
grips back at the truck. Mitch was frothing at the mouth, Steveo
could barely form meaningful sentences, and the local guys just
stared at the ground with their hands in their pockets. While Sara
Lee and I humped eighteen pieces of track, three crates of wedges,
and everything else needed to level the dolly shot, the rest of the
crew did nothing. It was time to play boss.

"Okay, listen up," I said. "Mitch, love to love ya, baby, but go
back to the hotel. *Now.* Steveo, get on the phone and find me a
new grip. You two, finish the towers. *Now.* Any questions? My
door's always open. Any comments or philosophical differences?
Save 'em for lunch. All right? *All right?*"

"This is such a fucking having."

"No shit, Steveo. So get used to it, or get gone. Okay? *Okay?*"

"Yeah."

"Mitch, c'mere for a second." I wrapped an arm around his
shoulder and walked him away from the truck. "I know this sucks,
but I'm buried right now, and I can't have you here stirring up the
rest of the crew. Don't worry, I'll make sure you get paid for the
rest of the week, but you have to get out of here. Okay?"

"Just tell me one thing."

"What's that?"

"What did I do wrong? Just tell me that. What did I do
wrong?"

"I don't know, and I don't have time to discuss it. I'll meet you
at the bar after dailies and we can talk about it then. All right?"

"Yeah, sure."

"Hey, Bobby."

"What is it?" I screamed, spinning around to face Steveo.
From his reaction, I could tell that I'd crossed the line from boss
to asshole. "Sorry, man," I said in a soft and sensitive voice.
"What's up?"

"How about hiring Sara Lee as the extra man?"

He had a point. Sara Lee was the only grip helping me, and the only grip not getting paid. I took a deep breath and tried to recall what was coming up on the schedule. There were some tough days ahead, and as much as I wanted to help Sara Lee, I had no idea how long Andrzej was going to fuck with me.

"I wish I could, but she's not ready yet."

Steveo nodded. "Yeah, you're right."

I slapped him on the back and said, "I know Mitch is your guy, and if you want to quit, I'll understand. All I ask is that you find me a decent best boy before you leave. Okay?"

"Sure."

I ran back to set and found Sara Lee sitting in Video Village. Andrzej had an arm around her shoulder and was feeding her a grilled cheese sandwich cut into bite-size pieces.

"Sara Lee, could you come here for a minute, please?"

She stood and Andrzej said, "That's all right, Sara Lee. Bobby will let you stay and finish your sandwich. Won't you, Bobby, darling?"

"Finish your sandwich, Sara Lee."

I laid out eighteen sections of dolly track, locked them together, and tossed a handful of wooden wedges near every joint. I turned and found Sara Lee standing next to me.

"Enjoy your sandwich?" I asked.

"Yes, I've never had provolone cheese before."

"That's terrific."

"Andrzej's a very nice man."

"Do you go to church, Sara Lee?"

"We're Church of Christ."

"Do you guys have Satan?"

"Do we ever."

"Good, because I'm about to do you a very big favor. You see that man over there?"

"You mean Andrzej?"

"That's not really Andrzej. That's the devil. And you stay away from him."

I could see she had no idea what I was talking about. "Forget what I just said. Let's talk about leveling dolly track. The first thing you gotta do is figure out which rail is highest. That's easy here because the ground slopes down. You with me so far?"

"I think so."

"Good."

I got down on my belly and put an eye to the high rail like I was aiming a shotgun. "Next, you find the high point on the high rail and raise everything up to it. That's what all the wedges are for. After that, you level the low rail with the high rail and you're good to go.

"I get it, it's like laying a brick wall."

"You know how to lay bricks?"

"No, but I've seen them do it on the Home and Garden Channel."

Reg ran up to us. "Yo, Bobby, Andrzej wants to know when the car rigs will be ready."

"That scene's not scheduled until after lunch," I said, climbing to one knee. "I'm not even going to start thinking about it for another couple of hours."

"I hate to break it to you, pal, but the car rigs are up first."

"What?"

"Andrzej flipped the schedule ten minutes ago. He said the light was better in the morning."

"It's two guys in a car. We could shoot it anytime."

"That's what I thought, but Andrzej insisted."

"Okay, how much time do I have?"

Reg checked his watch. "A half an hour."

"Can I leave this track here?"

"No, Andrzej says it's in the crane shot."

"What crane shot?"

"The one Andrzej added five minutes ago."

The morning blasted by in a blur of insanity as I tore down the track, mounted two cameras on a picture car, and assembled the crane. Movie cranes are like giant seesaws with a camera platform on one end and a weight bucket on the other. The two ends have to be perfectly balanced or the crane won't move. High-end cranes arrive preassembled and use hydraulic pumps and liquid mercury to balance the ends. Cheap cranes are a bitch to put together and are balanced with twenty-pound lead weights that you have to schlep up a ladder one at a time. Guess which kind we had. Like horses and helicopters, cranes are one of those cinematic thrill rides that every numb-nuts in Video Village feels the need to get his picture taken riding. Not only is this a major pain in the butt, it's also incredibly dangerous. Cranes may look warm and fuzzy as they glide through the air, but one mistake and they turn into a catapults.

My anger at having to sling a ton of lead was eclipsed by the memory of Carni going down on me the night before. Oral sex had long ago vanished from Natalie's bedroom repertoire, and I was surprised by how good Carni's perky little blow job left me feeling. Better still, I was saved from having to return the gift when the clock struck ten and Carni had to rush off to meet Frick and Frack.

The shot began high in the air and ended in a medium close-up of Ryan Donahue eating a sandwich. Steveo manned the back of the crane, and I had the front. Steveo started the move when Ryan Donahue walked out of a building and down a flight of steps. I took over as the camera reached shoulder height and eased it to the ground when Ryan sat down on a bench. It was an easy move, and as long as Steveo and I didn't blow the handoff, there was very little to distract me from thinking about Carni's oral antics.

"It's a nice shot," Sir Richard said from his seat next to Andrzej on the crane. "But Ryan, I'd like for you to reach for the sandwich with your left hand."

Ryan switched his turkey and Swiss from one hand to the other. "I don't know," he said. "It doesn't feel natural."

Here it comes, I thought. *A half-hour discussion about pulling a sandwich from a brown paper bag.*

"No, no, no," Sir Richard said. "You're missing the point entirely."

I heard a sharp metallic click, and fear shot through my body as I turned and saw Sir Richard unlocking the seat belt that was specifically designed to keep idiotic, overenthusiastic, first-time, fuckwad directors from jumping off the crane and killing the cameraman in the other seat.

"No!" I screamed, but Sir Richard was already on his feet. Andrzej saw what was happening and his mouth dropped open in disbelief. Worse, Sara Lee and Steveo were standing under the weight bucket and had no idea that five hundred pounds of lead were about to land on top of them.

Sir Richard took a step off the crane, and it shot into the air. I dove for the camera and landed on top of Andrzej. His knees slammed into my chest and forced the air from my lungs. My fingers turned to gummy worms, and I slid off of him as the crane continued to rise. I tried to grab his ankles, but everything was moving too quickly. The platform smashed into my chin and the world went white. I was sure it was over, but somehow Andrzej managed to get hold of my vintage Star Wars T-shirt. Han Solo raced up my back, followed by Luke Skywalker and Princess Leia. They were joined at my Adam's apple by Obi-Wan Kenobi, and together these four heroes from a galaxy far, far away began to choke me. I tried to tell Andrzej I couldn't breathe, but it's hard to form meaningful sentences when you're hanging by the neck. I wrapped my arms around the camera riser and pulled myself up.

"Let go!" I croaked. "I can't breathe!"

Sir Richard weighed forty pounds more than me, which meant the crane continued to rise, but not as fast. Sara Lee and Steveo jumped out of the way, and I was left dangling ten feet in the air.

"You saved my life, Bobby, darling," Andrzej said as we waited for Steveo and Sara Lee to let us down.

"Just doing my job."

"I guess that means I'll have to stop torturing you."

"It's your call."

He leaned in so no one else could hear and whispered, "Thank you, my friend."

Reg broke us early for lunch, and Andrzej headed straight to the camera truck for a drink. My chest felt like it had been run over by a grip truck, and my neck was on fire. Meg slapped a butterfly bandage on my chin, but I should have gone to the hospital for stitches. Unfortunately, we were a man down, and I didn't trust myself to just say no if the ER doctor offered me painkillers.

The grips were already eating when I arrived with my lunch tray. I took off my belt and noticed a piece of tape stuck to my walkie-talkie with the word *Mitch* written on it in black Sharpie. I had been wearing it all morning and nobody mentioned it. Thanks, guys. I peeled off the tape and threw it at a production assistant who looked way too happy.

The local grips were named Buzzy and Slocum. Buzzy was an Austin hipster, and Slocum was what I would call a New Age redneck. They weren't world-class grips, but I knew I could get more out of them than Mitch had. I watched Sara Lee listen to the guys tell war stories. Her mouth hung open, and whenever one of them mentioned a piece of equipment, she silently repeated the word over and over. I'd worked with a lot of freaks in my day, and it looked like Sara Lee was well on the way to claiming a choice spot in my Pantheon of Weird Grips. She was one of those women who covered her face in pancake makeup and did a terrible job applying it. Worse, she sweated like a linebacker and within an hour of call looked ready for a Halloween parade.

"Any luck finding another grip, Steveo?" I asked.

"Slocum's turned me on to a pal of his named George who can start tomorrow."

"That's great."

"You'll like George," Slocum said. "We've been doing the auto show together for years. That boy knows more about motor vehicles than anybody I've ever met."

"Thanks. Can I get you guys anything from the dessert table?"

The crew shook their heads.

I stood and said, "Oh, and by the way, if I catch another grip standing under a crane with his head up his ass, I'm firing him on the spot. I don't give a shit how short-handed we are." I looked each of them in the eye, and went to fetch dessert. On my way back to the grip table, I took a detour by the vanity crafts.

"If it isn't our new key grip," Georgette said as I sat down.

"That's me," I said. "Back like a bad check."

"Does Mitch have any idea why he was fired?" Georgette asked.

"No."

"Did you really hit Andrzej with a bag of laundry?" Medea asked.

"It was a laundry *memo*. And it barely touched him."

"Oh gawd, I just got off the phone with Tina Delblanco. She's day-playing on one of the *Law and Order*s—I can't remember if it's *SUV* or the one with the guy in the raincoat. Anyway, I just told her you hit Andrzej with a bag of laundry. In ten minutes everyone in New York is gonna hear about it."

"Thanks, Medea."

"Oh gawd."

"Can I ask you harpies a favor? You know my intern over there?"

"You mean Olive Oyl?" Georgette said.

"Yes, her. If things slow down could you do me a favor and give her a makeover? Or at least teach her how to put on makeup properly?"

"I don't know," Georgette said. "That's asking a lot."

"Pleeeeease."

"Okay. On one condition."

"What's that?"

"Tell us if Carni has stretch marks. She always wears those Capezio body suits in the gym, and I can't see anything."

"Oh gawd, Georgette. You remember after Genevieve Nichols lost all that weight? Her stomach looked like a freaking subway map."

"How would I know if Katherine has stretch marks?"

"Spare me. You two have 'just fucked' written all over you. You might as well tie a couple of tin cans to your asses. Why do you think Andrzej's busting your balls? He wanted to nail her."

"But Agnieszka and the twins are here this week."

"It's never stopped him before."

I got up from the table. "You two are terrible."

"Don't get all sanctimonious with me, Bobby Conlon. You want Olive Oyl to start looking like a natural woman, or what?"

"Okay," I sighed. "No stretch marks."

"I told you!" Georgette said, slapping Medea on the back. "Now you have to buy dinner tonight."

Medea shook her head. "I don't know why I always let you talk me into these gawddamn bets, Georgette. I always lose."

* * *

In addition to almost getting three people killed, Andrzej's flipping the crane shot with the driving scene totally messed up the schedule. We had to wait until the crane shot was finished before we could start lighting the night exterior. That meant it was going to be a very long day. To make life worse, it began to drizzle during the crane shot and pour while we were lighting the night exterior. On any other night, Reg would have called wrap and saved the scene for another time. Unfortunately, one of the actors had to fly back to LA for another job, and we needed to shoot him out no matter what. I didn't think a day could suck any more until I saw the first flash of lightning.

"Okay, folks," Dusty, the gaffer, shouted. "We're bringing down the genni. Be careful where you walk because things are about to get real dark real fast."

"What's going on?" Sir Richard asked.

"The generator attracts lightning, and the cables are like lightning rods," I said. "The electrics have to power it down and disconnect everything. Then we have to wait for the storm to pass."

"Oh my," he said. "We're never going to finish, are we?"

"The only way out of here is to shoot our way out."

Everything went black, and I pulled a Maglite from my pocket to give us some light. The rain started coming down in torrents, and Sir Richard and I huddled under the twelve-foot-by-twelve-foot grifflon I'd rigged over the camera. I held up my walkie-talkie and asked, "Would you like me to call someone to come and get you with an umbrella?"

Sir Richard shook his head and said, "No, thanks. I rather like the rain."

"I know what you mean."

"Though a man could use a drink on a night like this."

"Want a pop?"

"Can I?"

"You're the director."

"Then hell, yes."

I keyed my walkie-talkie and said, "Sara Lee."

"Go for Sara Lee."

"I need you to perform an important but top-secret mission. Get a couple of Cokes from craft service and go to the box on the truck marked *Spare Parts*. Inside you'll find a bottle of Jack Daniel's. Dump out a quarter of the Coke, replace it with the Jack, and bring the cans to camera. Tell no one what you're doing and get here as soon as you can. Copy?"

"Copy."

"Jack Daniel's and Coke?" Sir Richard asked. "Sounds sugary."

"It's called a Red Dog. The Jack Daniel's provides the buzz and the caffeine keeps you awake. It's the only way to drink on the job."

"You've got this all figured out, haven't you?"

"I don't do it very often, but I like to be prepared."

"No, not that. This film business, you seem to have it all figured out."

"Not really. I'm just good at one very small part of it." His words surprised me. My life was such a disaster, how could anyone think I had it together?

"I'm not sure if I'm cut out for it myself," he said.

"Why?"

"Everyone's so caught up in the schedule and the budget. Nobody seems to care about the performances. It's exactly the opposite in the theater."

"Putting on a play costs a lot less."

"I'm awfully sorry about what happened on the crane today."

"Don't sweat it. I guarantee you'll never make that mistake again."

"You're right. My agent thinks they're going to sack me."

"He told you that?"

"I asked him."

"Talk about undermining your confidence."

"I'd rather know where I stand."

Sara Lee materialized out of the darkness with a Coke in each hand.

"Thank you, Sara Lee."

"Is Sara Lee your real name?" Sir Richard asked. "Like the cake?"

Her face erupted into a huge smile. "Yes, like the cake."

"Cheers," Sir Richard said, taking a sip. "This is a big help."

"Happy to be of assistance."

Sara Lee walked out into the rain.

"You can stay here with us if you want, Sara Lee."

"No, thanks. I'll go wait in the truck with the other grips." She held out her arms and sang "Singin' in the Rain." As Sara Lee disappeared into the darkness she began to dance.

"I don't mean to be rude," Sir Richard said. "But is that girl touched or something?"

I took a long pull from my drink and said, "I'm still trying to figure that one out myself."

It rained and thundered for another hour, and by the time we were done shooting it was well past midnight. They canceled dailies, and since we were a man down I stayed to help wrap the equipment. Andrzej had jerked us around so thoroughly it took two hours of wet and muddy work to close the door on the truck. It wasn't the toughest day on my résumé—that would have been the time I worked seventy hours straight rigging Times Square for the millennium celebration, or the day I lit twenty miles of New Jersey coastline for a piece of junk called *Ghostbusters 2,* or the night of 9/11 when we rigged lights over ground zero for the rescue workers. No, this didn't come close to that, but it was still pretty damn hard. But it was something else too. A validation. I had thought I'd lost my chops, but I was wrong. The exhaustion, the camaraderie, the thrill of delivering the impossible again and again. After months being trapped in the gloom of my apartment it felt good to bust ass again. I piled into the fifteen-passenger van and basked in the satisfaction of a job well done.

Until someone mentioned Mitch, and I remembered that my night was far from over.

The bar was closed when we got back to the Omni, and Mitch didn't answer when I called his room. I was in no mood for a confrontation, but there was too much at stake to let him leave Texas without one last attempt at getting my money. The message light was blinking when I entered 619, and I expected it to be from Mitch. Instead, it was Carni calling to wish me sweet dreams. Images from the night before came rushing back, and all I really wanted was to fall asleep with visions of blow jobs dancing in my head. Maybe next time.

I was in the shower when I heard someone pounding on my door. I answered in a towel, and Mitch stumbled in, all drunk and stupid.

"Where have you been?" I asked, pulling on a pair of gym shorts.

"Troy and Dusty took me out for a drink."

"Where'd you go?"

"Antone's and the Yellow Rose."

"How is the Yellow Rose these days? They still have a no-silicone policy?"

"Not the girls we saw."

"Doesn't anybody have standards anymore?"

"Dusty said Andrzej fired me because you're fucking Carni."

"Her name is Katherine, man."

"You are fucking her! What happened to all that I-don't-need-another-woman-in-my-life horseshit you've been spouting off for the last nine months?"

"Hold on a second. Are we talking about my personal life or your professional life?"

"There's no difference when you're in bed with production."

I rubbed my eyes. "Look, Mitch, I don't want to get into a whole Us versus Them argument with you."

"Okay, but let me ask you one question. How come the first woman you sleep with after Natalie has the same job, wears the same kind of clothes, and probably goes to the same fucking gynecologist?"

"That's not true."

"How can you say that?"

"Because your mother doesn't dress like Natalie."

"Fuck you."

"That's not entirely true. Your mom does wear those black Natori thongs I like."

Mitch lunged at me, and I raised my hands to protect my chin. He got in two good punches before I rolled onto the bed and kicked him away.

"Goddamn it, Mitch. That hurt."

"It's supposed to," he said, collapsing in a chair.

I rubbed my ear and cheek and tried to remember the last time anyone had hit me.

"I don't get it, man," Mitch said. "I did everything Andrzej asked me to do."

"No, you didn't. You were never his slime."

"How can you say that? I kissed his ass all day long."

"You didn't do it hard enough."

"Well, screw him. I've got my pride. I've got a wife and a kid and an apartment on the Upper West Side. I don't need some fat fuck treating me like dog shit all day long. It's degrading."

"You think I like it? You think Troy and Dusty like it? I've got a house. Dusty's got kids. And God knows how many wives Troy has. It's all part of the job, so get used to it or find a new career.

Mitch, you're the best damn best boy I've ever worked with, but until you get better at sucking up, you're not going very far as a key grip."

"Between mortgage payments and tuition at Montessori, I can't make it as a best boy anymore."

"I don't know what to tell you, pal. You either have to scale back your extravagant lifestyle or master the fine art of ass-kissing. There are no alternatives."

"Maybe I could get on a soap. Ritchie Hanson clears over a hundred grand a year on *All My Children*."

"That sounds like a plan."

"But soaps are so boring. I'd go nuts working on a soap."

"Can I offer you one piece of advice?"

"What?"

"Quit smoking dope. Maybe when your head clears things will make more sense."

"That has nothing to do with it."

"Yes, it does."

"Believe me, it doesn't."

Yes, it did, and like every other pothead I knew, Mitch refused to admit it.

Chapter 14

Peter and Polly World

MITCH AND I stayed up all night swapping war stories and emptying my minibar. It cost a fortune in incidental charges, but by the time Mitch crawled off to bed, I had gotten him to swear on the lives of his wife and son that he'd get my money from his father.

My phone rang two hours later, and I didn't know if it was night or day.

"Yeah?" I croaked.

"Tell me you're not sleeping with Carni Bettencourt."

"Natalie?"

"I thought you had more class than that, Bobby."

"What time is it?"

"Seven-thirty your time, five-thirty my time."

"What are you doing up so early?"

"I'm meeting my trainer in an hour."

"Pilates?"

"Power yoga."

"Does that make you more calmly powerful, or more powerfully calm?"

"It keeps my ass from sagging pathetically. And just so you know, your movie is the studio joke. You're a day and a half behind schedule, the dailies are a snooze, and they're about to shitcan your director."

"Are you keeping tabs on me, Natalie?" A smile danced across my lips.

"Of course not. We're making movies for the same studio. Rumors hit me in the face the moment I walk out of my office. What else are people going to talk about around here?"

"I don't know. How about that you can't find a lead actor for your movie?"

"Did Carni tell you that?"

"Nope, just an educated guess. I figured that if you signed someone I would have heard about it."

"The script's out to a lot of big names."

"That's great, Natalie. Why did you call me?"

"Because I wanted to tell you to be careful. Carni's just using you to get to me."

"You're out of your mind."

"It's true, Bobby. Not to mention the fact that she's a lesbian."

"She is not."

"It's common knowledge. She had this quote roommate un-quote the entire time she was fat and dumped her the second she stopped shopping at Lane Bryant. And she drives a Volvo."

"You drive a Volvo."

"Not in LA. You know who would be perfect for you? Karen Greene. Why don't you sleep with her?"

"Sorry, Natalie. You don't get to micromanage my love life."

"Or what about Lori Watson? She's a total slut, and she's got those big boobs you like."

"You used to call her a cow."

"So milk her."

"No, thanks."

"You're sleeping with that bitch to get back at me, aren't you? That's exactly why you took that job in Austin."

"Take a deep breath, Natalie. Do you really think that my every action has something to do with you?"

"Unfortunately, yes. I was really, really hoping you'd get on with your life, Bobby, but it's obvious you're still obsessed with me. Oh, and Judith says we're supposed to have a corporate meeting to change the name of the business." Judith was our entertainment lawyer—not to be confused with Doris our tax lawyer, or Roz our divorce lawyer.

"Can this be it?" I asked.

"Sure."

"Okay, this meeting of the company formally known as Peter and Polly World is now open for new business. Have you come up with a new name for the business yet, Ms. President?"

"I was thinking of calling it Breakfasts by Tiffany, but after having to explain Peter and Polly World so many times, I'll probably go with something simple like Natalie Miguel Productions."

"Is that a subsidiary of Miguel-Simm Productions?"

"No, but we do have a strategic alliance."

"Is that what they call it in Hollywood?"

"See! I told you, you were totally obsessed with me. I've got to go, but I want to say one last thing before we hang up."

"What's that?"

"Carni does not have your best interests in mind."

"And you do?"

"Absolutely."

"I'll take that under advisement. This meeting is officially adjourned. Write up the minutes, and I'll sign off on them. Good-bye, Natalie."

* * *

We named our company Peter and Polly World after the director Peter Bogdanovich and his first wife, Polly Platt. Our principal business was film production, but the only photoplay we produced was a little bedroom video that Natalie made me erase immediately. We had big plans for Peter and Polly World, but there's nothing like working on other people's movies to keep you from making your own.

Why Peter Bogdanovich and Polly Platt? Because in the late sixties and early seventies they were everything we aspired to be— the perfect combination of marriage and movies. Peter Bogdanovich was the original film nerd. He was raised in New York City and watched more movies than any sane person should—ten, fifteen, twenty a week. The boy made copious notes on three-by-five cards of every film he saw, and his collection grew from the hundreds to the thousands. Peter grew up to become a journalist and wrote long, fawning articles on Howard Hawks, John Ford, and Orson Welles. These men weren't forgotten, but they were old and cranky, and their best work was long behind them. To Peter Bogdanovich, however, these men were giants. Not only did he know who they were, but he knew their movies inside and out. He called them legends and geniuses, and promised to write books and make documentaries celebrating their lives.

And he did it all with Polly at his side. Peter may have been the front man, but they were *a team.* Polly was a force in her own right—a smart girl with a tragic past who'd studied costume design at Carnegie Mellon and dressed like an Indian princess. Together, she and Peter were a two-person cinema studies department. They spent their days watching movies and their nights talking camera angles, performances, and directors until they passed out from exhaustion. Finally, when their bodies were so full of movies that they practically sweated celluloid, they got to make their first movie. Roger Corman, schlockmeister extraordinaire, had a few days left on a contract with Boris Karloff and called Peter to ask if he could throw together a movie for ten cents and a cup of coffee.

"Could I ever," Peter replied.

The result was *Targets*, a horror movie about a psycho with a high-powered rifle who picks off moviegoers at a drive-in. Peter and Polly wrote it together, Peter directed, and Polly was the production designer. The movie was a success, and they were on their way. Their next effort was *The Last Picture Show*, a bittersweet tale of love, friendship, and ennui set in a small Texas town. The movie starred a bunch of unknowns named Jeff Bridges, Cybill Shepherd, and Randy Quaid. Orson Welles told Peter and Polly to shoot it in black and white, and John Ford convinced Ben Johnson to play Sam the Lion, the role that won him an Academy Award. And the last movie shown in the picture show of the title? Howard Hawks's *Red River*. Talk about a pedigree!

But something happened during the production of *The Last Picture Show* that shook Peter and Polly's world straight down to its foundation the same way Elias Simm would shake Peter and Polly World, Incorporated, thirty years later. The little earthquaker's name was Cybill Shepherd, and during production of *The Last Picture Show*, she and Peter fell in love.

Imagine Polly's pain the night her husband and creative partner waltzes into their hotel room with the twentysomething scent of Cybill Shepherd wafting from his clothing. Picture Polly's torment as she takes Peter's shirt off the back of the hotel room chair, holds it to her face, and breathes in. Watch her eyes fill with tears as her worst suspicions are confirmed. In that anguished moment everything comes together: The dreamy glances across set. The sighs. The directorial hand dwelling too long on the lead actress's shoulder. Yes, it all makes sense. Too much sense.

Distraught as she was, there was no time for fights, no time for battles. Polly had sets to dress, and dailies to watch, and a thousand other decisions to agonize over because she and Peter were *making a movie*. And nothing else mattered. Not love. Not betrayal. Not pain.

Especially not her pain.

Peter and Polly made two more pictures together and both were huge. *What's Up, Doc?* was a thinly veiled remake of Howard Hawks's *Bringing Up Baby* and starred Barbra Streisand and Ryan O'Neal. Their final collaboration was a depression-era saga called *Paper Moon* that won little Tatum O'Neal an Academy Award. It was their third hit in a row. Peter graced the covers of magazines and was celebrated as the master of the medium in the grand tradition of his idols. And Polly? Well, there was only room for one genius per movie, and Peter sure looked spiffy in that tuxedo at the Oscars.

Peter and Polly World closed for business, and Peter Bogdanovich cast Cybill Shepherd as his new and improved Polly. They spent their days being fabulous together, and when it came time to make his next movie, it only made sense that Peter cast his lover and muse. Unfortunately, Peter and Cybill World's inaugural production, *Daisy Miller*, kind of sucked. As did their next movie. And the one after that. If you look at his filmography, there's no question that Peter made his best movies with Polly. Was this because Polly was the brains of the operation? Natalie and I gave this a lot of thought and decided that it was not. Peter Bogdanovich is nothing if not brainy. But Polly Platt was the soul of the operation. *Daisy Miller* and *At Long Last Love* aren't bad movies because they're Cybill Shepherd love fests. They're bad movies because they lack the detail, texture, and heart of *The Last Picture Show* and *Paper Moon*. That's what Polly brought to the table—detail, texture, and heart—and it was the glue that held those movies together.

When Natalie and I founded Peter and Polly World, Incorporated, we were two unique individuals with separate dreams, agendas, and neuroses. As our company grew, we passed opinions and habits back and forth like an old sweater. One of us would try on an idea or expression that had belonged to the other, wear it around the house, and it soon felt like it was part of us forever. After a while, it was impossible to tell where Natalie ended and I began.

"Oh my God," one of us said at least once a week. "I'm turning into you!"

The film business is an impossible way of life for a million reasons, and to have someone holding your hand while you stumble down its blind alleys is a gift. To have someone support you, and love you, and understand you is a blessing. For more than a decade, I achieved absolutely nothing on my own. It was all Peter and Polly World. And it was pure, man. Sure, Natalie and I spent our share of time behaving like rich New York assholes, but inside the corporate headquarters of Peter and Polly World life was innocent. It was a land of shared opinions and respect, of dancing dust bunnies and Cherry Garcia ice cream, of tenderness and love. That's what I lost when Natalie pranced off with Elias. Not the regular table at Balthazar, or the French bedding with the scandalously high thread count. Natalie didn't just betray me, she betrayed *us*—the world we had created together complete with our own private language and cast of imaginary friends.

After Natalie moved out, it was up to me to tell the other residents of Peter and Polly World that Mama wasn't coming home anymore. And when the Cherry Garcia ice cream and dancing dust bunnies asked why, I didn't know what to say. "Maybe," I told them, "if we cross our fingers and pray real hard, she'll come back." But I knew better. After all, there must have been a point, after years of directing crap like *Illegally Yours* and *To Sir, with Love II*, when Peter finally realized he needed Polly to make good movies again.

So, why didn't they get back together? Don't forget, these were two people who loved movies like nobody else before them. Who went to the funerals of John Ford and Howard Hawks and cried their eyes out at the world's loss. Didn't Peter want to make films as perfect and timeless as *The Front Page, The Searchers,* or *Vertigo*? Didn't Polly want to look up and feel the warm glow of her idols smiling down on her from heaven? Was any sacrifice too great? Any crow too putrid to choke down?

Alas, Peter and Polly never got back together. And knowing what had happened to them, I figured Natalie and I didn't stand much of a chance in the reconciliation department. I did not, however, tell this to the dancing dust bunnies and Cherry Garcia ice cream. For their sake, I sat in front of the TV night after night and waited for the keys to rattle in the lock that I didn't have the heart to change, no matter how many dry and empty days passed us by.

Chapter 15

Black and Blue Thongs

NATALIE'S WAKE-UP CALL left me too cranked up to sleep, and my mind filled with images of her and Elias playing hot oil tag in the backseat of our old Volvo. The light on my phone was blinking, and I punched in my code. In addition to the good-night message from Carni (which I had chosen not to erase), there was a less melodious message from Elvira telling me to call her at the production office.

"Hello, Romeo," Elvira said when I got her on the line. "What's your twenty?"

"I'm in my room."

"Alone?"

"Just me and the ghosts of my youth."

"Meet me in the hotel restaurant in fifteen minutes."

"Why?"

"I'll tell you when I get there."

I selected an outfit from the pile of T-shirts and cargo shorts fermenting in my suitcase and walked into the bathroom. Shit. In addition to the gash on my chin, there was a large purple bruise on my face from where Mitch had slugged me. It was too far gone for ice, and I wondered if I should tell people what really happened. It was only Wednesday and already I needed a day off.

The restaurant's big-haired hostess sighed when she saw my face and attire, but she had to seat me because the movie was dropping a ton of money at the hotel. The worst she could do was exile me in the back corner of the restaurant as far away as possible from the businessmen yakking on cell phones. I was the proud owner of a cell phone myself and whipped it out to check my voice mail. There was a two-day-old message from Roger saying that he and Bess had arrived in New York and the apartment was "wonderful." He didn't mention anything about snow globes or Vicodin bottles, but he couldn't help but notice the kitchen smelled like pinecones every time they used the garbage disposal. Cheers. The second message was garbled, and I had to listen to it twice before I realized it was from a bunch of grips on the set of *CSI: NY* congratulating me for "kicking the shit" out of Andrzej.

I closed my phone and thought about quitting the film business for the millionth time. I couldn't believe it. Here I was, as far away from New York and LA as you could get, and my every action was common knowledge on both coasts within hours. Why couldn't everyone just leave me alone so I could pull my life back together? Or at least let me get some sleep.

"Aren't you a vision?" Elvira said, sitting down across from me.

"Thanks."

"I assume Mitch did that to the side of your face."

"How'd you guess?"

"Because he took up residence at my desk for two hours yesterday and whined about how you stole his job."

"Did you tell him that it was all Andrzej's bullshit?"

"No, I told him it was completely your fault."

"Elvira!"

"Of course I told him you had nothing to do with it, but he was too stoned to listen. What shape is he in, by the way?"

"I didn't lay a finger on him."

"Sorry you missed your opportunity."

"What are you talking about?"

"The insurance company rejected the claim for your truck. They're not paying anybody. You or Mitch."

"Can I appeal?"

"You can't, but Mitch can. The problem is, Mitch keeps telling me to call his father, and old man Markham won't return my calls. Something weird is going on."

"Let me go talk to him," I said, getting up.

"Don't waste your time. He left for the airport twenty minutes ago."

"Shit."

"Want me to call Southwest and cancel his flight?"

"I have a better idea." I handed Elvira my cell phone.

"What's this for?"

"Take my picture." I turned my bruised face toward the camera phone and extended my middle finger.

"How flattering," she said and snapped the photo.

"Wait until I start sending him action photos of my bowel movements. Just out of curiosity, do you think Katherine could help me out with the insurance company?"

Elvira stared me, and I could feel her scanning my soul with X-ray vision. She said, "I've almost forgiven you for turning me down in my moment of sexual need, but if I find out you're fucking Katherine for the insurance money, I'll kick your ass so hard your mother will bleed."

"Jesus, Elvira, what kind of feelingless asshole do you think I am?"

"You tell me, city boy."

"Forget I even mentioned it. Do you have any advice on how I should deal with the insurance company?"

"You want my honest opinion?"

"Duh."

"The best thing you can do right now is order breakfast." She handed me a menu and stood. "I recommend the Hungry Texan Special. It's gonna be a long day."

I watched Elvira march off and wondered how much damage she could inflict on my plan to get Katherine to intervene with the insurance company. Plenty, if she set her industrious little mind to it. This complicated things, but there was no way I was going to give up trying to get my money. Not after what I'd been through. I would, however, have to postpone things for a couple of weeks. That was about the time my divorce papers were supposed to arrive, and I figured the odds were now fifty-fifty whether I'd have to sleep with Katherine. There had to be easier ways of making a movie.

I scanned the menu and saw that the Hungry Texan Special was a chicken-fried steak with two eggs, biscuits, and a side of grits. I'm not a breakfast person, but when the waitress arrived I ordered it anyway along with a pot of coffee, an *Austin American-Statesman*, and a *New York Times*, and charged it to Mitch's room. It was the least I could do. As the waitress walked away I noticed Katherine sitting at a table with Frick and Frack and Hank Sullivan, who had just arrived from LA. I didn't exactly feel trapped, but I didn't want to put Katherine in a position where she felt obligated to talk to me when I was dressed like a bum and my face looked like a veal chop. I'd been in similar positions with Natalie, and Mitch's words from the night before came rushing back.

Okay, so maybe I did receive oral pleasure from someone who had the same job as Natalie, but so what? I hadn't planned on it happening, it just happened. Was I *not* supposed to sleep with Katherine because she had the same job as Natalie? Of course not. And when you got right down to it, every woman in the film industry had something in common with my soon-to-be-ex-wife, starting with their gender and chosen profession. *So fuck you,*

Mitch, I thought. *Not only is it your fault that I'm trapped in this restaurant with a raspberry on my face, you still don't know what the hell you're talking about.*

"I'll go fire the bastard right now," Frack shouted. "Just say the word."

Hank put a hand to his head, and Katherine glanced around to see if anyone from the movie was within listening distance. She spotted me before I could cover the bruise on my face, and her eyes grew wide before she turned her back to the meeting.

My coffee and newspaper arrived, and I wondered if Hank was Natalie's source about the somnambulistic powers of our dailies. It was hard to say. Hank had a big mouth, but it was never a good idea to trash-talk your movie to anybody. Not that this movie was Hank's baby. It was more like his punishment for going so far over budget on the first picture in his deal. Our job was a kind of Frankenfilm cobbled together from odds and ends lying around the studio: a director who had done a play in London Julia Roberts flipped over, a book the studio paid too much for, and a classy gig for Frick and Frack after *Scooter and Timmy's Acapulco Vacation* grossed a zillion bucks on DVD.

"What happened to your face?"

I lowered my paper to see Katherine standing in front of me.

"Mitch punched me."

"Why?"

"I told him his mother wore black Natori thongs."

She burst out laughing. "You're kidding me."

"Nope. Black Natori thongs."

"Are you going to press charges?"

"Of course not. Mitch was drunk, and I was being an asshole. I'll tell people I smashed myself in the face with a highboy. It's less scandalous. How are things over at the producers' table?"

"Lousy. Joe and Jeff ran out of stuff to tell their friends in LA and are going to fire Sir Richard for telling them to shut up at dailies."

"They should fire Sir Andrzej for flip-flopping the schedule and making us work an extra five hours yesterday."

"They could care less about what happens on set. Unfortunately, Ryan found out about them wanting to fire Richard and is making all kinds of noises. He actually likes the little poof and thinks firing him will have a negative effect on his performance."

"And who will be replacing our late director?"

"Sebastian Shane."

"Who's that?"

"Some TV hack Jeff used to represent."

"What's he done?"

"Cable porn."

"Really?"

"No, but just about." Katherine rubbed her neck. "Waa, I want my back cracked."

I checked my watch. "We have forty minutes until call."

"I have to go watch dailies with Hank and the editor."

"I thought the editor was Sir Richard's guy."

"That's the problem with this fucking movie. Nobody's anybody's guy. Except maybe for you, Troy, and Dusty. And after the way Andrzej treated you yesterday, I'm not sure about your status."

"Don't worry about Andrzej. He's indebted to me for saving his life. By the way, you'll never guess who called me at seven-thirty this morning."

"Natalie?"

"How'd you know?"

"Just a hunch. Hank said Natalie was chock-full of questions about our movie."

"How come?"

"You tell me."

I shrugged.

"Do you mind if I ask what you and Natalie talked about?"

"Nothing much. She said I should sleep with Karen Greene or Lori Watson."

"Why those two?"

"Something about breasts. Oh yeah, she also said you were a lesbian."

"What?"

"And that you drove a Volvo. Is it true? Do you really drive a Volvo?"

"Yeah."

"What model?"

"The Cross Country wagon, but as soon as the lease is up I'm going to get one of those new SUVs."

"I'm starting to get pissed that everyone on both coasts is talking about us, Katherine."

"I'm sorry, Bobby."

"It's not your fault. I just wish people would leave it the fuck alone."

"I have an idea."

"Yeah?"

"Let's get a house together. That way we can leave all the washerwomen behind at the hotel."

Living together? The muscles in my chest squeezed tight. There was no way I could avoid sleeping with Katherine if we were trapped under the same roof. "I'll think about it," I said.

The smile fell from her face, and I could see that I'd given the wrong answer. I began backpedaling. "I didn't say no. I just want to think about it, that's all. I'm still recovering from my last live-in situation."

"Do what you want, but I'm having the locations department rustle up some houses for me to look at. You're welcome to come along."

"Okay."

"There's Hank, I gotta go."

Katherine leaned over and kissed me. As she walked away, I wondered if the kiss was for my benefit, or if she was sending a message to Natalie through Hank.

Chapter 16

■■■■■■■■

Family Values

Tomorrow is Skirt Day. Show some team spirit and wear a skirt! If for some reason (fellas), you do not own a skirt, the wardrobe department will be happy to lend you one. Please note that while not required, boxer shorts, tighty-whities, and black Natori thongs are strongly recommended.

—From "Elvira's Notes" on Day 7's call sheet

WE WERE SHOOTING at Don's Depot, site of the infamous Sex Rodeo. The scene was two pages long, and from past experience with Sir Richard Davis's directorial process, this meant we were in for a long first rehearsal. It was a beautiful day, and we emptied the truck to let our equipment dry from the previous night's deluge. I sent Sara Lee to the Hair & Makeup trailer for her makeover and went to craft service for another B_{12} shot. The crew seemed to be buying my story about smashing myself in the face with a highboy until Georgette appeared with fury in her eyes.

"C'mere," she said, digging her fingernails into my biceps.

"Jesus, Georgette. What the hell's going on?"

"Just come with me."

I did as I was ordered and followed her to the Hair & Makeup trailer. The door was locked, and Georgette let herself in with a key. Inside, Sara Lee had her shirt off and when she saw me she crossed her arms over her chest.

"You said you wouldn't tell him!" Sara Lee shouted and began to sob.

I looked at Medea for a clue, but she refused to make eye contact with me.

"Did you do this to her?" Georgette asked.

"Do what?"

Georgette leaned down to Sara Lee and whispered. "It's okay, honey, just let him see." Sara Lee lowered her arms to reveal dark bruises on her chest and stomach.

"Oh my God," I said. "Are you okay? Should we take you to the hospital or something?"

"I'm fine," Sara Lee said, grabbing her T-shirt and pulling it over her head.

Georgette dragged me out of the trailer.

"So?" she said.

"What?"

For perhaps the first time in the history of cinema, Georgette said nothing.

"You think I did that to her?" I said. "Are you out of your fucking mind? How could you even think that?"

"She said she smashed herself with a highboy at wrap last night. That sounds a lot like what you said to describe that thing on your face. So what happened? Did she hit you defending herself?"

"Mitch did this to me, you moron."

"Why?"

"It was nothing. Just bullshit."

Georgette stared at me.

"Okay, he was drunk and I told him his mother wore a black Natori thong."

"What's the matter with Natori thongs? I'm wearing one right now."

"Mitch obviously has lingerie issues to work out." I rubbed my eyes. "How'd you find out Sara Lee had those bruises?"

"Why do you think she wears a quarter inch of base all the time? Her cheek looks just like yours."

"And when you asked her what happened, she said she hit herself with a stand?"

"Doesn't win many points for originality, huh?"

"Okay," I sighed. "Let me go talk to her."

Georgette and I marched back into the trailer

"I'm sorry for causing all this trouble, Bobby," Sara Lee said. "I didn't mean for this to happen. You've showed a lot of faith in me, and I know you've got a lot on your mind, being the new key grip and all."

"Sara Lee, you're not causing anybody any trouble. Would you like to tell me what happened?"

"Do I have to?"

"You don't have to do anything you don't want to."

She thought about that for a moment and said, "On Sunday, my father was watching a football game, and I was talking too much, so he hit me. But it was my fault. I should have left him alone, but I was so excited about all the cool names for the equipment and the knots you guys taught me. I just couldn't help myself."

Sara Lee looked down at her feet and said. "And then he told me I was shit, because that's what I was getting paid. And I said no, that I was an intern and that's how people got started in the business. Then he told me I was stupid and hit me."

I thought about Sara Lee working so hard the day before and felt sick. If Andrzej was in the trailer I would have hit him with a laundry truck.

"What happened after that, Sara Lee?" I asked.

"I left, and I haven't been back since."

"Where are you living?"

"In my car. But it's okay. I've done it before."

I left Georgette and Medea to finish Sara Lee's makeover and tried to figure out my next move. It wasn't like I could rescue Sara Lee from her shitty life, but I had to do something. I hated getting involved in my crew's personal lives, but the image of her bruised stomach and chest burned in my brain. How could a father do that to his child? My first impulse was to pile the grips into a fifteen-passenger van and pay Daddy a little midnight visit, but the guy probably slept with a twelve-gauge shotgun under his pillow.

I found Steveo hanging out near the dolly and told him what had happened to Sara Lee.

"Her *father*? That's such a fucking having."

"I know. It's like out of *Deliverance* or something."

"What are you gonna do about it?"

"She doesn't want to press charges, but I'm going to let her crash in my room so she doesn't have to sleep in her car anymore."

"That's cool."

"And let's try and turn her into a real grip before we leave Texas. Maybe then she can support herself and not have to move back in with that asshole."

"You are *so* having me."

"Why?"

"I was thirty seconds away from telling you I was out of here. Now I've got to stay on this pig fuck and see it through to the end. Goddamn it."

"Sorry, Steveo. At least it's for a better cause than another shitty movie on your résumé."

"Okay, but I want to rent a house. George and Slocum live way the hell out near Bastrop, and I don't want them falling asleep on their way home from work. If you and I move out of the hotel, we can pool our housing allowance and rent a place for the entire department including Sara Lee."

"Sounds good, but you don't need a room for me."

"How come?

"Because I'm moving in with Katherine."

Steveo whistled. "Man, oh man. This job is getting more interesting by the second."

Chapter 17

Screwed

TWO HOURS LATER Sara Lee looked like Julia Roberts, and Sir Richard and the actors were still in Don's Depot. I glanced over at Video Village, and Andrzej was talking to a well-groomed gentleman in an expensive suit who had materialized out of nowhere. My instincts said agent, and I tapped Reg on the shoulder.

"Who's the suit?" I asked.

Reg turned toward Video Village, and his eyes grew wide. "Holy shit. When did he get here?"

"I don't know. Who is it?"

"Dan Berg. He runs Bryant/Berg."

Bryant/Berg was the biggest management company in Hollywood. Angelina Jolie big. Tobey Maguire big. Leonardo Di-Caprio big.

"That's Dan Berg?" I said. "What's he doing here by himself? I heard those Bryant/Berg guys traveled in packs like wolves."

"I heard they studied hapkido and could kill people with their bare hands."

"You're the ranking adult on set, Reg. Go see what old Danny Boy wants."

"Fuck that," he said. "I'm calling Carni and Hank. Let them deal with it."

Reg walked away. I whipped out my cell phone and hit number 3 on the speed dial.

"Miguel-Simm Productions," came a snippy female voice.

"This is Bobby for Natalie."

"Bobby who?"

"Conlon."

"What is this in reference to?"

"I'm her husband."

"And ..."

"And, duh, I want to talk to her."

"Hold, please."

"Thanks," I said, feeling deflated. For fourteen years my name had been a master key granting me access to production offices from Maine to Mexico. Now I was just another Joe Jerk.

"I'm sorry, but Ms. Miguel's in casting right now. Can I take a message?"

"Yeah, tell her Dan Berg is standing fifteen yards away from me."

"The Dan Berg?"

"Apparently so."

"Hold, please."

Natalie was on the line in a heartbeat.

"Is Dan Berg really there?"

"Swear to God. But none of the producers are here, and Reg is shitting a brick."

"Where are Hank and Carni?"

"Watching dailies, but they should have been here by now. What do you think Dan Berg is up to?"

"He's there to sign Ryan Donahue. The reviews for *Trail of Broken Hearts* just came out, and *Variety* is calling him the next Paul Newman. This is a disaster."

"Why?"

"If Ryan finds out Dan Berg is there to sign him, he'll make keeping Sir Richard part of his deal."

"Can Dan Berg do that?"

"Dan Berg can stop a tsunami with a phone call. You've got to keep him away from Ryan until Hank and Carni get there. Tell Reg to throw him off set."

"Reg won't listen to me."

"Let me talk to him."

I ran over to where Reg was talking on his cell phone.

"Here," I said, jamming my phone in his face.

"Who's that?" Reg asked.

"Natalie."

"Here," Reg said, jamming his phone in my face.

"Who that?" I asked.

"Katherine."

Reg and I swapped phones

"What's going on?" Katherine asked.

"Natalie thinks Dan Berg is here to sign Ryan Donahue, and that Ryan will use Dan Berg to keep Sir Richard on the movie."

"He can't do that! We just hired Sebastian Shane. Joe and Jeff are on the phone with *Variety* and *The Hollywood Reporter* right now telling them it's a done deal. Shit. We can't let Dan Berg get to Ryan."

"How long until you guys get here?"

"Fifteen minutes. Put me back on with Reg."

"It's Katherine," I said.

"It's your ex-wife."

Reg and I swapped phones.

"How'd it go?" I asked.

"I don't think Reg has the balls to throw Dan Berg off set. How long until Carni gets there?"

"Fifteen minutes. What should we do?"

"Ask Carni if you can do whatever it takes to keep Dan Berg away from Ryan, then do it."

"Gimme that," I said, grabbing Reg's cell and holding both phones to my head.

"It's me," I said to Katherine. "Can I do whatever it takes to keep Dan and Ryan apart?"

"Absolutely!"

"Okay, get here fast."

I said good-bye to Katherine and told Natalie I got the green light.

"Good luck," she said. "But you better call me back the second you're done, otherwise I'm going to wet myself."

"Give me ten minutes."

I grabbed my walkie-talkie and said, "Okay, listen up. I want a twelve-by grifflon on set *now* and somebody bring me my Makita and the bag of screws. Now."

A minute later, Buzzy ran up to me with a screw gun and a bag of screws.

"What's going on, chief?"

"How much longer until that grifflon is ready?"

"Another couple of minutes."

I grabbed my walkie-talkie and shouted, "Do I need to be more specific here? I want a twelve-foot square of white reflective material tied to an aluminum frame on set *now*! I don't care about stands or tie lines or sandbags or anything else. You hear me? I want to see a twelve-by grifflon in thirty seconds."

Ten seconds later George and Slocum ran on set carrying a twelve-by grifflon at waist level.

"Over here, boys," I shouted. "Hold it up vertically."

The grifflon now blocked Dan Berg's view of Don's Depot.

"Okay, Buzzy. Shoot a dozen screws into that door so no one can open it."

"Ten-four."

"I'll take your place, George. Come back with two highboys as soon as you can."

"Steveo's got 'em already."

I turned and saw Steveo rolling two highboys toward us. Sara Lee followed ten steps behind him with a cartful of sandbags.

"Good work, lady and gentlemen. Stand it, bag it, and tie it off."

Reg appeared at my side. "Did you just trap our director and lead actor on set?"

"C'mon, let's hit craft service for some Twizzlers."

"If Sir Richard tells the Directors Guild, I'll be fined like a thousand bucks."

"If you were Sir Richard, wouldn't you be a bit embarrassed to tell anyone about it?"

My phone rang, and I flipped it open to hear, "Nice picture, asshole."

"Mitch, darling, how are you?"

"Peachy. I'm sending you a picture of my own, but you better not look at it in mixed company."

"The insurance company just turned down the claim, and Elvira said that your dad won't return her calls. What the fuck is going on?"

"Don't sweat it. My father doesn't return my calls half the time."

"I am sweating it, Mitch. I'm sweating it one hundred fifty thousand dollars' worth."

"I said I'd take care of it, and I'll take care of it. How are things going on set?"

"Frick and Frack hired a new director, and I just trapped the actors and director in Don's Depot."

"Same old shit, huh?"

"It's still early."

Frick and Frack arrived ten minutes later. Joe slithered all over

Dan Berg like a snail, and I unscrewed the front door of Don's Depot. Reg escorted the actors off set, and Jeff went inside to fire Sir Richard. By the time Hank and Katherine arrived, our former director was on his way back to the land of tea and crumpets. Mission accomplished. I felt bad about Sir Richard getting the old heave-ho, but that's showbiz. Reg called wrap, and the movie went on hiatus for the rest of the week. Not only was our equipment dry, but Sara Lee's makeover improved her appearance one hundred percent, and we got three days off with pay. When Katherine appeared at the back of the grip truck I figured she wanted to thank me for saving the movie from embarrassing articles in *Variety* and *The Hollywood Reporter*.

"What's up?" I asked as we walked toward her car.

"Why did you call Natalie when Dan Berg arrived?"

"I . . . I don't know," I said, stopping in my tracks. "I really don't."

"I'd appreciate it if you kept your ex-wife's nose out of my movie. Every other word out of Hank's mouth is 'Natalie this' and 'Natalie that.' I'm so over it."

"Look, Katherine, I'm sorry I called Natalie, but— You know something, I'm not sorry I called Natalie. And you know why I did it? Because I've been calling Natalie for fourteen years. I thought what happened the other night was great and everything, but I can't extract myself from the last third of my life with the snap of your fingers. If those are your expectations, we might as well stop this thing now before somebody gets hurt."

Katherine stared at me. "Do you remember that tomato sauce commercial we did all those years ago?"

"Sure."

"Do you remember how Ritchie Gillardi made me cry?"

"Kind of."

"You wouldn't believe what he called me. I remember walking out of the soundstage and thinking, *Fuck this*. I mean, that was back in the eighties when an MBA from Wharton was a license to print money. And here was this retard who hadn't even graduated high school calling me a fat hairy pig cunt. I was literally walking away from the film industry when you came out and talked me down. So I guess this is all your fault." She kissed me and stepped back to inspect my face. "I can't believe you told Mitch his mother wore a thong."

"It seemed like the right thing to do at the time. How come you never hired me again after that tomato sauce job?"

"I was fat. You were married. It hurt."

"Does that mean you hired me on this movie because you were skinny and I was getting divorced?"

"Hank hired you. I had nothing to do with it."

"But a girl's got to have her dreams, right?"

"I don't know what you are. The jury's still out."

"Let's start with housemate, and we'll take it from there."

"You want to move in with me?"

"If the offer's still open."

Chapter 18

Playing House

THE LOCATIONS DEPARTMENT gave us three options, and by
noon we had the keys to a house. Two-twenty-five Nickerson
Street was a bungalow in the Travis Heights section of Austin, a
block off of South Congress. The Continental Club was at the
bottom of the hill, as was an excellent bakery and a hipster coffee
stand where the last of the dot-com cowboys sat sucking on cell
phones. The house was in immaculate condition and stocked
with everything from dish towels to a half bottle of Campari in
a cabinet above the fridge. As perfect as it was, I could not ignore
the tingle of guilt knowing that it was exactly the kind of place
Natalie and I would have bought if we'd chucked it all and moved
to Texas. It was a thrill making one of my dreams come true, I
just figured I'd be doing it with Natalie instead of Katherine. The
weird part was, when compared to these two strong-willed lasses,
I thought of myself as a jellyfish drifting in their wake. But as I
stood there in my Texas dream home, I realized I was stronger
than I had believed. I was the one—not Natalie, not Katherine—
who had wound up getting what he'd wanted.

Yeah, I know it was insane moving in with a woman I had no

intention of sleeping with, but if marriage had taught me any-thing, it's that the physical act of love takes up about as much time in a relationship as going to the dry cleaner's. You may tell your-self you're doing it all the time, but that mountain of pantsuits on the credenza tells a different story. What I missed most about my marriage going south was the companionship—the little words and shared experiences that hold you together like epoxy. I wanted a friend, not a lover, and I figured the combination of long days and separate bedrooms would keep Katherine from taking me to the cleaner's.

The weekend presented a bigger challenge, and when Kather-ine mentioned having Hank over for dinner on Sunday, I called him up immediately. He arrived with a raspberry cheesecake and a headache from dealing with Sebastian Shane. Typical for a direc-tor, Sebastian said the screenplay was in perfect shape before he had the job, and demanded a page-one rewrite thirty seconds after he signed his deal memo. He wanted to bring in his own writer, an annoying little dweeb who had nothing on his résumé except a little TV. The writer was acting like a jerk and not returning Hank's phone calls while his agent demanded the kind of fee only an A-list writer got on his best day. Good luck.

"My guess is he's hiding in his garage and rewriting the entire screenplay regardless of what we've shot," Hank said.

"Why would he rewrite stuff that's already in the can?" I asked.

"He has to make substantial changes to the script or he won't get screen credit. Not to mention that Sebastian Shane won't want another director's footage in his movie."

"There's no way we can get Julia Roberts back to reshoot her scene," Katherine said.

"For the time being, yes," Hank said. "But who knows?"

I thought about the bruises on Sara Lee's chest and stomach and the crane shot that had almost killed Andrzej. All that work and pain flushed down the toilet just to satisfy a writer's greed and a director's ego. I tried to tell myself that it didn't matter. It was not my movie, and not my money, and I just had to reach the finish line. But that didn't make me feel any less disgusted. I knew the drill, and by Hollywood standards what Sebastian Shane and his little writer chum were up to barely qualified as gossip. Ten minutes after the hacks at the Directors Guild finished expressing their outrage at the studio for firing Sir Richard Davis, they'd start applauding Sebastian Shane for "saving the movie" and "sticking up for his vision." It was bullshit, and everyone from the lowliest slime up to the two intelligent and well-educated souls across the table from me were part of the same jolly conspiracy. We called ourselves filmmakers, but our jobs had little to do with making good movies. Our mission was to keep the cameras rolling at all costs. It didn't matter what we shot as long as everyone made a comfortable living. The only people not in on the joke were the poor suckers lined up at the multiplexes who got tricked into watching a piece of crap. Maybe that was why box-office receipts were down.

Katherine excused herself to use the bathroom. The moment she was out of earshot Hank leaned forward and whispered, "What the fuck are you doing, man?"

Hank was my friend, but he was not the kind of guy who would stick his neck out for anyone. That was why I didn't ask him to intervene with the insurance company. If he thought it might hurt his business, he'd put the kibosh on it. I couldn't tell him the truth.

"What are you talking about?" I asked.

"Spandex Sally back there," he said with a jerk of the thumb. "I understand getting your rocks off, and I understand doing crazy shit after your wife dumps you, but Jesus, pal, *Carni Bettencourt*? If you fucked some dude I'd be less shocked."

"Funny you should mention that. I was just thinking how awesome you looked in those jeans. What are they, Diesel?"

"Spare me. C'mon, what's going on?"

"Nothing. Katherine and I like each other. What's the big deal?"

Hank laughed. "If you gotta ask, there's no way I can help."

"Who says I need help?"

"I do."

Hank's phone rang. He checked the number and said, "This is it."

"Is that the box-office numbers?" Katherine called from across the house.

"Yeah."

She rushed in to join us, and we waited as Hank finished his call.

"That's great. Thanks, Paul." Hank closed his phone and said, "*Trail of Broken Hearts* grossed twenty-two-point-three million dollars and was number one at the box office. It's official. Ryan Donahue is a movie star."

"Wow," Katherine said.

"That's terrific," I said.

"No, it's not," Hanks said. "It's a fucking disaster."

"What are you talking about?" I said. "I thought *Trail of Broken Hearts* hitting a home run was good for us."

"A single? Great. A double? Fabulous. But a home run?" Hank shook his head. "After today, Ryan can do whatever he wants and we'll have to smile and say yes."

"And you just fired his favorite director," I said.

"Exactly."

"Sebastian Shane better learn to kiss ass fast," Katherine said.

"We all better," Hank said. "This movie just turned into a vehicle for America's newest heartthrob, and we're all along for the ride."

Hank and Katherine grew quiet, and I could feel the Hand of Blame coming to rest on my shoulder. No jury would convict me, but Hank and Katherine were slipping into ass-covering mode, and it would be a lot easier to blame me and my little screw-gun Watusi than take responsibility for pissing off Mr. Twenty-Two-Point-Three-Million-Dollar-Opening-Weekend. I had gone from hero to schnook with one phone call.

"It's getting late," Hank said. "And we have a big day ahead of us tomorrow."

"I'm exhausted," Katherine said. "Was that the shortest weekend on record, or what?"

"Thanks, Bobby, dinner was awesome."

"The pleasure was mine, dude." I held out my hand to see if Hank would shake it. He did, but I could tell he was worried some of my stupidity might rub off on him.

"I'll walk you out to your car," Katherine said.

Hank and Katherine left, and I went into the kitchen to cut myself an extra-large slice of raspberry cheesecake. An hour earlier, my dinner companions had said that raspberry cheesecake was their single most favorite food on the planet, but *Trail of Broken Hearts*'s big opening weekend had had a profound effect on their taste buds. This was good and bad. It was good because Katherine would be in no mood to put the moves on me when she was finished talking to Hank. It was bad because I had trapped a movie star in a bar with a screw gun. Firing me would be like swatting a gnat.

Hank's cheesecake tasted like plastic, and I felt like a chump. Sir Richard Davis was a decent man who had gotten in over his head. He was the only person on the movie who cared about making a good film, and I'd played a starring role in getting him fired. He said I had it all figured out, but I was as lost and selfish as the rest of them. I'd convinced myself that moving into the bungalow was what I really wanted. It wasn't. What I really wanted was the cinematic equivalent of capturing a tornado.

Capturing tornadoes is damn near impossible because you

never know where one will touch down. Even in that tornado alley called Hollywood, chances are that if you rush around desperate to catch one, you'll find yourself in the wrong place at the wrong time. The best way to capture a tornado is to stay put until you see one coming. But patience is not rewarded in this business, and frantic effort is. That's why we were doomed to set up the same shots over and over despite the cost, aggravation, and pain. What Sir Richard Davis never understood was that movies are not about long rehearsals and finely crafted performances. Movies are about chasing tornadoes and trying to catch something magical before the trailer park is destroyed.

I heard the screen door slam and listened as Katherine walked into the bathroom to brush her teeth. She was in there for a long time—deciding my fate, I assumed—and I dumped my cheese-cake into the trash. The bungalow had a dishwasher, but I needed to perform a mindless task to clear my head. Compared to every-thing else in my life, washing dishes made perfect sense. They were dirty, and when I was finished they'd be clean. This may not seem like much, but in the face of so much bullshit, simple accomplish-ments are worth their weight in unfulfilled dreams. The water was running, and I didn't hear Katherine walk up behind me. She slid her arms around my waist, and I felt the crackle of static electric-ity as her shirt attached itself to my back.

"Want to dry?" I asked.

"Sure," she replied.

I handed Katherine a dishrag, and we set to work. Neither of us said much because we were caught up in thinking about what was in store for us the next day. Katherine would still be line pro-ducer, and I (hopefully) would still be key grip. But we'd be some-thing else too. Starting tomorrow, we were all Ryan Donahue's slime.

Chapter 19

Captain Bingo

SEBASTIAN SHANE WAS tall and thin. The hair on his head was the same length as the hair on his face. He wore rimless glasses, a peach-colored Ralph Lauren polo shirt, and a shiny new viewfinder around his neck. He was a director.

"Okay," he said, strutting onto set. "Let's shoot the master from here with a thirty-five-millimeter lens, and—excuse me, what's your name?"

"Uh, Bobby Conlon."

"Well, Bobby Conlon, are you going to mark down the camera position or not?"

"Oh, Andrzej usually . . ." I turned to Andrzej, but his face was a block of concrete.

Sebastian said, "I set up my own shots, okay?"

"Sure thing, Sebastian," I replied and marked an X on the ground.

"Okay, next we'll shoot a tight two from here."

I marked the camera position.

"Thank you, Bobby. After that, we'll shoot the singles from here with the fifty. Don't bother marking those. I'll set them with the camera." He took the viewfinder away from his eye and turned to face us as if we were his audience. "And bingo, that's the scene. Any questions?"

No one said a word.

"Oh, Andrzej?"

"Yes."

"I'd like you to shoot a few inserts. Trees, birds, architecture— that kind of stuff. You never know when those kinds of details will save your ass in the cutting room."

"Yes, Sebastian."

"Reg, I'll be in my trailer working on the script with Donald. Come and get me in a half an hour. By then I expect the scene to be lit and the actors to be out of makeup. Okay?"

"You got it, Sebastian."

Sebastian pranced off. The moment he was out of earshot Andrzej turned to Troy and said, "Set up the shot. I'm going to take a nap. Somebody wake me up when that fuckhead comes back."

Andrzej walked away and Troy, Dusty, and I looked at each other.

"Is it just me," I said, "or did this just turn into a TV movie?"

"*And bingo, that's the scene?*" Troy said. "He didn't even rehearse with the actors."

"Yo, Bobby, thread up a couple of twelve-by grifflons, and we'll wheel them around when the actors show up," Dusty said. "If he wants this to look like *The Wide World of Sports,* he's got it. Anybody want a Red Dog? I'm buying."

No one said anything.

"Suit yourselves," Dusty said and walked away.

I turned toward Video Village. Hank and Katherine were silent as Frick and Frack drooled all over themselves.

"Is that kid fast or what?" asked Frick.

"Yeah, no more of those fucking two-hour rehearsals. Just watch, we're gonna wrap this picture by lunch," answered Frack.

Half an hour later the actors were out of makeup, Andrzej was back from his nap, and Sebastian appeared with a pale, tubby guy who reminded me of a toy koala bear.

"Everyone? This is my good friend Donald Rasmussen. He's going to be doing a little work on the script. When you start seeing those colored script pages in your mailboxes, you'll know who to blame." Sebastian slapped Donald on the back and said, "Go hang out by the monitor, Donny. I'll be there in a minute."

"You got it, Seb."

Seb and Donny. Donny and Seb. What a couple of fucking nerds. If Moose was around I would have bet him fifty bucks that Donny and Seb made Super 8 movies together in middle school.

"All right, Reg, let's get A Team in here and shoot this puppy."

"Sure thing, Sebastian."

Ryan Donahue eased out of his director's chair and strutted onto set with all the confidence of a twenty-two-point-three-million-dollar opening weekend.

"Where would you like me to stand, Sebastian?"

"Right over by that pay phone. Is Carlo around? Oh, there you are." Carlo was an actor pal of Ryan's who had arrived the week before when it looked like *Trail of Broken Hearts* was going to be a hit. "Carlo, your cue is when Ryan hangs up the phone. Slap him on the back, run your lines, and bingo, that's the scene."

Sebastian walked up to the camera. "Troy, right?"

"Yep."

"I want to watch the first couple of rehearsals through the camera. Keep an eye on the video monitor, and do what I do. Okay?"

"Sure," Troy said, climbing off the dolly.

Sebastian got behind the camera and looked through the lens. "Is everyone set? Great. Let's try one. And . . . action."

Nothing happened.

Sebastian pulled his eye away from the camera and said, "Is there a problem?"

"I'm sorry," Ryan said. "I'm just trying to get into the right frame of mind here. The scene before this one is when I have that shouting match with the professor in the lounge, right?"

"Riiiiiiight." Sebastian turned to Video Village and called to the script supervisor, "Mindy, could you come here for a sec, please?"

"Yes?" Mindy said, walking up to camera with the thick binder containing her notes on the movie.

"We're double-checking that the scene prior to this one is where Ryan gets into the fight with the other professor."

Mindy flipped a page and said, "That's correct."

"Great. Everyone back to one, please." Sebastian watched as Ryan sauntered back to his first position. "And . . . action!" Sebastian put his eye to the camera.

"I'm sorry," Ryan said, walking back to Sebastian. "I'm just wondering, if I just had a screaming match with another professor, would I really start off a telephone conversation by asking someone how his wife is?"

"Good point." Sebastian turned back to Video Village and said, "Donny, could you join us, please?"

Donny dribbled over to camera and Sebastian said, "Ryan's concerned about how he starts off the conversation with the department chair. You know, after he just had the fight with Rossi in the faculty lounge?"

"Uh-huh," Donald said.

Ryan said, "Instead of talking about his wife, wouldn't I just cut to the chase and say that I wasn't going to put up with any more of Rossi's bullshit?"

"Absolutely," Donald said.

"I agree completely," Sebastian said.

"But then again . . ." Ryan said, "there's that whole subplot in the book about the chair's wife having cancer."

"As good as the book is, it's not the movie," Sebastian said.

"What do you think, Donald?" Ryan asked. "Will that subplot with the chairman's sick wife have any bearing on your next draft?"

"Oh shit," Katherine whispered to Hank. I turned and saw the color had drained from her face.

Donald swallowed hard, scratched his leg, and finally said, "I think we could work that in, don't you, Seb?"

"Yeah." Sebastian nodded. "I think that could add a nice texture to the story."

"You sure?" Ryan asked.

"I sure am," Sebastian said.

"Absolutely," Donny said.

"Hold on a sec, will ya?" Ryan walked to his director's chair and pulled a paperback copy of *Aquarena Springs* from the side pocket. He handed it to Sebastian and said, "There is no subplot about the chairman's wife in the book. You haven't even read the book, have you? *Have you?*"

Neither Seb nor Donny said a word.

Ryan turned to Frick and Frack. "You fired Sir Richard for *this* loser? What the fuck were you thinking?" He turned back to Sebastian and said, "Call me when you have your shit together, Captain Bingo. I'll be in my trailer. C'mon, Carlo."

Ryan and his sidekick walked away as Sebastian climbed off the dolly.

"C'mon, Donny," he said, marching up to the producers as if nothing were his fault. "I'm the director of this movie, and I will not have this kind of prima donna bullshit on my set!"

I turned to the crew and said, "Show of hands. Who's read the book?"

No one raised their hands.

I shook my head. "Are we a bunch of illiterate retards, or what?"

"What do you mean?" Dusty asked. "When I did *The Long Goodbye* with Altman nobody read the book. Not even the big man himself. He said it was incomprehensible, and that was that."

"Are you comparing Robert Altman to this jerk-off?" I said.

"Of course not," Dusty said. "I'm just saying that Altman was a hell of a lot smarter."

"No shit," Troy said.

"Dusty, darling, would you care to join me at the camera truck for a beer and a nap?"

"Captain Bingo," I said. "That has a pleasant ring to it."

"More like Captain Douche Bag," replied Troy.

Dan Berg arrived so fast he must have been circling Austin in his Gulfstream. And this time he was not alone. At his side were four "associates" who looked like the talent agency equivalent of Yakuza hit men. While Dan Berg disappeared into Ryan's trailer to hold his client's twenty-two-point-three-million-dollar hand, the associates set about grinding Frick and Frack into a powder so fine you could have used them to cut baby laxative.

I felt the urge to call Natalie and fill her in on the latest gossip, but my last call to her had almost cost me my "relationship" with Katherine. Instead, I climbed into a fifteen-passenger van with the rest of the crew and headed to the Salt Lick to eat barbecue. I ate enough brisket to put a man twice my size into a cholesterol coma, but not as much as Andrzej and Dusty, who got into a rib-eating death match. Andrzej won by a couple of ribs, but I could tell that Dusty took a fall. This was confirmed when Andrzej went to the can, and Dusty spied an uneaten sausage link on the plate of the electrician sitting next to him.

"You gonna finish that?"

"All yours, boss."

"Nobody tell Señor Polack, okay?" Dusty said, spearing the sausage with his fork.

We returned to set and the entire Bryant/Berg posse were jammed in Ryan's trailer and Hank and Katherine were the sole inhabitants of Video Village. Someone had rigged a pair of rabbit ears to the monitor, and Hank and Katherine were watching a soap opera. Katherine waved me over.

"You didn't bring us back anything from the Salt Lick?"

"They didn't have Chinese Chicken Salad on the menu. Did I miss anything fun?"

"Donny's gone," Hank said with a smile. "His agent cut his asking price to Writers Guild minimum, and we still said no."

"That was fun," Katherine said.

"That was great," Hank said.

"What about Captain Bingo?"

"Gone. Joe and Jeff too."

"Talk about a palace coup."

"Yep," Katherine said. "You're looking at the new producer of *Aquarena Springs*."

"Cool, and who'll be directing our little photoplay?"

"That's a little more complicated," Hank said.

"Why?"

"The studio wouldn't let us shut down again. We needed someone familiar with the material who could start first thing tomorrow."

"I'm available." I said it like a joke, but I was dead serious. "And Andrzej would jump at the chance to—"

"We hired Elias," Katherine said.

Cut to a close-up of Bobby Conlon as his world comes crashing down. Betrayed by his friends, Bobby does his best to keep his composure when what he really wants to do is gobble a handful of

Vicodin and smash everything in sight. He looks down, feigning interest in a blade of grass, then looks up and says:

"Is Natalie coming too?"

"Nope," Hank said.

"Good luck keeping her away."

Katherine shook her head. "No Natalie. It was part of the deal."

"Natalie's got her hands full prepping *Ant Eater*," Hank said. "Besides, what better way to find out if Elias can really direct?"

"And if he can't?"

"If you're still available, maybe we can work something out."

Hank and Katherine went to go talk with Dan Berg and I wandered back to camera. Ryan's copy of *Aquarena Springs* was lying on the dolly where Sebastian Shane had left it. I picked it up and saw that Ryan Donahue had written his name on the title page and scribbled notes in the margins. I slipped the book into my cargo shorts. Maybe, if *Aquarena Springs* was a hit, I could get a few hundred bucks for it on eBay. I spied a couple of the Bryant/Berg boys standing around Video Village and wondered if they had seen me steal the book. Not a chance. My hair could have been on fire and they wouldn't have noticed me. I was the cinematic equivalent of a janitor to them. A fucking nonentity. I reached for my Xanax, and by the time I remembered I didn't have any more, I'd punched 3 on my speed dial.

"Miguel-Simm Productions."

"This is Bobby calling for Natalie."

"Hold, please."

Natalie came on the line saying, "I only have a minute. What's up?"

"You fucking cunt," I hissed. "You fucking hairy pig cunt. You *played* me. You made me look like an asshole in front of Dan Berg and Katherine and now you got Elias to direct this movie. Well, fuck you. Fuck you big time. Remember what I said about not contesting the divorce? Forget it. Tell Roz she can jam those divorce papers up her ass 'cause I'm hiring a new lawyer and I'm going to fucking *rape* you. I'm going after the house, and your pension, and everything else I can get my hands on. If you try to stop me, so help me God, I'll drag every one of your friends into court to give depositions. And you think that's bad? Remember that little videotape we made on my birthday? I didn't erase it like I said I did. Don't be surprised when it shows up on the Internet. So fuck you, bitch. I never want to talk to you again for the rest of my life!"

"Bobby, I—"

I didn't want to hear it. I was sick of Natalie's bullshit. Sick of lies. Sick of palace intrigue. I was sick of everything there was to be sick about—especially the ring tone on my cell phone, which I smashed against the dolly again and again. By the time I was finished, there was nothing left but a broken pile of plastic and my hand was covered in blood. As wonderful as that made me feel, it wasn't half as rewarding as looking up and seeing the two Bryant/Berg boys staring at me. *Ooh,* I thought, as I went to jam my throbbing fist into the beer cooler. *Maybe I'm not so invisible after all.*

Chapter 20

The Killer Instinct

ELIAS'S FLIGHT LANDED at 8:17, and our producers met him at the airport. It was Katherine's job to bring him back to the production office to prep with Andrzej for the next day's shooting. And it was Hank's job to meet me at the Omni for a drink and make sure I didn't beat Elias to death with a grip stand. It was flattering to be thought of as such a loose cannon, but I never would have done anything so obvious. I'd be far more sneaky and slip horse laxative into his coffee like Eric Roberts did to that cop in *The Pope of Greenwich Village.* Or I'd leave a horse head in his bed like they did to John Marley in *The Godfather.* At the very least, I could roll myself into a drooling, Vicodin-addicted ball of misery like I had when Elias ran off with Natalie. There were so many options.

A smarter production team would have fired me on the spot. But Hank was my friend, and Katherine was the woman who had waited sixteen years to take advantage of me. By my third Jack Daniel's, I had exhausted every movie revenge fantasy I could think of and had moved on to other, more productive flights of imagination. Hank had said that if Elias screwed up I could finish directing the movie. Maybe he hadn't used those exact words, but he'd joked about it, and that was enough for me. I mean, why not let me direct? I knew the script, was friends with the producers, and was already in Austin. What more did they need? Wackier things had happened, and I had no doubt that I could do a better job than the first two dorks they'd hired.

But the real reason they should have let me direct *Aquarena Springs* was *I deserved it*. I had earned the right on a hundred movie sets and for countless hours worked. If you added it up, I had dragged a dolly the size of the Taj Mahal around the world and back. I had pushed the White House across the ocean floor. I had circumnavigated the globe with a thousand movie cameras strapped to my back. I'd worked in the rain. I'd worked in the cold. And I'd worked through some of the gloomiest fucking nights you can possibly imagine. Why?

To earn a living? To make a buck?

Fuck that. I'd rather sell crack to preschoolers than to work on movies just for the money. I did it because movies were my life. And movies destroyed my life. I'd guzzled the Kool-Aid and was gacked to the gills. Remember when I said I'd always been faithful to Natalie? I lied. Movies were my mistress and had been all along. They got me up in the morning and tucked me in at night. I didn't have blood in my veins. I had celluloid, and it was pumping through my body at twenty-four frames a second. But I'm frail. I'm weak. I know I should turn my back on movies. I know they'll break my heart and leave me begging for more. But I can't say no. Movies have me. Movies own me. I believed their lies. I embraced their truths. Horse laxative in Elias's coffee? That was *nothing*. I would have ripped out his spleen with my stubby little fingers for a chance to direct.

Hank arrived looking tired and wired. He ordered a drink and sat down at my table.

"How's Elias doing?" I asked.

"Scared shitless," Hank said with a twisted grin.

"How are you doing?"

"Exhausted. What happened to the days when you hired a director and he stayed around to finish the movie?"

"Not to worry. When we make my movie, I promise to hang around for the whole shoot."

"I'm not sure my sanity will hold out that long."

"Just hang on for another couple of months. We go into production the first of the year."

Hank leaned forward. "You got a script for me to read?"

"No, but the important thing is I'm moving forward."

"What about financing?"

"My mom's brother died and left me a hundred and fifty thousand dollars."

"Don't do it."

"What?"

Hank put down his drink and said, "Don't waste your money. Buy an apartment or invest it in something. Don't make a movie."

"Why not?"

"Because you'll lose every penny and rich uncles don't come around that often."

"So what? I'll be a director."

"You want to be a director?" He waved an imaginary magic wand over my head. "Boom, you're a director. Now save your money and go back to being a grip."

"Wait a second, you four-eyed fuck. What happened to all that stuff about you helping me make my movie? Was that bullshit?"

"Nope."

"Then what was it?"

Hank stood. "I need another drink. You want something?"

"Yeah, a fifth of Jack Daniel's."

Hank walked to the bar and ordered. He flirted with the bartender, and it took all my strength and maturity not to throw an ashtray at him. When our drinks were ready, he brought them back to our table and said, "Somebody should have told you this a long time ago, but you don't have what it takes to be a director."

If he had said that I had only three months left to live it wouldn't have hurt more.

"How can you say that?" I sputtered.

"Because in all the time I've know you, you've never done anything more than talk about making movies. You haven't even finished one screenplay."

"Then why did you say you'd help me?"

"Somebody had to get you off those fucking pills."

"You mean this was all some kind of intervention?"

"And it worked, right? When was the last time you took anything stronger than a couple of Advil?"

"It doesn't matter."

"The hell it doesn't. When was it?"

"The day after I got here."

"Congratulations, that's over a week."

"Big fucking deal."

"It is a big deal. Six months ago you were a mumbling gob of pus. Now look at you."

"What? I'm a forty-four-year-old failure with a blown-out back and a wife who's fucking the guy who gets to call 'Action' tomorrow morning."

"Yeah, but you're clean."

I didn't have a snappy response for that one and said, "You're wrong about me not being able to make a movie. I know more about the nuts and bolts of filmmaking than anybody you know."

"I'm not talking about knowing stuff. I'm talking about that drive, that fire in the belly that'll make you do anything to get your movie made. Sorry, pal, I've seen the Killer Instinct in action, and you don't have it."

"The Killer Instinct? What are you talking about?"

"The world's full of people who say they want to make movies, but only those willing to chew off their arms to escape the bear trap of failure ever see their names in the opening credits, my friend. Look at Elias and Natalie. Look at Carni. You think she got that operation just to sleep with your pathetic ass? That was a career move. It's okay to be a chunky monkey when you live in New York and work for John Sayles, but that shit doesn't fly in LA. Out there, if you're too big a pussy to stick your fingers down your throat to get rid of a few extra calories, no one will trust you to jam your fist down your enemy's throat and tear off his balls. In LA fat is weakness without glamour. And glamour counts. You look good in Prada and Jil Sander, and nobody gives a shit what you're hooked on as long as you hit your marks and show up on time."

Hank kept talking, but I stopped listening. He was a sharp cookie when it came to making movies, but he didn't know shit about women, and he didn't know me. As he sat there rambling on, I made two important decisions. The first was that Hank could never find out that my rich uncle was really Katherine and the insurance company. If he didn't think I had the goods to be a director, he would never take a chance on committing fraud, or doing whatever it took to get my money. The second was that I had to sleep with Katherine. I needed a producing partner who believed in me, and Katherine fit the job description. But there was more to it than that. Hank had left me second-guessing myself, and if I could sleep with Katherine I could do anything. Killer Instinct, here I come.

"Here we go," Hank said, waving someone over. I turned and saw two women approaching our table.

"Who are they?"

"The blonde is an extra, and the brunette is the woman who's going to clean your clock tonight."

I grabbed his arm. "I'm not ready for that, Hank. I haven't been with anyone since Natalie."

"What about Carni?"

I shook my head.

"You mean that crap you told her about holding off until you signed your divorce papers was true?"

I nodded.

"Damn, boy, Natalie messed you up worse than I thought."

Chapter 21

Whores,
All Shapes and Sizes

THE NEXT MORNING a pale and exhausted Elias Simm stood in front of the crew and made a little speech. "I know this has been a difficult shoot," he began. "But that ends today. From now on we're going to make our days, break on time, and produce a terrific movie to boot. As some of you may know, this is my first show, and I'm going to be relying on all of you for your experience and enthusiasm. Feel free to offer any suggestions, and if there's anything I can do to help make this a better experience, please let me know."

Steveo's hand shot up.

"Yes?"

"Could you ask them to stop serving so much chicken at lunch?"

Everyone cracked up, and Steveo won the bottle of Cuervo Gold I'd offered to the first person to humiliate our director in front of the crew. Technically, Elias deserved this prize for making his dumb speech in the first place, but he was unaware of the little war I was waging behind his back. While I appreciated his honesty, standing up and announcing you're the least experienced person on the crew is not the best way to instill confidence. Elias could have scored a lot more points by keeping his mouth shut and tossing a hundred bucks into the beer kitty. I would have been happy to tell him that, but I was too busy wishing he'd die of a brain embolism.

We were shooting the same scene as the day before, but this time around Andrzej set up the shots because our director didn't know the difference between a fifty-millimeter lens and a two-liter bottle of Diet Sprite. His speech completed, Elias climbed behind the video monitor and didn't say another word for the rest of the morning. We got our first shot off in forty-five minutes and were ahead of schedule for the first time since we landed in Texas.

Frick and Frack would have been thrilled, but I was unimpressed. Sitting back and letting the machine do your work for you might have been great for the schedule, but it sucked for the movie. You can't defer everything to crew. The speed of a dolly shot or the color of a hair clip may not seem like much, but those choices add up. The results are called either talent or style, and that's what makes a good director. Jealousy and hatred aside, Elias did not have what it took to make a good movie. This was why Katherine made a strategic mistake when she barred Natalie from set. Natalie had taste and style in spades, and if Katherine had let Elias rely on Natalie the way that Peter had relied on Polly in their glory days, Elias had a shot at making a good movie. But with Natalie back in LA, Elias had about as much of a chance of turning our movie into something special as I did winning the Irish Sweepstakes.

As we were setting up the second shot, Troy turned to me and said, "So tell me about that honey you slept with last night."

"What honey?"

"Don't try and deny it. We saw you two piling into the elevator last night and her hands were all over you."

I looked around to make sure Katherine wasn't around and said, "We saw? As in you and who else?"

Troy leaned in and whispered, "Elvira, and man, is she pissed off at you. What did you do to her?"

"Not sleep with her."

"Hell hath no fury, my friend. I had to listen to her trash you for like a half an hour before she'd take off her girdle."

"She wears a girdle?"

"I believe the technical term is a corselet. For somebody with so much personality, she's sure insecure about her body. She wouldn't even let me see her naked."

What is it with all the sagging flesh on this job? I thought as a wave of nausea washed over me. I couldn't tell if it was from the previous night's Jack Daniel's, or the thought of seeing Elvira in a girdle. It was probably the booze, but the girdle came in a close second.

"So what was that honey's name?"

"Deirdre."

"And what does she do?"

"She manages a couple of stand-up comics, but mostly she's a hooker."

"Really?" Troy said, visibly impressed. "Was she on or off the clock?"

"On."

"What did she charge?"

"I have no idea. It was a gift."

"You wouldn't happen to have her phone number, would you?"

"Why? You're the last person I know who would need to see a hooker."

Troy shrugged. "Some nights I feel like pizza and other nights I feel like Chinese food. What can I say?"

I had never slept with a whore before—unless you count Natalie after she started banging Elias. The experience was weird, especially because I didn't realize Deirdre was a pro until halfway through the evening. I just thought she found me charming and attractive. The funny thing is, I think we would have gotten along great in another life. A life that didn't include Natalie, the film business, or Deirdre taking money for sex, of course, but I did feel a certain connection between us. Then again, maybe she was just good at her job. When I asked Deirdre what Hank told her when he booked her services, she said that he needed her for "an intervention."

"What's the deal?" she asked. "Are you like one of those guys who pretends to be straight, and then sneaks off to have sex with other men?"

"Nope."

"Well, you're not a junkie because I don't see any track marks, and you obviously have no trouble getting it up. So what kind of intervention is this?"

I told Deirdre the tragic tale of my life. I had been itching to get it off my chest, and Deirdre seemed as good a choice as any.

"That's pretty low," she said when I was finished. "This Katherine woman waits sixteen years, gets her stomach cut in half, and you're gonna fuck her for the insurance money."

"Putting it like that takes all the romance right out of it. Besides, it's a lot of cash."

"How much?"

"A hundred and fifty thousand dollars."

"I'll tell you what. You stay here. I'll go fuck her."

"You see my point."

"Maybe you could talk her into a double girl thing and we can split the money three ways."

"You do that kind of stuff?"

"If the price is right."

"What's the weirdest thing someone's asked you to do?"

"I don't talk about that stuff." She reached over and rubbed my dick. "Is that thing coming back to life anytime soon? One of my comedians is performing at the Velveeta Room tonight, and I'd like to catch his show."

"Is he very funny?"

"You like Aggie jokes?"

"What are Aggie jokes?"

"They're kind of like redneck jokes, but a lot more regional."

"Naw, that whole blue-collar comedy thing leaves me dry."

"Then Harlan's definitely not for you. You like political comedy? This other guy I handle does this bit about Barbara Bush and Hillary Clinton in bed together that I swear is gonna get him on *Letterman* one day."

"Is he performing tonight too?"

She shook her head. "He's in Houston doing a showcase."

"Then I guess it's going to have to be Aggie jokes," I said, climbing out of bed.

"Is that it? Harlan doesn't go on for another hour and the club's just a few blocks away."

I pointed at my shriveled-up member. "This thing's dead. And besides, I could use a few laughs."

"It's your call. Fucking. Comedy. It's all the same to me."

Back on set, Elias grew more passive with each shot, and by the time Reg called lunch, Andrzej was directing the movie. Lucky for me, I hadn't wasted a lot of energy tracking down horse laxative or decapitating an innocent Clydesdale to slip between Elias's sheets. He was going down on his own, and faster than I could have hoped. The Killer Instinct? The guy barely had survival skills. He just sat there with a bemused expression on his face like it was cocktail hour on the Cape. After a while, even I found myself wanting Elias to crawl out from behind the monitor and at least make an effort. But no, he just sat back and let it all blow by. What a tool.

No one else seemed concerned that the director of our little photoplay had been replaced by a life-size stuffed animal. Katherine was knitting a sweater, Hank was buried in a crossword puzzle, and the two remaining guys from Bryant/Berg were studying an L.L. Bean catalogue that had been making the rounds. If any of them cared about the movie we were making, they were doing an excellent job of hiding it.

"What the hell's going on?" I asked Hank when I caught him walking away from Video Village.

"I'm going to the honey wagon to take a dump. Why?"

"Why? I don't know. I just thought you'd be a little more concerned that our director is out to lunch and Andrzej is directing the movie."

"We're on schedule."

"Big fucking deal."

"What do you want me to do? Start telling Elias how to direct? If he wants to hand over the reins to Andrzej, that's fine by me. At this point, as long as Ryan's happy and the rest of the crew is playing nice, then I'm happy."

"And what's up with Ryan? I can't believe he's being so easy on Elias after he gave Sebastian such a hard time."

"If Ryan gets a second director fired, he'll come off looking like an out-of-control egomaniac. He's stuck with Elias just like the rest of us. And who knows? Maybe the Ivy League fuck will wind up making a good movie."

"That's it? That's all you've got to say?"

"Actually, there is one thing." Hank pulled a folded-up newspaper out of his back pocket and asked, "Who's the god of fire? I thought it was Prometheus, but that doesn't fit."

"Greek or Roman?"

"It doesn't say, but the third letter is a *p*."

"Hephaestus."

Hank counted the letters and said, "No, that doesn't work."

"There's a silent *a* after the *ph*."

"That's it! You're a genius, Bobby."

"Then let me finish directing this movie."

Hank slapped me on the back. "Such a kidder."

Chapter 22

Compression

WITHOUT A DIRECTOR to slow us down with pesky distractions like vision and ability, we wrapped in eleven hours. To celebrate, Katherine canceled dailies and slipped into something more comfortable. I was in an easy chair reading the latest issue of *American Cinematographer* when she appeared wearing a silk dressing gown over a champagne-colored garment I had not seen before. I would never forget it, though, because when Katherine sat on the couch I spied a thatch of brown pubic hair where the crotch should have been.

"Uh, your leotard is showing, Katherine."

"It's called a compression garment, actually."

"Is that so?" I said, thinking that somewhere in the world there was a person who sold crotchless compression garments for a living. I pictured her as a middle-aged woman named Gladys with gray hair and granny glasses. In addition to compression garments, she was the world's leading purveyor of erotic stump covers and naughty colostomy bags.

Katherine patted her lap and said, "C'mere, big boy."

I did as I was told and stretched out on the couch with my

head in her lap. I could feel the static gluing my hair to her robe, and Katherine looked down at me and said, "From this angle you look like Ed Harris."

"It must be my ruddy complexion."

"It's more like the hair line."

The scent of L'eau d'Issey wafted up from Katherine's gown and filled my nostrils. She had anointed herself in my honor, and despite my oath to remain faithful to Natalie, Katherine was determined to nail me then and there. And for the first time since she threw open her robe and offered herself to me, it didn't seem like such a horrible idea. Hank thought he was doing me a favor when he hooked me up with Deirdre, but the results were much worse than favorable. Afterward, alone in the Omni, I felt like a man condemned to life with no chance of parole, and without any medication to tamp down my addled brain, a flood of painful memories took control. Every failed relationship from third grade on came back to remind me of how empty my life had become. *I've waited sixteen years for you, Bobby.* Women didn't say stuff like that to me very often, and to be desired with such enthusiasm was more than I deserved. Katherine was everything I wanted in a woman except for one sagging detail. Could I get beyond that? I didn't think I was that accepting a person, but there was only one way to find out.

But first there was a little business to take care of.

"Do you know Greg Allen?" I asked.

"From the insurance company?"

"Yeah, Elvira said he's the one who turned down the claim on my truck."

"I've known Greg forever. He used to work for me as an accountant, and now we go to Lakers games together."

"I don't know what his problem is, but he's trying to screw me out of my money."

Katherine leaned down and kissed me. "I'll take care of it."

"Really?" I said, thinking that if it was going to be so easy I would have asked for a raise too. "I wasn't going to bug you about it," I whispered between kisses. "But I really need that money to make my movie."

"You're making a movie?"

"It's now or never. I'll tell you what, if you can get that money out of Greg I'll give you a producer's credit."

"Who else is on board?"

"Just you so far. Hopefully, I can find a couple of other people to do the heavy lifting."

"That shouldn't be too hard."

Mission accomplished. I slipped a hand under Katherine's gown and wrapped my arm around her waist. It felt like a gallon of warm Jell-O sealed inside a Ziploc bag, and I tried to concentrate on her more alluring qualities. Like her eyes. Katherine had spectacular eyes. They were deep and brown and had this innocent twinkle that a quarter century in the film business had not extinguished. And her smile. Katherine's lips weren't full in the Kim Basinger sense, but they were plump and soft and a pleasure to kiss. And the way she breathed. In the quiet of the bungalow I could hear her taking in air through her mouth in short, strong puffs, and when I rolled over and buried my face in the spot liberated by Gladys, that evil genius of orthopedic unmentionables, Katherine's breaths increased in speed and volume.

I followed Katherine into her room. She slipped off her robe, and when I tried to remove her compression garment she whispered, "Believe me, it'll be better for both of us if I kept this thing on."

We climbed into bed, and I was inside her within seconds. I grabbed her hips, and she ran her fingers along my shoulders, but it wasn't what either of us had hoped for. She was embarrassed about her body, and I had way too much Natalie on my mind. We moved around to try and get comfortable, but we couldn't get the

rhythm right. I kept slipping out of her, and we had to keep starting over accompanied by the never-ending crackle of static electricity. We both wanted this first time to be special, but we couldn't
get it together. When I popped out of her for the fourth time she
looked up with an embarrassed smile and whispered, "Try coming
at me from behind."

She climbed onto her knees and buried her face in her pillow.
I slipped inside her and, just like that, everything was right with
the world. I could heard her moaning into the pillow, and it made
an incredible feeling feel even better. My eyes followed the bumps
of her spine up to where her hairline began. Her neck arched. I
watched her squeezing the pillow with the rhythm of my thrusts.
Something shifted inside of me, and the world that I'd been
trapped in for the last year began to fade away. Natalie and Elias
and Ziploc bags filled with warm Jell-O were no longer an issue,
and Katherine and I were alone in a wonderful place.

Later, as we lay in each other's arms, I asked her why she had her
stomach stapled shut.

"Have you ever been addicted to anything?" she asked.

You mean besides Xanax, Vicodin, Anexsia, Lorcet, and every
other Vicoprofen I could get a doctor to write me a prescription
for? "I smoked for a while," I said with a shrug.

"Did you have a hard time quitting?"

"Just the first thirty times. After that it was a breeze."

"Then you know about the games you play with yourself. The
endless inner negotiations. When you're fat, it's even worse. It's
not like quitting other stuff because you still have to eat. What
happens is that every single thing you put in your mouth is sus-
pect. Flavor, taste, nourishment, everything gets turned upside
down." She sighed and said, "Do you really want to hear this?"

"Yeah. I do."

"You wouldn't believe what it's like to have your back and knees hurt all the time. And the crappy clothes. And the hormonal shit. And having to look at yourself in the mirror. And knowing that it's all . . . your . . . fault . . ."

"Hey." I touched her shoulder.

"You asked for it, huh? And you know what's really gross? The creepy guys who are into fat girls. Or the jerks who think they're doing you some kind of favor by hitting on you, and then freak out when you turn them down. But you know what finally made me get the operation?"

I shook my head.

"Ella Fitzgerald. When I was a kid my father took me to see her with the Count Basie Orchestra. She had these thick, thick glasses and sang 'A-Tisket, A-Tasket' and 'My Funny Valentine,' and it was like watching my father's record collection come to life. Then, years later, her diabetes got so bad they had to cut off her feet. I just couldn't believe it. With all the doctors and medicine in the world, they couldn't save Ella Fitzgerald's feet. And I thought, how will she ever be able to sing again after that?

"Then my blood sugar started going wacky and the doctor said I had type two diabetes. That's all I needed to hear. The funny thing was, it had nothing to do with losing weight. I was just scared of losing my feet. But after my operation, it was like Christmas when you're a little kid and you get so many presents at once, you don't know which one to play with. The diabetes went away and I could wear normal clothes, and people stopped looking at me like I was a freak. I felt like a new person. It was the best thing that ever happened to me."

So it wasn't the Killer Instinct after all, I thought as Katherine stroked my chest. Hank had been wrong. Katherine's actions weren't part of some Machiavellian scheme to take her to the top of the cinematic mountain. She was just a nice girl who didn't want to lose her feet. And here she was in bed with a flaming ass-hole who was going to use her like a piece of grip equipment and dump her the minute his movie won the grand prize at Sun-dance.

She would have been better off with the Killer Instinct.

Chapter 23

Backseat Director

It's not my movie. It's not my money.
It's not my movie. It's not my money.
—The Grip's Mantra

I WAS PULLING THE dolly off the truck the next morning when somebody called my name. I turned around and it was Elias. It was the first time we had been alone together since I had found out about him and Natalie. And, yes, I thought about killing him.

"Can I help you?" I asked.

"We need to talk."

"Okay."

"Not here."

I followed him out of the grip truck and toward his trailer. Just for fun, I grabbed the eight-pound sledgehammer we used to pound in stakes. Elias glanced back and, spotting the sledgehammer, asked, "What's that for?"

"To bash in your skull."

"Okay, but just so you know, if anything happens to me, my attorney has a letter implicating you in my death."

"Really?"

"Of course not."

Elias ran a hand through his hair and said, "This is kind of tough for me to say, but I need your help."

"What kind of help?" I asked, dropping the sledgehammer on the ground between us.

"I'm completely out of my depth here. I have no idea how to direct this movie, and if things stay on their present course Andrzej will take over completely."

"Sucks for you."

"No, it sucks for both of us."

"What do you mean?"

"Because Hank will pull the plug on my movie and then everything that's happened with Natalie will be for naught."

"For naught?" I snorted. "Who the fuck are you supposed to be? Nobody says naught in regular conversation."

"Naught's a perfectly acceptable word."

"Maybe in Harvard Yard it is, but not on a movie set."

"Forgive me. I'll to stick to the vernacular."

"Goddamned right, bubba," I said, picking up the sledgehammer and using it like an imaginary golf putter. "Now what's this shit about Natalie?"

"Do you think what she did was easy for her? Do you think she's not torn to pieces by it?"

"Do you think I give a shit? Don't try and make me feel guilty."

"I'm not trying to make you feel anything. I'm just saying that if my project falls apart, there's a strong chance Natalie will too."

"Good thing she's got a guy like you to take care of her, huh? A word of advice. When her depression kicks in and she can't get out of bed in the morning, don't let her have any asparagus. Otherwise things can get mighty funky." I rested the sledgehammer on my shoulder and smiled.

"There's another reason you should help me."

"What's that?"

"Because it's the closest you'll ever come to directing."

"That's what you think. Katherine and I go into production on my movie as soon as we wrap this job. And at the rate Andrzej's going, that shouldn't take more than a few weeks."

"Your own movie? What's it about? I'd love to read the script. Have you started writing it yet?"

"Fuck you," I said and threw the sledgehammer at him. I meant for it to land at his feet, but I underestimated my anger.

"Hey!" Elias shouted, jumping out of the way. The sledge landed where he had been standing and left a two-inch divot in the ground. It was more of a statement than I had intended to make.

"I could get you fired for that!"

"You're the director, dipshit. You could get me fired if you didn't like the way I said 'Good morning.'" I picked up the sledge-hammer. "But then who would direct the movie for you?"

"Then you'll do it?"

I slung the hammer over my shoulder. "Absolutely not, but I will give you a word of advice. No more speeches to the crew. It makes you look like a pussy."

I walked back to the truck and found Steveo sitting on the dolly eating a breakfast burrito. "This just arrived," he said, handing me a letter. "The office PA said it came registered mail. Elvira had to sign for it."

"It must have something to do with my divorce," I said, feeling a twinge of anxiety in my gut. Natalie must have taken what I had said about raping her seriously. This was not good.

Except the letter had nothing to do with my divorce. It was written notification from the DeSalvo Brothers Salvage Company saying that the contents of my truck were being auctioned off to pay for their storage fee of one hundred dollars a day.

"What the fuck?" I handed Steveo the letter.

"This sucks," he said after reading it.

"That's an understatement."

"No, this really sucks."

"What are you talking about?"

"Remember what I said about Moose tossing that half pound of dope in the river?"

"Yeah."

"I lied. It's still on the truck."

I grabbed the letter and read it again.

"What's today's date?" I asked.

"The twelfth."

"I am so incredibly screwed. It says here that the day after tomorrow the DeSalvo Brothers are doing an inventory of my truck, and that a member of the Bucks County Sheriff's Department will be on hand to ensure a 'fair and accurate' record of the contents."

"What are you going to do?" Steveo asked.

"I better go talk to Katherine."

"Could I ask you a favor?"

"Yeah?"

"Don't tell her I had anything to do with the dope."

As I made my way across set, images of every prison movie I'd ever seen, from *I Am a Fugitive from a Chain Gang* to *Ernest Goes to Jail,* burned through my brain. None of them were the whiz-bang, good-time hours that I was hoping to ease into once I got over the whole Natalie thing. On the positive side, the skills I had acquired in the film business would come in quite handy in prison: I'd be excellent at honing silverware into weapons, navigating mail carts around impossibly tight corners, and building birdcages out of toothpicks. And when it finally came time to hang myself, I was going to have a hell of a time choosing just the right knot for the occasion. Fucking dope smokers. Why couldn't they just drink themselves to death like the rest of us law-abiding losers?

Okay, I'll admit it. I was worried. I was more than worried. I was scared. I thought my luck had turned around, but the streak of bad juju that had cost me a wife and a truck had not run its course. Whatever deity I'd pissed off was still very much into messing with me. This was confirmed when I got to Video Village and saw Katherine talking to Elvira. Katherine's eyes were filled with tears, and if I had been packing a gun, it would have been a tough decision who to shoot first, Elvira or myself.

"Speaking of weasels," Elvira said as I approached. "If it isn't Romeo Conlon."

"Oh, hi, Elvira. You look *fabulous* this morning, is that a new girdle you're wearing?"

"Go to hell," she said and marched off.

"Give my best to Desmond," I called after her.

Katherine climbed out of her director's chair and looked me in the eye. "Is it true?" she asked.

What could I say? That it was all Hank's idea? That Deirdre was only a hooker and meant nothing to me? The same horrid feeling I got when I found out about Natalie and Elias grabbed hold of my insides and twisted me up like a pretzel. It was worse this time because there was no one to blame but myself.

"Yeah," I said. "It's true."

Katherine looked at her feet and said, "I thought you were different."

"Different from who?"

"All of them."

    Q: What's the difference between a grip
       and a bucket of shit?
    A: The bucket.

Chapter 24

▮▮▮▮▮▮▮

Aquarena Springs

LUCKY FOR ME, room 619 was available when I returned to the Omni that night. After a few fun-filled nights in the house of my dreams, it felt good to be back in a cold and impersonal hotel room again. Katherine wouldn't let me anywhere near the bungalow, and I was forced to wash my T-shirt and cargo shorts in the bathroom sink. I had no clothes, no place to go, and nothing was on television. I toyed with the idea of renting a pay-per-view movie, but the accounting department examined our hotel bills with a high-powered microscope, and I had no desire for Katherine to find out that I'd rented *William Shakespeare's The Merchant of Penis* on the night she'd kicked me out of the bungalow. With nothing else to do, I picked up the copy of *Aquarena Springs* I'd stolen from Ryan Donahue and began to read.

The novel opened with the wife of a middle-aged writer named Robert Marcus dumping him for his best friend. Robert is devastated and takes the first job away from New York that he can find, which is a gig teaching creative writing at Texas State University in San Marcos, Texas. Adjacent to the university is a run-down amusement park named Aquarena Springs. Once famous for an underwater diving show starring Ralph the Swimming Pig, the park has gone bankrupt and been taken over by the university.

Depressed by the loss of his wife, Robert finds himself unable to write. He becomes so desperate to crack his writer's block that he tries his hand at the creative writing assignments he assigns to his students. Robert's ego eventually gets the better of him, and he submits his work to be read anonymously in class. The students trash his writing as being too depressing, and when he tries to defend himself, they realize what he has done. They complain to the administration, and Robert becomes the laughingstock of the university.

Not only is he humiliated, but he can't quit because he's flat broke from his divorce. Meanwhile, Robert's writer's block grows so bad that his nose bleeds every time he picks up a pencil. He wanders the grounds of Aquarena Springs, watches the water show from a hill overlooking the lagoon, and falls in love from afar with one of Ralph's costars, an overweight water ballerina named LeeAnne. Robert is too smitten to speak to her, and pours his feelings into a journal with a handkerchief held to his bleeding nose. It takes him weeks to gather up the courage to speak with her, but Robert eventually asks LeeAnne out on a date, and she says yes. Their romance blossoms, as does Robert's writing. His breakthrough comes when he realizes that the observations in his journal are more interesting than anything he's written in years, and he turns them into a novel.

On the same day that he mails the novel to his agent, the head of the English department informs him that they are not renewing his contract and the university announces that they are closing Aquarena Springs. Robert and LeeAnne have no other work options, and their desperation tears them apart. Just when it looks as if all is lost, Robert's agent sells his book. The sale gives him the money he needs to marry LeeAnne and to leave San Marcos forever. The novel ends with Robert and LeeAnne buying

Ralph from the university and driving him to a farm in the Texas Hill Country.

I was shocked. *Aquarena Springs* was really good. Frick (or was it Frack?) was right. It was like *The Bridges of Madison County* without all those fucking bridges—a sweet and salty confection that, once you got over the guilt of enjoying it, was totally satisfying. The literary equivalent of ketchup. What made it so good—and what was completely missing from the script—was the tone of the writing and Robert Marcus's self-depreciating humor in the face of repeated humiliations. By page three, it was obvious why the book had become a best seller, and why so many readers responded to this gentle tale of a man trying to pull his life back together. What I didn't understand was why Ryan Donahue, a thirty-two-year-old actor with a washboard gut and a jaw you could park a Buick on, was cast as Robert Marcus.

Choosing Ryan Donahue to play Robert Marcus drove a steaming garbage truck through the heart of what made *Aquarena Springs* special. In the book, when Robert Marcus gazes down at LeeAnne, you totally feel for the guy because he doesn't have a shot in hell of hooking up with her. But when you swapped out Ryan Donahue for Robert Marcus, you had no problem picturing him ripping off his shirt, doing a triple gainer off the side of the mountain, and ravishing LeeAnne in front of Ralph, God, and a busload of Canadian tourists. The casting destroyed the story. They could have picked any older actor from Clint Eastwood to Robin Williams to play Robert Marcus, and *Aquarena Springs* could have been a great movie. Instead, they chose Ryan Donahue, and we were doomed to make a piece of crap.

And I know a little something about pieces of crap. You can't imagine how many bad movies I've worked on. When I started out in this business, home video had just taken off and the Asian market bought any movie with a gun in it. I used to work for this guy named Charlie McGruder who directed movies starring whatever piece of military equipment he could get his hands on. One time, Charlie found a guy in New Jersey who owned a tank, so we made *Tank Commandos,* the climax of which took place in front of a VFW hall in Bergen County because they had an old cannon parked out front. Charlie didn't even ask permission. We just pulled up in full commando gear and started shooting. And when a bunch of drunken old vets piled out suffering from Greatest Generation flashbacks, we bought them a case of beer and put them in the movie too.

My mother once tried to rent *Jeep Attack!*—a masterpiece shot on Rockaway Beach after Charlie met this closet Nazi who restored WWII Schwimmwagens—at her local video store, but the clerk said he couldn't do it because the movie was so bad.

"But my son worked on it," my mother pleaded. "I want to see his name in the credits."

"Tell you what," the twerp replied. "Go find it on the shelf and I'll fast-forward to the end so you can see his name. That way I won't feel guilty for taking your money. But next time you talk to that son of yours, tell him that he should be ashamed of himself for working on a movie that bad."

The kid had a point. The world would be a better place if there were fewer bad movies on the video store shelves. Working on a bad movie makes a hard job twenty times harder. Every sandbag feels two pounds heavier and every hour lasts seventy minutes. I got into this business because I love movies, and working on a piece of garbage makes me feel guilty and cheap. I can name a dozen movies where I should have pushed the camera into the Hudson River instead of letting them use it to violate the laws of art and taste.

And I'm not talking about *Tank Commandos* either. Charlie

McGruder, for all his lack of talent, went out every morning convinced he was going to shoot the greatest movie ever made. Sure, he wanted to make a buck, but Charlie wasn't cynical. He loved movies and lived to blow shit up. Working for Charlie was exhausting, frustrating, and dangerous, but it was never dull, and it was always fun. But God please forgive me for some of the *American Playhouse,* independent film, actor-turned-director, Sundance Festival, rich-kid-as-auteur, renowned-Eastern-European-director-making-his-American-film-debut *crap* I've worked on. Self-Indulgent. Postmodern. Artsy-fartsy. Cinema of Poetry. Dogma 95. *Garbage.*

May a band of avenging angels swoop down from heaven and smite every last copy of these cinematic atrocities from every video store on the planet. And when they're done with the video stores, I hope they head straight to the film vaults and dump the negatives for those pretentious pieces of shit straight into a sacred vat of Clorox. When the time comes to meet my maker, I'm not worried that I'll be judged for walking past homeless people on the street, but I'm terrified that I'll be sentenced to push a dolly through the sizzling corridors of hell for working on *Men of Respect,* a Mafia version of *Macbeth* starring Rod Steiger and John Turturro.

"So Robert," I fear God will say to me on Judgment Day, "I have one question for you. What the fuck were you thinking? That movie *sucked.*"

And lo, I will feel shame.

I asked the front desk for a five o'clock wake-up call and tried to sleep, but there was too much stuff bouncing around in my head: Natalie, Katherine, Deirdre, Andrzej, Elias, my truck, the insurance company. Where to begin? I turned on the light and picked up the copy of *Aquarena Springs* on my nightstand. Something was bothering me, and I turned to the passage describing LeeAnne's "generous thighs and Botticelli" belly. The description reminded me of Katherine, whose thighs and belly I had never actually seen or touched except through her compression garment. This hardly mattered, as images from the night before came rushing back. I was transfixed by the memory of her eyes, the bumps of her spine, and the mouthwatering combination of flesh and Lycra.

Overcome by emotion, I climbed out of bed and rubbed my feet on the carpet. I touched a floor lamp and a spark jumped off my fingertip, igniting a craving deep inside me. I tore the cover off the bed and dragged it across the floor. A symphony of electrostatic crackles filled the air. I pulled off my shirt, stood near the wall, and watched with perverse fascination as my chest hair reached toward the wall like a drowning man grasping for shore. I leaned in closer, and my right nipple touched the wallpaper. A spark lit up the room, and a shiver of ecstasy rushed down my spine.

What the hell was happening to me?

Chapter 25

Hell to Pay

Aquarena Springs was a real place. Located half an hour south of Austin, it had fallen on hard times, and with the exception of a glass-bottom boat tour, they had let it rot. The lagoon was covered in algae, the resort hotel boarded up, and the overhead cable ride rusted and still. It would have been a great place to shoot a zombie movie.

Filming underwater may sound like fun, but it's actually a big fat pain in the butt. Every shot takes four times longer than normal, and no matter how many members of the crew claim to be certified divers, some numb-nuts always runs out of oxygen in the middle of the best take of the day. With so many people flopping around, the crystal-clear water of Aquarena Springs grew cloudy with silt, and we had to wait ten minutes between takes for it to settle. On the upside, it was pleasant to see the female crew members in bathing suits, and Andrzej never grew tired of pushing people into the lagoon. Being a terrible swimmer, I handed the job of babysitting the camera over to Buzzy, who was so graceful in the water he could have been a dolphin in a past life. This freed me up to prep other parts of the park and avoid Katherine's acid stares.

Not to mention that I was exhausted. My little foray into electroerotic stimulation the night before had left me too aroused to sleep, and I had stayed up half the night worrying about how to get a half pound of dope out of a bonded storage facility over a thousand miles away. You'd think that after seeing *Ocean's Eleven* and *Mission Impossible* so many times on cable, I would have been an old hand at planning intricate heists from impregnable fortresses. Sadly, this was not the case. And it wasn't just the pit bulls and video cameras that worried me. With a name like DeSalvo Brothers Salvage, it was probably a safe bet that the guys "guarding" my equipment had more than a passing connection to the Corleone family. I was trying hard not to panic, but by eleven o'clock that morning I had exhausted every possibility I could think of for getting the dope out of there.

Except one.

"Is that thing charged yet?" I called to Steveo.

"Just about," he said, handing me the cell phone I'd bought to replace the one I'd smashed against the dolly.

I looked down at my new top-of-the-line Motorola. Cousin Roger was sending my address book from Brooklyn, and the next week was going to be all about entering numbers into this complicated device. There was, however, one number I knew by heart, and with heavy finger I punched it in.

"Miguel-Simm Productions."

"This is Bobby calling for Natalie."

"She's in casting right now."

"I'll try again later." I hung up and wondered how many times I'd have to say "I'm sorry" before Natalie spoke to me again. I checked my watch and saw that time was running out. In less than twenty-four hours the DeSalvo Brothers would start going through my stuff, and Sheriff Billy Bob would be issuing a warrant for my arrest.

"Steveo!"

"What!

"Here," I said, tossing him the phone. "Hit SEND, and tell the receptionist you're Sammy Michaels calling for Natalie."

"Sammy Michaels?"

"Yeah."

"Do you want me to disguise my voice or something?"

"Your regular voice is fine."

Steveo did as I asked, and Natalie got on the line immediately.

"What's the matter?" she asked in a tone devoid of emotion.

"I need your help. Mitch stashed a half pound of weed in Gerti, and a sheriff is supposed to be there when the salvage company inventories it tomorrow."

Natalie let out a laugh. "Sorry, Bobby, but that's not my problem. Why don't you have your big-time divorce lawyer take care of it after he's through raping me?"

"I'm sorry I said those things, but I'm in trouble here."

"And . . ."

"And I'm really, really sorry."

"And . . ."

"And as soon as I get off the phone I'll call Mark's Garden and order you the biggest bouquet imaginable."

"With peonies?"

"With peonies."

"And Queen Anne's lace?"

"And Queen Anne's lace."

"And then you'll start helping Elias direct the movie."

"No fucking way."

"Then have fun in prison, butt boy."

"C'mon on, Natalie. Stop acting like ten-year-old."

"*I'm* acting like a ten-year-old? You're the one who threw a sledgehammer at him."

"Elias told you that? God, he's such a little tattletale."

"What's it gonna be, Bobby? Jail or backseat directing?"

"The latter."

"Excellent. I knew you'd see things my way. Now call Moose."

"And do what?"

"Have him take care of the dope for you. Duh."

"That's it? I could have thought of that without having to promise you anything."

"But you didn't, did you?"

She was right.

"Now tell me," Natalie said, "why did Miss Goody-Two-Shoes kick you out of the house?"

"Because she found out that I slept with a hooker."

Natalie said nothing. I tried to wait her out, but she was better at that kind of stuff than I was. "You still there?" I finally asked.

"Yes. I'm just really disappointed. That's all."

"Coming from you, that really means something."

"What happened to you, Bobby? You used to be the most faithful person I knew."

"I think something busted inside of me."

"A broken heart is no excuse."

"It's not my heart. It's like my soul is out of whack. Nothing's the same anymore."

"Fix it. You're too good a person to turn into an asshole."

"Thanks, I guess."

"And speaking of being an asshole . . . you're not really going to sue me for my house and pension, are you?"

"Of course not."

"Good, because Roz FedExed the divorce papers to you. They should be arriving this afternoon."

"How efficient."

"It's what I do."

I hung up and felt the obligatory wave of sadness wash over me. I wasn't ready to call Moose and wondered for the thousandth time what my life would have been like if I hadn't taken the job where I'd met Natalie. Back then, I slept beside milk crates filled with grip equipment and scoured the floors of movie sets looking for stray bits of rope and gaffer's tape to take home. While other guys my age were working on Wall Street and buying German beer and oysters, I lived in shitbox apartments and survived on peanut butter and ramen noodles. But I was working on movies, and that was all that mattered.

I became a dolly grip because it was as close as I could get to the action. By the end of most gigs, not only did the actors and director remember my name, but they sometimes asked my opinion. Thanks to my close proximity to the camera, I'd improvised lines of dialogue on a handful of movies, and my name appeared on FBI badges, newspaper headlines, and door buzzers in a dozen more. I was there when actors gave performances that won Academy Awards, and had my picture taken with everyone from John Travolta to Meryl Streep.

In the midst of all this glittering activity, it was easy to pretend my participation mattered. Comparing notes on the opening crane shot of *The Man with the Golden Arm* with Marty Scorsese or asking David Mamet about his script for *The Untouchables* made me feel like an honest-to-God filmmaker. The only problem was, I was full of shit. Pushing dolly—even for cameramen as talented and sadistic as Andrzej—was a waste of time. Hanging out with actors and directors was a contact high that provided little more than cocktail chatter. They were distractions from my real job, which was supposed to be writing and directing.

"A little help, please," Steveo shouted from inside the truck.

"What?"

"The spindles they sent us are too big for the size cable we have. Should I send them back?"

I picked one up and said, "Yeah, these are useless. Swing by Home Depot after lunch and get the proper ones. Better yet, go to that fancy hardware store on Anderson and bring back some of those chocolate-covered espresso beans that Andrzej likes."

"Okay, but you're going to have to pay for the beans yourself."

"Just slip it in your petty cash."

"Didn't you read Elvira's latest memo?"

"Which one is that?"

"The one that says production has to approve all petty cash expenditures over five dollars."

"What's the point of having petty cash if you can't blow it on stupid shit like chocolate covered espresso beans? I'll talk to Dusty about it."

"Don't bother. We're the only department that got the memo. I checked."

"How come?"

"You tell me, Casanova. My guess is it has something to do with you hanging out here instead of at Video Village with our beloved line producer."

"Katherine's not like that," I said, rubbing my tired eyes. "It's probably Elvira taking matters into her own hands."

"Either way, it sucks."

"It'll blow over by the end of the week."

"It better. Who's Sammy Michaels, anyway?"

"Years ago, Natalie and I went to Mexico City when all these kidnappings were taking place. Our travel agent told us to make up code names in case one of us got abducted. If we used the code name, it meant it was time to mortgage the house for ransom money."

"That's very James Bond of you. Who's Sammy Michaels?"

"Ever see a movie called *Targets*?"

Steveo shook his head.

"It's Peter Bogdanovich's first film. He also plays a small role as a movie director. The character's name is Sammy Michaels."

"That has to be the most obscure movie reference I've ever heard in my life."

"Stick with me, pal. There's plenty more where that came from."

"I thought this was supposed to be your last show."

"Not at the rate I'm going. Do you have Moose McMahon's number?"

"Check the crew list in the road box."

There was an envelope with my name on it sitting on the road box. I tore it open to read:

> Dear Bobby,
>   Since your housing allowance has been reallocated toward the rental of "Griphaus," you are personally responsible for picking up the cost of Room 619. That said, you are still eligible for the production's special room rate of seventy-nine dollars per night plus all applicable taxes. This represents a genuine savings of over twenty-three percent off of the Omni's standard rack rate! If you have any questions, please don't hesitate to call.

Elvira had scribbled *You little shit!* across the bottom of the memo with a red Sharpie. That was one of the things I liked best about the film business—the way people kept their opinions to themselves.

I crumpled the memo, threw it at Steveo, and found Moose's number in the road box. It listed his real name as Aloysius, which was news to me. I was tempted to call him that the next time I saw him, but decided that I also enjoyed having a full set of teeth in my mouth.

This is Moose. State your business after the beep.

"Moose, this is Bobby Conlon. I'm in a jam and need your help."

"Yo, Bobby, what's up?"

"Oh, hi, Moose. I thought I was talking to your voice mail."

"I just answer like that when I don't recognize the number of the person calling. By the by, I'm sorry about what happened to your truck. I was so worried about them shutting down the movie that I never got to take a nap. Pretty fucked up, huh?"

"Don't sweat it, although that's kind of why I'm calling."

"Talk to me."

"Certain people who shall remain nameless stashed a half pound of weed in the grip truck before you left for Texas. I just got a letter from DeSalvo Brothers Salvage Company saying they're going to auction off my equipment and that a member of the Bucks County Sheriff's Department will be there when they inventory it tomorrow."

"Half."

"What?"

"I want half of whatever you get for your stuff."

"Is that fair?"

"It's too late for fair. To put it bluntly, you're fucked."

"Good point. What do you plan on doing?"

"Don't ask. Don't tell. Where's the dope?"

"Hold on a second." I put a hand over the phone and yelled, "Hey, Bob Marley, where did you and the Wailers hide your ganja?"

"In the twelve-by butterfly bag."

I took my hand off the phone. "It's in an orange bag marked Twelve by Twelve Silk."

"Consider it done. And one more thing. You tell Mitch Markham that the next time he uses me to haul dope without making it worth my while I'm breaking his fucking skull."

"It'll be a pleasure."

Chapter 26

Directing 101

Tomorrow is Greek Waiter Day! Show some team
spirit and wear black pants and a white short-
sleeve shirt. Souvlaki is optional.
    —From "Elvira's Notes" on Day 11's call sheet

I GOT BEHIND ELIAS in the lunch line and whispered, "When you're finished eating meet me at the grip truck."

"Okay."

"What'll it be, Elias?" Joe the Cook asked as Elias slid his tray up to the catering truck window. "Chicken and dumplings or chicken parmigiana?"

"I'm sorry, but thought I asked for there to be less chicken."

"You did, but I gotta work through the five cases I have in the cooler before I can move on to something else. That's why I doubled up on it. You know, to get it over with quick."

"I appreciate it, Joe. I'll have the chicken and dumplings."

He handed Elias a plate, and I slid my tray up to the serving window. When Elias was out of earshot, Joe said, "What'll it be, Bobby? Shepherd's pie or lobster?"

"What about chicken and dumplings?"

"I only got a few servings left, and I'm saving those for the director."

"I'll have the lobster."

"Lobster it is."

I choked down my lunch and rushed to meet Elias. As pissed as I was at having to help the man who stole my wife, I was jazzed to think of the afternoon's work as a directorial challenge instead of as a burden to endure before I cracked open my first wrap beer.

"The most important thing," I told Elias, "is that Andrzej doesn't find out about this. He wants to direct Hank's third movie more than you do, and if he figures out I'm helping you, I'm dead."

"Can't I just have him fired?"

"You can fire anyone, but firing Andrzej would be a major mistake. He may be a prick, but he's also the best cameraman you'll ever work with. You let Andrzej pick the shots, and you'll finish ahead of schedule, and the movie will look great."

"Then what am I supposed to do?"

"Two words: Ryan Donahue. Concentrate on his performance and everything else will fall into place. And don't feel like you have to direct the hell out of him. Ryan's already got his character figured out. Your job is to make him feel comfortable and confident. Never give him a line reading, and always go straight to him after a take. Actors hate it when directors leave them flapping in the breeze to go talk to the cameraman. And if you really want Ryan to love you, get the hell out of Video Village. Watch a couple of rehearsals from behind the monitor, then stand near camera for the takes. Concentrate on the performances. Troy will tell you if there's a problem with the shot, and if there's any doubt you can always check the playback."

"What if Ryan does something I don't like?"

"The last thing you want to do is get in a pissing match with a movie star. If Ryan does something wrong, just explain the problem as simply and pleasantly as you can. You're a charming fuck, that shouldn't be too hard for you."

"Hey."

I pulled the script pages for that afternoon's work from my cargo shorts. It was a short scene between Ryan and the elderly groundskeeper he befriends at the park. I handed the pages to Elias and asked, "Anything about this scene strike you as out of the ordinary?"

Elias read the scene and said, "Not really."

"Me neither. Just a couple of guys on a bench drinking coffee. Let them rehearse it a couple of times, pick something to compliment them on, and shoot it. Do three or four takes, ask Peter if it was good for him, and we're on our way back to the hotel. Piece of cake."

"It can't be that easy."

"For this scene it is." Then I remembered something Ryan had underlined in his copy of *Aquarena Springs* and said, "Remember how before there were Starbucks you had to tear that little plastic triangle off the top of Greek diner coffee cups to drink it?"

"Sure."

"That might be a nice piece of business for the scene. Have Ryan tear off a triangle, start to throw it away, then stick it in his pocket when he remembers it's the groundskeeper's job to pick it up. Actors love that kind of shit."

An hour later, thirty-five seasoned professionals and a half million dollars' worth of motion picture equipment were pointed at two actors on a bench in south-central Texas. The crew was still logy from lunch, and a couple were asleep on their feet. Those who were paying attention watched as the actors ran through the scene and the cameraman made the final adjustments to the lighting.

"All right," the assistant director called. "Let's have hair and makeup in for last looks and we'll try shooting one."

"Hold it for a second, Reg," came an unfamiliar voice from the wilderness. The crew turned, and Elias Simm rose phoenixlike from behind the monitor.

"What the hell does *he* want?" someone whispered as Elias dashed to the bench and sat between the actors.

Andrzej glared at Reg, and Reg shrugged as if to say, *Hey, it's not my fault.*

"That's a great idea," Ryan said, slapping Elias on the back. "When I read that in the novel, I thought it would go great in the scene, but I totally spaced on it."

"Reg," Elias called, waving to his assistant. "Could you do us a favor and track down a couple of those Greek diner coffee cups and a bunch of plastic lids? We'd like to use those instead of these Styrofoam ones."

"Props!" Reg shouted.

After that, all Elias needed was a gin and tonic, and he could have been at a cocktail party on the Cape. The old Simm charm came rushing back, and when Elias announced he preferred to stand near the camera instead of behind the video monitor, I thought Ryan was going to plant a big juicy one on his cheek. You could feel the mood rise as Elias took charge, and with the exception of Andrzej, who looked like he wanted to beat Elias to death with his viewfinder, everyone fell under our director's spell. I, of course, derived exactly zero pleasure from my pupil's success. The entire time he was winning over the crew with his prep school bonhomie, I was secretly hoping he'd get into a fight with Ryan so I could say, *I told you so.* Not a chance.

Elias's success was too much for me to take, and I headed back to the grip truck. There was a present from Roz Chaffman waiting for me on the road box. I tore open the FedEx Pak and sat down on the lift gate. Seeing Natalie's and my name on the first page of the decree filled my pockets with stones. I saw her walking down the aisle and wondered what had gone wrong. So many dreams, so many plans, so much pain. I reached for my cell phone, but stopped short of dialing her number.

"Those look legal," Slocum said, hopping onto the lift gate.

"My divorce papers."

"Sorry, brother," he said, reaching into his back pocket and pulling out a round tin.

"What's that?"

"Skoal. You want a hit?"

"Sure."

Slocum filled his lower lip and tossed me the can. "Ever dipped before?"

"Years ago, but my wife made me stop."

"There's one benefit of getting divorced. Is it costing you a fortune?"

"Not too bad." I fished out some Skoal and stuck it in my mouth.

"Got any kids?"

"Nope."

"Then you're getting off easy. My divorce was hell. I thought I married a reasonable individual, but brother, was I wrong. I should of known she was nuts by the kind of wedding she wanted—hundreds of guests, a ten-piece orchestra, and a honeymoon in Waikiki. You ever been to Hawaii?"

"No, just the Caribbean."

"It's paradise, man. Did you know that they consume fifty percent of all the Spam in the world there? They even use it to make sushi."

"No way."

"Swear to God. I even tried it."

"What did it taste like?"

"What the hell do you think it tasted like? It tasted like Spam.

I've done a lot of dumb shit in my life, but dropping forty-seven bucks on Spam sushi has to top the list. That and marrying Daisy."

"Your wife's name was Daisy?"

"Daisy Louise Winesap. Sounds like something out of *Dukes of Hazzard,* don't it? We almost made it too. We had a sweet little place near Town Lake, and I had a steady gig installing T1 lines for all them dot-com dummies. My big mistake was letting Daisy handle the finances. I thought we were doing okay, but she kept buying more and more shit and throwing it on the credit cards."

"Those things are evil, man."

"Tell me about it. I still haven't paid off that damn honeymoon, and it kills me to think that eating Spam sushi near the ocean may be the high point of my life. When the Internet bubble burst I did everything I could to get by: landscaping, cashier in a convenience store, I even sold jerky on the side of the road. The thing is, you can work five jobs, but if your wife's buying sixteen ThighMasters a day, there's no way you can dig yourself out."

Slocum shook his head. "Sorry brother, didn't mean to drop my hard-luck saga into your lap. You got your own problems to deal with."

"Don't sweat it."

"I got an idea. Why don't you come by Griphaus tonight and get shit-faced?"

I didn't feel like explaining that I'd be taking up permanent residence in Griphaus that evening and said, "I've been doing a little bit too much of that lately."

"We have a saying in Texas: If a little bit's good, then a lot's better. I'll get some steaks at that Mexican supermarket, George can mix up some Short Arm Margaritas, and we'll blast Neil Young till the cops shut us down."

"Sure. Why not?"

"Great. I'll tell the ADs to put Divorce Party on the call sheet. Who knows? Maybe some of those bathing beauties will show up."

I was about to tell him that it would be months before the court granted my divorce. Then I remembered something Elvira had mentioned and said, "Thanks, pal."

"Believe me, chief, you won't thank me tomorrow."

Buzzy's voice burst from our walkie-talkies, "Hey, Slo-cum! Where the hell are those cheeseboro clamps?"

Slocum sighed. "Can you do me a favor and tell Napoleon I'm on my way?"

"Sure, and thanks for the Skoal."

What I remembered was that Elvira faxed the call sheet to the studio every night. The way gossip flew around that place, I figured Natalie would learn about my divorce party within minutes.

Okay, maybe I was acting like a ten-year-old, but I couldn't help myself. Peter and Polly World had closed for business, but the Peter and Polly World in my head refused to die. I continued to send Natalie messages through call sheets and housing choices, and no matter what happened, I could not let go of the paper-thin possibility that we might get back together. *Maybe*, I told myself, *the only reason she was with Elias was for the career opportunities. Maybe while she was asleep Natalie concocted elaborate fantasies where she and I fought crime, saved Third World countries, and protected the rain forest.* Then again, maybe I was crazier than Slocum's ex-wife.

Chapter 27

Divorce, Party of Two

BESIDES THE BEER cooler, the most important piece of equipment on a grip truck is the grip stand. Also called a C-stand—short for Century stand, the long-defunct company that originally manufactured them—a grip stand has three legs, three telescoping risers, and a circular clamp on top called a gobo head. Through this clamp you slip a forty-inch piece of steel tubing called a long arm. If space is tight, a twenty-inch short arm is used instead. Short arms can do almost anything a long arm can as well as one important task a long arm can't. Short arms are the signature ingredient in that glorious concoction grips have been using to lure the panties off female crew members since the days when Jolson sang "Mammy"—the Short Arm Margarita. Alas, many younger grips have expressed little interest in mastering the fine art of blending the perfect Short Arm Margarita, and many older grips have consumed so many that they can't remember how to make them. As a service to the greater good of mankind—and to alleviate my fear that Short Arm Margaritas will go the way of three-strip Technicolor and double-time after twelve—here's the recipe for any and all who are interested:

SHORT ARM MARGARITAS

1 bag of ice

1 garbage bucket (preferably clean)

1 big bottle of tequila (the cheaper the better)

Margarita mix to taste

1 short arm

1. Dump the ice into the garbage bucket and cover it with the tequila.

2. Add enough margarita mix so that women will drink it, but not so much that it tastes like crap.

3. Stir the ingredients with the short arm.

4. Repeat until wasted.

PLEASE NOTE: If you forget to remove the mud from inside the short arm or clean the garbage bucket, you *must* wait for the dirt to settle before serving. Otherwise, women will not drink the margaritas and have no reason to sleep with you. Enjoy!

Griphaus was located in East Austin in what was once a dicey section of town until Austin got expensive and the poor folks had to find somewhere else to be poor. According to the locations department, my new home was owned by a Dell millionaire who bought houses all over town, fixed them up, and made a killing renting them to University of Texas students. His contractor missed the start of the fall semester, and my grips were the perfect short-term tenants. They hadn't been living there very long, but the place already smelled like the inside of a laundry hamper. I felt embarrassed that Sara Lee had to stay in such a pit until I snuck a peek in her bedroom and . . . let's just say Ralph wasn't the only pig working on our movie.

Mid-shoot parties sound good in theory, but I find them a big snooze. After being trapped on set with sixty sweaty crew members for thirteen hours, it takes more than a few Hawaiian shirts and some free hooch to make me want to party with them. But Slocum was on a mission, and I didn't want to piss on his parade—especially when I was the guest of honor. We stapled a copy of my divorce decree over the bar, covered the lamps with titty-pink gel, and blasted Neil Young on three different boom boxes. Unfortunately, all anyone wanted to talk about was their divorces, and I kept getting suckered into conversations about ex-wives, outrageous alimony, and bloodsucking divorce attorneys. It was like a long, bad country-western song.

"There he is!" Slocum said, finding me on the backyard patio. "Guess who's here?"

"Ralph the Swimming Pig."

"Try again."

"I give up. Who?"

"Look," he said, pointing into the house. I followed his finger and saw that the water ballerinas had shown up as promised. The only problem was, without their costumes they looked more like strippers than mermaids.

"C'mon," Slocum slurred. "Let's go talk to them."

"I better go freshen my drink."

"Good idea. Bring some back for the ladies."

The Short Arm Margaritas were burning my stomach, and I walked into the kitchen to find some milk. I was drunker than I wanted to be, but not so far gone that I wanted a night of passionless passion with a water stripper. It would have been a snap to squeeze into one of their thongs by playing the sympathy card or saying that I was friends with the director and could get them more screen time. Sleeping with Deirdre had turned out to be a major mistake, and I was in no mood to repeat this blunder. Not to mention that I had a lipful of Skoal, and if Natalie was to be believed, most women considered this a turnoff.

I found Troy in the kitchen examining my divorce papers with the eye of a seasoned professional.

"Conjugal abandonment?" he asked with a raised eyebrow. "Does that mean what I think it does?"

"Let's just say it's one crime you'll never be accused of."

"Not in a million years, my friend." He pulled the papers off the wall and said, "You are aware that these are part of the public record? Do you really want the whole world knowing that you refused to sleep with your wife for a year?"

"It's not a big deal," I said, opening the refrigerator. "New York State doesn't have no-fault divorce, and conjugal abandonment is the quickest way to get it over with. Besides, I found the irony appealing."

"Irony or not, what happens if you get famous? This could end up in *Vanity Fair*."

"I sincerely doubt *Vanity Fair* will ever be interested in the intimate details of my love life."

The only dairy product in the kitchen was a handful of creamers lifted from the local IHOP. The thought of doing half-and-half shooters turned my stomach, and I began searching for some baking soda.

"What the hell are you looking for?" Troy asked.

"My stomach's killing me, and I'm trying to find something to chill it out."

"You want to walk down to that supermarket at the end of the block?"

"Sure, but what about them?" I nodded toward the bathing beauties in the living room.

Troy closed his eyes and took a long, luxurious breath through his nose. He smiled and said, "Don't worry. They'll keep."

* * *

Make no mistake. It might not have been conjugal, but I did abandon my wife. The original plan for Peter and Polly World was to use Gerti to cover our expenses while Natalie and I worked on our own projects. This sounded good in theory, but what really happened was my truck became the perfect excuse for postponing those projects indefinitely. There was always an apple box to varnish, a stand to repair, or a piece of paper to shuttle over to the accountant. Meanwhile, Hank Sullivan continued to live on ramen noodles and produce movies for people with half my talent and ten times my ambition. Indie cinema, New Queer Cinema, Black Cinema, Hank was there for it all. I occasionally played grip emeritus on his shoots, but after I joined the union and started working on "real" movies, Hank's projects seemed a little too rinky-dink for a grip of my stature. That changed the night Natalie and I walked past the Angelika Film Center and saw a line for one of Hank's movies stretching down Houston Street. Overnight, Hank started hanging out with Jim Jarmusch and Wim Wenders, and I started having a hard time telling people I was a filmmaker.

The moment of truth arrived when I trashed a tendon in my leg and took some time off to recover. I dropped three grand on an awesome laptop, filled it with the best screenwriting software available, and spent the next eight weeks playing Tetris. I wanted to write—so help me God, I wanted to write—but every time I tried to coax some words onto the page my nostrils burned from the stench of that foul river of screenplays that had been flowing through our apartment for years. I could barely breathe, the air was so thick with smash cuts, bad dialogue, and characters "shooting" each other looks. Everywhere I turned I saw serial killers, Mafia hit men, and suitcases jammed with drugs or money. It was suffocating. By the time I reached the sixteenth level in Tetris, I convinced myself that the only thing separating me from that swarm of no-talent wannabes was the fact that I hadn't written a screenplay. My failure was really my success. Plus, I had an image

to maintain. I had a great gig standing behind the dolly and trad-
ing quips with famous filmmakers. But as soon as I tried slipping
one of them a screenplay, I'd be stripped of my grip-hipster status
and be just another aspiring asshole.

So I gave up. I bailed. I quit. I thought I'd feel terrible, but it
was more like a forty-pound tumor had been removed from my
consciousness. I felt nimble and refreshed, and the world smelled
great and glorious. Or it did until the morning I unlocked my
truck and realized that my equipment business was no longer a
distraction or a way to pay the rent. It was my life.

Vicodin was two years away.

Troy and I were halfway to the supermarket when I saw the white
Crown Victoria driving toward us.

"Oh, Christ," I said.

"Who's that?"

"Our director."

"Do I need to point out the irony of him showing up here tonight?"

"Please don't. I've had my fill of irony for one evening."

The car pulled over and Elias hopped out. "Can I speak to you
for a sec?" he asked.

"Sure."

"Hi, Troy. Thanks again for your excellent work today. That
little pan you did on Ryan's over-the-shoulder shot was terrific."

"My pleasure."

Elias dragged me out of earshot and waved a videotape in my
face. "Here, you've got to watch this."

"What is it?"

"An old musical from the forties called *Neptune's Daughter*. It
stars Esther Williams. She was this Olympic swimmer who made a

bunch of movies for MGM with these amazing synchronized swimming sequences."

"I know who Esther Williams is. Where'd you get that tape?"

"Natalie sent it to me. This is exactly what we need for the water ballet scene. Let's go back to the production office and watch it right now."

"Sorry, pal. I'm a little busy tonight."

"With what?"

"The crew's kind of having a party for me."

"Oh, right. Uh, congratulations."

"I couldn't have done it without you. Look, why don't you pick me up tomorrow morning, and we can talk about it on the way to set?"

"Sounds good," Elias said, climbing into his car. He rolled down the window and shouted, "How do you take your coffee?"

"Black."

"Black it is."

"What was that about?" Troy asked as Elias pulled out.

"Nothing a lead pipe to the head wouldn't cure."

"I take it you don't care for our director very much."

"What gave you that idea?"

"Just a hunch. Oh, Deirdre says hello, by the way."

"You went for it, huh?"

"I couldn't resist. She said that the reason you hooked up with Carni was to get your money out of the insurance company. That's pretty low, Bobby."

"I can't believe she told you that!"

"Dude, never tell anything to a hooker that you don't want broadcast to the general population."

"I thought you were supposed to tell hookers your life story."

"Only in the movies."

"Then what's the point of going to see one?"

"Anal sex."

Troy and I entered the supermarket and headed straight for the dairy case. I grabbed a quart of milk off the shelf and guzzled half the carton. The burning in my stomach faded away, and I wiped my chin with the back of my hand.

"Let's grab a shopping cart," I said. "I want to pick up some stuff for the kids back at the ranch."

Troy and I cruised the aisles, and I filled the cart with a delectable assortment of beer, snacks, and frozen food.

"You're right about Katherine," I said. "I feel terrible about it. And the sad part is, I really started to like her."

"Then send her some flowers and get back together."

"It's more complicated than that."

"Then give her a pair of earrings."

"Not complicated for her. Complicated for *me*. Divorce or no divorce, I still feel like a married man. I can't buy a woman a drink without winding up in a discussion about what color to paint the spare bedroom."

"You have to let go of your preconceptions."

"I'm not like you, Troy. I'm not just looking for a one-night stand."

"Oh, I'm sorry. I didn't realize you were after a long and meaningful relationship with Deirdre."

"That was a mistake. Besides, I was drunk."

"Drinking doesn't make you do stuff. It just gives you permission."

"Enough with the platitudes. I'm trying to figure something out here." I picked up two jars of salsa to compare and said, "You remember the day Mitch got fired?"

"Yeah."

"After he went out with you and Dusty he stopped by my room."

"And punched you in the face."

"Right before that he said Katherine was just another version of Natalie. You know, the same job, the same clothes, that sort of thing."

"So?"

"So, I don't know if I'm attracted to Katherine because I really like her, or because she's so much like Natalie."

"Does it make any difference?"

"Isn't it supposed to?"

"Not necessarily. Some guys like blondes, some guys like brunettes, some guys like line producers. If you like her, you like her. What's the big deal? This is love we're talking about, not psychotherapy."

"I just don't want to screw things up again."

"Is it that, or are you still carrying a torch for your ex-wife?"

A jar of salsa slipped from my hand and crashed to the floor. I looked down at the mess and back up to Troy.

"Okaaaay, then," he said, scraping the salsa off his leg with a sandal. "I guess we've answered that question."

Chapter 28

Pit Bullshit

Bobby?"

Someone pinched my big toe.

"Bobby. Wake up."

"Go 'way," I croaked.

"There's someone here to see you."

"Who is it?"

"He says his name is Moose."

I opened my eyes to see Sara Lee hovering over me. She was wearing a pink velour running suit and hadn't put her face on yet. *Oh God*, I thought, *make it go away.*

"How does he look?" I asked.

Sara Lee thought about it a moment and said, "Desperate."

"Great."

I sat up and a bucketful of bad margaritas smashed against the side of my head. I was wearing only undershorts, and wrapped the covers around my waist.

"Don't worry," Sara Lee said. "I've seen men in their underwear before."

"How do you know I'm even wearing underwear?"

"Who do you think put you to bed last night after you passed out in the bathroom?"

"Thanks," I said, trying hard not to picture Sara Lee undressing me. "Is there any coffee around here?"

"We usually get it on the way to set."

"Shit." I made a mental note to buy a coffeemaker. It was number two on my list right after *Never get mixed up with Teamsters.*

"Um, have you seen my shirt and shorts?"

"They're in the dryer."

"You washed my clothes?"

"They were filthy."

I was touched. It was the first time someone had done my laundry since I'd moved out of my parents' house. Need I mention that washerwoman was not a skill listed in boldface type on Natalie's résumé? "Thank you, Sara," I said.

"I'll go get them."

Sara Lee went to fetch my clothes, and I crawled to the front door. Moose took one look at the sheet wrapped around my waist and said, "Who the fuck are you supposed to be? John Belushi?"

"What brings you to Texas, Moose?"

"Things didn't go so good at the DeSalvo Brothers'. I slipped their pit bulls some sleeping pills, but they wore off while I was still searching for the dope."

"How do you slip a pit bull a sleeping pill?"

"You stick it in a Big Mac and toss it over the fence. Chopped meat works better, but I couldn't find a supermarket with a drive-through. Anyway, the little four-legged fuckers cornered me in the warehouse, and I had to take them out."

"You shot the DeSalvo Brothers' dogs?"

"It was them or me. But it turns out that Crazy Joey DeSalvo is like some kind of world-class pit bull breeder. Those fucking dogs were like children to him, and he put a contract out on me."

"How did he find out it was you?"

"He hasn't. Yet. I figured it was a good idea to get out of town for a while, so here I am. You think I could crash with you for a while?"

I pointed toward a corner of the living room. "You could put an air mattress over there."

"Great. That'll do until I can get production to put me up at the Omni."

"But you're not working on the movie anymore."

"I will be after I talk the local drivers into betting on some football games. Just watch, I'll give Dallas and Houston a couple of extra points and those Texas pricks will be owing me their houses by Monday."

Elias strolled through the front door. He glanced at the sheet wrapped around my waist and said, "*Et tu, Brute?*"

"*In vino veritas,*" I replied.

"That must have been some party."

"Elias, this is Moose. Moose, this is Elias, our new director."

"What happened to Queen Richard?"

"He got the hook," I said.

"Taking too long to get the shots off?"

"That and almost killing Andrzej."

"Wait a second," Moose said, pointing at Elias. "I heard of you. You're the one banging Bobby's wife, right?"

"Natalie and I have a relationship, yes."

"A relationship, huh?" Moose cocked his head in my direction, and the gleam in his eye seemed to ask, *You want me to fuck with this guy?*

I nodded.

Moose turned back to Elias. "You went to Harvard, right?"

"For a little while."

Moose grinned. "Then I bet that makes you a Patriots fan?"

* * *

It took no time for Moose to talk Elias into putting two hundred bucks down on Sunday's Miami–New England game, and we were soon headed south on I-35. Elias drove while I sat in the passenger seat and reviewed his storyboards for the water ballet scene. While the good Lord may have blessed our director with good looks and charm, He had definitely shortchanged him in the visual arts department. Elias's drawings were a joke, and I had to turn them upside and sideways before I realized the brown and green squiggles at the bottom of the pages were supposed to be mermaids.

"What do you think?" Elias asked.

"It's . . . ambitious."

"I want to shoot the whole thing live action with no computer-generated effects."

"Why no CGI?"

"Because that's the way they did it in the old days. I don't care what anyone says, effects are soulless. It's like what Walter Benjamin talked about in 'The Work of Art in the Age of Mechanical Reproduction.' They lack an aura."

Soulless? An aura? *What the fuck do they teach you dipshits at Harvard?* I wanted to scream. *You've directed exactly one scene, and now you want to tackle something Steven Spielberg would find challenging.*

"Maybe you should talk to Andrzej and Katherine about this," I said.

"Fuck Andrzej. I'm so over his 'Elias, darling' this and 'Elias, darling' that. I'm the director, and he'll do what I say."

What was it about sitting in a director's chair that turned reasonable human beings into fire-breathing assholes? I'd seen it happen dozens of times, but Elias was on his way to setting the land speed record for directorial assholery. A huge synchronized swimming scene with a dozen water ballerinas, a diving pig, and two hundred extras? It was insane. It was also super-expensive, incredibly time-consuming, and I could feel my soon-to-be-ex-wife's fingerprints all over it.

It was classic Natalie. Katherine had barred her from set, so Natalie was getting even by filling Elias's head with the most expensive and over-the-top cinematic horseshit she could think of. Natalie knew that Katherine had been brought up in the John-Sayles-is-God school of filmmaking, and it was a safe bet that Katherine would stick her neck out to do whatever her director wanted. Even if it meant going over budget. Even if it meant screwing up her career. Natalie's plan was pure genius, and if it didn't disgust me so much, I would have called her up to congratulate her on the depth of her craftiness.

"This is all very impressive and well thought out," I said. "But it might be a good idea to come up with a couple of alternate strategies for shooting the scene so you don't wind up locking yourself into something."

"Locking myself into something is exactly what I want. That way, once I get the studio to commit to my vision there's no going back. In for a penny, in for a pound."

In for a major fucking disaster was more like it. Natalie was letting her hatred of Katherine cloud her judgment. If Elias blew the swimming scene, it would not only mean the end of Katherine's career, but of Natalie's and Elias's too. Was I the only one who could see this? Then again, if Natalie wanted to risk her little stud muffin's future on some over-the-top aquatic extravaganza, that was her business. I was just some grip, after all. Who was I to question his "vision"? In for a penny, in for a pound.

I held up one of the drawings and said, "How many extras do you think you'll need in this shot?"

"No more than two hundred."

"Better make it four hundred."

* * *

We got to set fifteen minutes early and piled into Elias's trailer to work on the storyboards. The trailer was tricked out with a satellite dish, a wireless laptop, and an espresso machine so complicated you needed a master's degree from Starbucks to turn it on. The shelves were stocked with much better munchies than we ever saw on the craft service table, and there were a twelve-pack of Sam Adams and a case of Pellegrino in the fridge. It's good to be the king.

"Can I get you something?" Elias asked as we sat down.

"No, thanks, I'm still working on my coffee."

"Would you like me to heat it up in the microwave?"

"I'm cool."

Elias popped *Neptune's Daughter* into the VCR.

"I want to open with Ralph running along the gangplank, diving into the water, and us pulling back, back, back, back, back to reveal the water ballerinas, the lagoon, and the audience. Do they make a crane that goes that high?"

"Sure. I mean, they're really expensive, and somebody has to drive it all the way from LA. But for a shot like this it's *totally* worth it."

There was a knock on the door.

"Who is it?" Elias called.

"It's Andrzej, I want to go over this morning's shot list."

"Shit," I whispered. "If he finds me here I'm dead."

"Just a second, Andrzej," Elias shouted. And then, in a lower voice, "Here, take the storyboards and go hang out in the bedroom. I'll try to make this fast."

"Thanks. Can I borrow your laptop to check my e-mail?"

"Sure."

I dashed to the back of the trailer as Elias opened the door for Andrzej.

"What took you so long, Elias, darling? Are you fucking some little PA in here?"

"No, Andrzej, darling. Just finishing up in the WC."

The trailer's bedroom wasn't large, but it had a full-size bed and a mirrored vanity. Just the place for a key grip to put on his face in the morning. I opened the Web page for my e-mail account and waded through the spam and forwarded bullshit. From the tone of the conversation in the next room, it sounded like I was going to be in here for a long time. With nothing better to do, I opened a search engine and typed in "compression garments." Dozens of pages came up, and I was soon swimming in a sea of liposuction girdles, abdominoplasty recovery kits, and cotton support bras designed for women who had experienced "massive weight loss." Oh joy.

I typed in "plastic surgery before and after," but all that came up was a bunch of stuff about Botox. "Gastric bypass surgery before and after" was a much better phrase, and I was rewarded with multiple photos of fat ladies in flowered shirts. The real score was a site maintained by a woman named Sandy Beemer who had transformed herself from a 400-pound hippo to a 165-pound goddess. Sandy was so proud of her weight loss that she included nude photos of her shrinking body with a little pink heart drawn over her pubic hair. The first one hundred and fifty pounds of weight loss were just gross, but after that, things got interesting fast. Sandy looked best at a hundred and eighty-nine pounds, and I thought she should have stopped there. But you can never judge a person until you've walked a half block in her sagging flesh, and who was I to say what Sandy Beemer's proper weight should have been?

Elias and Andrzej were still going strong when I noticed the lump in my cargo shorts. *No,* I told myself. *Don't even think about it.* Shocking your nipples in the privacy of your own hotel room was one thing, but whacking off with Andrzej and Elias in the next room? That was insane. If I got busted, Andrzej wouldn't have to kill me for colluding with Elias. I'd die of embarrassment. But I couldn't help myself. I mean, there was Sandy Beemer at a mouthwatering one hundred and eighty-nine pounds practically begging for it, and here I was with nothing better to do than obey her brash and saucy desires. Was I not human?

Sandy and I were deep into it when the loud *ping* of Elias's e-mail program almost made me scream in surprise.

"What was that?" Andrzej asked, freezing me in midstroke.

"Just my computer."

"Do you think I could check my e-mail when we're done?"

"Certainly."

I exhaled slowly and clicked on the blinking envelope on the lower right-hand corner of the screen. A window popped open informing me that there was a new e-mail from someone named miguelinator@hotbox.com. My erection deflated immediately. Natalie had always used natalie.miguel@aol.com as her e-mail address, but I had no doubt who this miguelinator@hotbox.com was. That explained why I never found any e-mails from Elias on Natalie's computer. She'd been using a sex name! The old feelings of anger and betrayal bubbled up inside me, and I felt horrible and desperate all over again.

I clicked on miguelinator's e-mail and read:

> E:
> Been thinking about the swimming scene
> again. In the cold light of dawn, trying to shoot
> the whole thing live action is probably too
> ambitious. Let's go with CGI, and save the big
> battles for OUR movie. Don't know about you,
> but I'm freaking exhausted. New rule: No more

phone sex on school nights!

N

That fucking bitch! In all my lonely years on the road Natalie and I had had phone sex a grand total of zero times. And whenever I brought it up, she always made me feel like a desperate loser for asking. I hit the REPLY button and typed:

You goddamned whore!!! I hope your fucking

clit falls off!!!!

I was a millimeter away from pushing the SEND button when I regained my senses. I hit the DELETE key and typed:

N:

I was thinking the same thing about the CGI.

It could have been great, but it also could have

been a disaster. And as far as no phone sex on

school nights . . . I'm not sure if I'm that strong.

E

I pushed SEND and erased all evidence of Natalie's e-mail and my reply. I was glad to see that Natalie was thinking straight again. Using the synchronized swimming scene to get even with Katherine was far too big a risk. Still, I was disappointed that she had put her own petty careerism over the artistic integrity of her lover. Lucky for him, I had nipped that one in the bud.

Thank God someone was looking out for Elias's vision.

Chapter 29

Shit Kicker

A dolly grip dies and goes to Hell. He arrives at the craggy gates and is shocked to discover that Hell is one big film shoot. The hours are endless, the set's an inferno, and the cameraman is a complete dick. Centuries go by, and one morning the dolly grip looks up and sees that a door to Heaven has materialized on the far side of set. *This is it,* he thinks. *My ticket out of here.* He throws down his tool belt and races across set as fast as he can. The closer he gets, the better it looks: green fields, cool streams, and happy people lying in hammocks. It's Paradise, man. He gets to the door and glances back for one last look at Hell. To his surprise, the entire grip department is staring at him and shaking their heads.

"What's the matter, pussy?" one of them shouts. "Can't take it?"

BY MY SECOND week in Griphaus, Troy was threatening to call the health department and have my cargo shorts declared a biohazard. Using Steveo as an intermediary, Katherine and I set up a time when I could swing by the bungalow and pick up my stuff. Despite her refusing to talk to me, I still hoped we might patch things up. This had nothing to do with getting my money from the insurance company, by the way. If there was one thing I'd learned from making love to hotel room carpets and jacking off to fat girls on the Internet, it was that I could have a full and meaningful relationship with a woman whose abdominal region sloshed around like a half-filled waterbed. It's amazing the stuff you discover on location.

Still, I couldn't get Natalie's e-mail out of my mind, and every time Elias got within ten feet of me I wanted to slug him. No matter how hard I tried, I could not escape the thought of him cooing in Natalie's ear while she touched herself in ways she never had for me.

Fuck it, I thought. *I should just quit this damn movie while I still have a sliver of sanity left.*

Quitting *Aquarena Springs* would have solved only one small part of my problems. There was no way I could stay in the film business and not feel the pain of my past life. Natalie and the movie industry were so intertwined in my being that I could not have one without the other. The only way to truly separate myself from her would be to find another career.

But what else was there besides movies?

I thought about the guys in my building in New York who worked on Wall Street. Their lives seemed so much more stream-lined compared to mine. All they needed was a firm handshake and a pack of breath mints to make it through the day, while I re-quired a forty-foot tractor-trailer and a crew of dysfunctional film pirates to accomplish the most simple task. The sad part was, I knew I was smarter and more hardworking than every one of those pin-striped business monkeys I lived beside. If only I had focused my energy and intelligence on a real career, I could have been wildly successful. The only problem was that with the exception of astronaut, secret agent, and rock star, every other job was boring as hell.

Who was I trying to kid? I wouldn't have lasted one pay period in a company where quarterly performance and arcane corporate hierarchies determined who got the choicest slice of cheese. While my neighbors sold their souls for security and a comprehensive benefits package, I'd sold mine for hope. Despite a lifetime of evidence to the contrary, I could not stop believing that my next gig would be *the one*—the job where I got yanked out of the chorus line and handed a director's viewfinder. And if not that job, then the one after that. Or the one after that. I knew the legends about grips marrying movie stars, and production assistants selling scripts for millions of dollars. *That could be me,* I told myself each morning as I girded my loins for another fourteen-hour day. It was only a matter of time till somebody saw me for the talented and world-class individual I was. And what better place for that to happen than on a movie set, that magical place where dreams came true?

There was no one home when I arrived at the bungalow, and I let myself in with my key. I half expected to find my belongings in a shredded pile in the middle of the living room, but either Katherine wasn't that vengeful or she didn't have the time to rent a tree chipper. The first thing I went for was the bottle of Absolut Citron in the freezer. I poured myself an adult dose and leaned against the counter. My plan was to write Katherine a note apologizing for what I had done and beg for her forgiveness. I hadn't run the odds by Moose, but I figured I had a fifty-fifty chance of getting her back. I looked around for something to write on and spotted a box of Hostess cupcakes on top of the refrigerator.

"Oh shit," I said, setting my drink on the counter. The only rule Katherine laid down when me moved in together was no junk food in the house. Soda, snack cakes, and potato chips were

like crack to her, and once she got started on them she was pow-
erless to stop. I opened the pantry and saw it was filled with
boxes of Ring Dings, Twinkies, and Funny Bones. Katherine was
using again. I debated taking her stash with me, but it was pointless. After the countless lies and scams I'd come up with to keep
my veins flowing with Vicodin, I knew that it didn't matter how
good your intentions were, anyone who got between a junkie
and his stash was the enemy. It made no difference whether your
drug of choice was Scooter Pies or heroin, the results were still
the same.

And it was all my fault. Okay, maybe not all of it, but enough
to make me feel crappy in a hundred new ways. I heard the front
door open, and Katherine rushed by without even seeing me. She
grabbed the box of cupcakes off the refrigerator and pulled out a
two-pack. Her fingers were sweaty and she had to tear it open with
her teeth.

"Hungry?"

"Jesus Christ!" she screamed and the cupcakes fell to the
floor.

"Don't worry. If those are dirty there are plenty more in the
cupboard."

"Then you know." She reached down and picked up the cupcakes.

"I put two and two together."

"Goody for you." She jammed the cupcakes into her mouth
one after the other. Crumbs fell down her shirt and her cheeks
puffed out as she squeezed the last of them past her lips. She tried
to swallow, but the cupcakes backed up in her pint-size stomach
and Katherine began to choke. I thought she was just pretending
until she started making these jerking motions with her arms. I
got up to give her the Heimlich maneuver, but she kept pointing
to her back, so I gave her a karate chop between the shoulder
blades. She coughed up a huge wad of cupcake, and it flew across

the room, hitting the refrigerator and leaving a chocolaty trail as it fell to the floor.

"You have to be really careful about giving the Heimlich maneuver to somebody who's had a bypass." She coughed. "It could tear their stomach apart."

"I didn't know that."

"There's a lot you don't know," she said and began hitting and punching me. "You asshole," she screamed. "You fucking, fucking, fucking asshole!"

Her punches didn't hurt very much. I figured I deserved it, until her vintage Gruen watch caught the side of my face and tore into my cheek.

"Hey!" I said and grabbed her right hand. She kept going with her other hand, and I grabbed that one too.

"Let go of me."

"Not until you calm down."

"I am calm!"

"No, you're not."

"You're right," she said and kneed me in the balls.

It was a dead-on shot, and I crumpled to the floor. Katherine went back to punching and slapping me, and I slid against the wall and covered my head with my hands. Big mistake. Like Frick and Frack, the first thing Katherine did when she arrived in Texas was buy a pair of five-hundred-dollar Lucchese cowboy boots. Nice ones. With very pointy toes. The first kick landed on the upper part of my thigh and gave me a killer charley horse. The second kick hit my left kidney and hurt so bad it almost made me forget the throbbing in my crotch.

"Enough!" I screamed.

"No way. I have sixteen years of longing to kick out of you, and I'm just getting started."

Her third kick would have taken my head off if I hadn't slid a chair between us and knocked her off balance. She landed on the floor in a pile of chocolate and tears.

"All I wanted was a boyfriend," Katherine wailed. "My whole fat fucking life that's all I've ever wanted. Every other girl in the world gets to have one, why not me?"

I grabbed the kitchen table and pulled myself to my feet. "Grow up, Katherine. I don't care how fucking lonely you are. You're a movie producer. You have responsibilities. Trying to kill yourself with a pack of cupcakes is beyond pathetic." I stepped over her and walked out of the kitchen.

"I hate you!" she screamed.

I entered my soon-to-be-ex-bedroom and pulled my duffel bags out from under the bed. I could hear Katherine whimpering in the kitchen, but I didn't care. The kicks, the choking, the cupcakes, it was all too much. Yeah, I slept with a hooker, but so what? Katherine wasn't my wife, and she wasn't my girlfriend. I never said I loved her. Was I sorry that she waited sixteen years and I had turned out to be a dud? Sure, but what I really felt was relief.

I'd gone there intending to throw myself at Katherine's feet and beg for her to take me back. If she had said yes it would have been a disaster. I had been blinded by her desire for me and a new-found fascination with sagging flesh. What I didn't see until then was that Katherine was a little girl. She had never learned to love someone like an adult and was stuck in a teenage girl's idea of what it was like to be in a relationship. She didn't love me, she had *a crush* on me.

"Some of your stuff is in the dryer."

I turned and Katherine was standing in the doorway.

"You didn't have to do my laundry."

"I didn't. I'm paying the house cleaner extra to do laundry. You owe me five bucks."

I pulled out my wallet, but Katherine ignored it.

"Was it my body?" she asked. "Did it sicken you? I was supposed to have a second operation to get rid of all the extra skin, but I had such a horrible reaction to the anesthesia the first time that I kept putting it off. Then I got a job, and another one, and I'm still like this."

"You're beautiful, Katherine."

"No, I'm not. But thanks for saying so."

"You're welcome."

"I'm going to take a shower. If you could be out of here by the time I'm done I'd appreciate it."

I went into the laundry room and pulled my clothes out of the dryer. A pile of Katherine's laundry was sitting on the washing machine, and I spotted the crotchless compression garment at the bottom. I pulled it from the pile and held it to my cheek. Maybe things could have worked out between us, but we would never find out. If I had learned anything from my marriage it was that relationships required more than just love. I needed a partner, not someone who jammed cupcakes down her throat the moment things didn't go her way. That kind of drama lost its appeal when I graduated from high school. What I needed was a person to share my future with who understood that life wasn't easy, fair, or pain-free. And unfortunately, that person was Natalie. And she was with Elias. Having lots of phone sex while I slept on a couch and quelled my desire with wall-to-wall carpeting.

And you know what the saddest part was? I would have taken Natalie back in a heartbeat. I had learned something that Katherine would never understand, and that was when you really loved someone, you'd do whatever it took to be with her. Even if she did things with her boyfriend that she had never done with you. Even if it meant sacrificing every last bit of pride and self-respect you had left.

I slipped the crotchless compression garment in my duffel bag and went back to Griphaus to crash on the couch.

Chapter 30

Pig Fest

You'd think that with all the resources of a major motion picture studio at our disposal it would have been easy to find a swimming pig. It was not. Animal gags are tough, and a well-trained animal can make the difference between backslapping success and endless, grinding failure. Our first Ralph was as cute as a Chia Pet and would have put that old Arnold from *Green Acres* to shame. He was smart, well trained, and did whatever Elias wanted. Until he dove into the water; and then all he did was float there like, well, a fat pig. Our second Ralph could swim like Mark Spitz and dive like Greg Louganis. Unfortunately, Ralph the Second developed a nasty case of piggy pneumonia and had to be shipped back to LA with an oxygen mask strapped over his snout. Ralph number three was a nonstop porcine shit machine. And believe me, you have not lived a full and meaningful life until you've seen a two-foot-long trail of pig crap as photographed by Toby Landsman, the most renowned underwater cameraman since Philippe Cousteau. The good news was that Katherine had not skimped on hiring a first-class effects team, and their remote-controlled robotic swimming pig worked flawlessly. The bad news was that we didn't have a hero Ralph to match, and the effects guys didn't know what color to paint their bionic bacon maker.

Week eight of *Aquarena Springs* was supposed to kick off with Elias's show-stopping synchronized swimming scene featuring Ralph and a dozen mermaids. It was easily the most complicated sequence any of us had ever worked on, and thanks to my interception of Natalie's e-mail, Elias was determined to film it without any computer-generated effects. It was a stupid, egotistical decision, and like passengers on a runaway train, everyone went along for the ride. Andrzej saw disaster looming in the distance, but was happy to give Elias all the rope he needed to hang himself. He watched every Esther Williams movie he could get his hands on, and to re-create the look of *Neptune's Daughter,* Andrzej ordered a dozen arc lights, a Techno crane, and two additional camera operators from LA. I spent a week rigging thirty-foot-tall scaffolding towers for high-angle shots and, despite Elvira's memo that every grip expense over five dollars had to be approved in writing, managed to drop over a thousand bucks on specialty hardware. The biggest coup by far, however, was Katherine finding Barbara Delmar, the woman who had choreographed the original Aquarena Springs water show. She was close to ninety years old and needed a cane to get around, but once she got in the water, the old gal moved like a gleeful, glistening otter.

The insanity in all this was that we still didn't have a swimming pig. Those who weren't in total denial on the subject were banking on the second Ralph recovering in time for the big number. Elvira lived on the phone and when she wasn't talking to Ralph's vet in LA she was calling every petting zoo, circus, and traveling minstrel show in the country in search of a replacement Ralph. Three days before we were scheduled to shoot the scene, pigs from seven states were winging their way to Austin. But there's an old saying in our business that goes: "You can lead a pig to water, but you can't make him swim." None of the pigs were acceptable, and two hours before call Katherine pulled the plug.

There was not enough time to cancel the hundreds of actors, extras, and water ballerinas, and everyone descended on Aquarena Springs in one slow-footed mass of shouting confusion. Worse, the ADs plugged so many extra walkie-talkies into the gift shop's power outlets, they blew the circuits. Not one of their walkie-talkies charged, and an AD without a walkie-talkie is as effective as a hammer without a head. They had no way to talk to the extras, or each other, and had to communicate through cell phones. Unfortunately, there was no comprehensive phone list, and the cell towers overloaded as soon as the extras arrived and began calling their friends to tell them how boring it was to work on a movie. Lucky for us, Steveo charged our walkie-talkies at Griphaus, and we communicated with the same ease and charm for which grips are known the world over.

"Goddamn it," I screamed into my walkie-talkie as I slogged through a river of screaming grade-schoolers. "We've been in for almost a half an hour, and I'm the only grip on set. How hard can it be to roll two carts a hundred feet?"

"Sorry, chief," Steveo squawked back. "Our stuff is spread out all over the place, and everybody keeps asking where they can get Ryan Donahue's autograph."

"Gosh, Steveo, I had no idea your job was so interesting. Now unspread the fucking equipment and get it down here."

"Thanks for the positive feedback. Things would go a lot faster if you could give us a hand."

"I'd love to," I said, "accidentally" pushing an extra into the water. "But there are so many people in the way it would take me twenty minutes to get there."

Our cover set was located at the far side of the park in an abandoned building that used to be a hotel. The Aquarena Springs Spa & Resort was a putrid pus hole of a place that looked like half the rats, snakes, and armadillos in South Texas had been living in it since the Johnson administration. When I got there, Troy and a bunch of electricians were blocking the entrance.

"What's going on?" I asked.

"It's fucking Ebola Central in there," Troy said. "I'm not going in without a respirator and a hazmat suit."

"It can't be that bad."

"Take a whiff for yourself."

I opened the door and was overwhelmed by the raw stench of decay. "Jesus Christ." I gagged. "Somebody get the shop steward over here. This has to violate some OSHA regulations."

Andrzej arrived with Dusty at his side and said, "Dusty, darling, why are your electricians standing around like a bunch of lazy fuckwads and not running power to our cover set?"

"Damned if I know, boss." Dusty turned to his best boy. "Hey, Gizmo, what the hell?"

"Space is tight in there, Dust. Just wanted you and Chiefie to sign off on it."

"Jesus Christ," Andrzej said, reaching for the door handle. "Do I have to do everything for you battery-operated dildos?"

"Watch this," Troy said with a low chuckle.

Andrzej opened the door and took one step inside before he jumped back. "*Kurwa!*" he screamed in Polish. "It smells like a whore's asshole in there."

Katherine and Elias arrived, followed by a trail of PAs. Katherine's hair was a stringy mess, and she looked like she hadn't slept in a week. But the most frightening thing was the bottle of Dr Pepper in her right hand. After spending a lot of time on plastic surgery Web sites, I knew that carbonated beverages were a major no-no for people who've had gastric bypass surgery. The pressure caused by the bubbles can rupture their stomachs and cause all kinds of internal nastiness. Katherine had really lost it.

My cell phone rang, and I took a step back from the insanity. "Yeah?" I said.

"You owe me six G's."

"Moose?"

"And what the fuck's the matter with the cell phone service out there? It took me like ten times to get through."

"The extras are hogging up all the phone lines."

"Fucking parasites."

"Wait a minute. Did you say I owed you six grand?"

"That would be correct."

"That means they only got twelve thousand bucks for my entire truck's worth of equipment." I ran the numbers in my head. Twelve grand meant that after I paid Moose and the DeSalvo Brothers I'd end up with, well, nothing.

"It would have been less if we hadn't bid it up."

"We?"

"Jimmy Briscoe had to do a run near Philly and happened to drop by."

"Jesus Christ!" Katherine screamed. "Who do I have to fuck to make a phone call around here?" She threw her cell phone at a PA and shouted, "Keep pushing REDIAL until you get through."

I turned around so Katherine could not see I had a functioning cell phone and said, "Did a lot of people bid on the equipment?"

"Not really. Mitch and Jimmy were the only ones who knew what it was worth."

"Mitch was there?"

"Who do you think won the auction?"

"You're fucking kidding me."

"And boy, did he get pissed when Jimmy started bidding against him."

My hands began to shake, and I heard myself say, "Just out of curiosity, how much would it cost to send Mitch on a very long vacation?"

Moose laughed. "You're not serious?"

"Not unless you know somebody who takes American Express."

"Sorry, buddy, it's strictly a cash business. But look at the bright side. Imagine how pissed off Mitch is gonna be when he finds out his dope is gone. That ought to be worth six grand easy."

"Almost. I'll give you the money as soon as the DeSalvo Brothers' check clears."

"You're the man, Bobby."

A crowd of extras surged forward and Ryan Donahue appeared. He wasn't in the water ballet scene and was scheduled to have the week off. Ryan wore dark glasses and was accompanied by his pal Carlo. From their slumped shoulders and wrinkled clothing it looked like they'd been up all night partying.

"Thanks for coming on such short notice," Elias said. "You really saved our asses here. Just so you know, the set's a little, uh, fragrant. Katherine's going to order some air purifiers or something as soon as she can get through to Elvira."

"Whatever." Ryan belched.

Elias held the door for Ryan, who took a step inside before reeling back as if shot. He put a hand over his mouth and shook his head. "No fucking way, man. You can order a thousand air purifiers, and I'm not going in there. I can already feel my asthma acting up."

"You tell them, R.," Carlo chimed in. "You gotta protect your instrument, man."

"Asthma!" Troy whispered in my ear. "Why didn't I think of that?"

"Maybe because you don't have asthma."

"Here," the PA said, handing Katherine her cell phone. "It's ringing."

Katherine put the phone to her ear and said, "Elvira? Wake up Hank Sullivan and the head of production in LA and conference me in with them right now. And whatever happens, *do not* hang up on me."

Someone jammed a piece of paper in my face, and I turned to see the Douglas Sirk–loving office PA who had given me so much attitude on my first day in Texas. He wore the same smug expression and appeared to be waiting for someone to ask him to direct the movie. Too bad I was ahead of him in line.

"What's this?" I asked.

"A memo from Elvira."

I grabbed the paper and read:

It has come to our attention that certain crew members are chewing tobacco. Feel free to indulge in this filthy and disgusting habit until your teeth turn brown, but as of today all spit cups, jars, and cans are banned from set. Happy swallowing.

I jammed the memo in my cargo shorts. "This your first day on set?" I asked.

"Yep."

"Some first day, huh?"

"Beats hanging around the office. I didn't drop fifty grand on film school to spend my life running to the bank for the accounting department."

"Tell me about it. What's the point of working on a movie if you're not near the action, right?"

"Absolutely."

"Good. Now go and get me a Diet Coke."

The smile fell from his face. "What?"

"And bring me back a couple of Advil while you're at it."

For a moment I thought he was going to cry, then he turned

and headed toward craft service like a good little doggie. I pulled my walkie-talkie out of the holster and said, "Hey, Steveo, you still need help?"

"Now more than ever."

"There's some slime in a purple shirt headed your way. Feel free to abuse the shit out of him."

"Excellent."

"And if you really want to mess with his head, tell him he looks just like John Gavin."

"The pitcher from the Cubs?"

"No, the actor from *Imitation of Life*."

"What's *Imitation of Life*?"

"Never mind."

Katherine handed her phone back to her PA and said, "Under no circumstances hang that up." She chugged the rest of her Dr Pepper and announced, "Okay, people, listen up. Here's the deal. We're flying back the first Ralph and using him for the shots on land. For everything in the water we're either going animatronic or computer-generated. Reg, release the extras and have them come back Wednesday morning. Elias, someone from Digital Domain will be here this afternoon to supervise the CGI. I need you to go over your shot list with Andrzej and figure out which shots need effects and which ones don't. And everyone else . . . I don't know. Make yourselves look busy."

"You've got to be kidding," Elias said. "What happened to shooting everything live action?"

"Sorry, Elias. But we can't wait any longer for the perfect pig. Maybe if we had a couple more months to train one . . ."

"*You people,*" Elias hissed. "I try to do one thing my way, and you won't even let me do that. You don't care about this movie. All you care about is your budget."

"That's not fair, Elias. Look around. Do you think any of this was cheap?"

"I'm not talking about what's fair. I'm talking about what's right. You promised we'd do this my way, and now you're breaking that promise, you two-faced bitch."

One of the problems with going to film school is that you're taught to believe in the auteur theory of filmmaking, which is basically a French intellectual's way of saying the director is always right, even when he's wrong. Especially when he's wrong. If I were a real man—or at least the man I fancied myself to be in the non-stop monologue in my head—I would have jammed my walkie-talkie so far down Elias's throat he would have farted static for a week. Instead, I stared at my Nikes and wished I were in Kansas. The only real man in our midst turned out to be Andrzej, who stepped forward and put a hand on Elias's shoulder.

"That's enough," he said in a low voice.

"You're one to talk," Elias shouted. "You walk around like you're God's gift to the light meter, but all you are is a fucking studio hack."

Elias fell to his knees so fast it took a moment to realize that Andrzej was digging his fingers into his collarbone. So much for the auteur theory of filmmaking.

"Stop it," Elias screamed.

"Stop what, Elias, darling?" Andrzej said, removing his hand.

Elias climbed to his feet and looked Andrzej in the eye. "Go fuck yourself."

"As you wish. Now be a good boy and go work on your shot list."

Elias looked around for support, but, seeing no one in his corner, stomped off muttering, "I'm calling the guild."

Chapter 31

Spousal Abuse

The devil walks into a producer's office and says, "How would you like to produce the biggest movie of all time? It'll star Tom Hanks, Jennifer Aniston, Will Smith, Reese Witherspoon, Owen Wilson, Ben Stiller, and Vince Vaughn. Madonna will do the music, Ralph Lauren the costumes, and Steven Spielberg wants to direct. You can start shooting tomorrow, and all you have to do is sell me your soul."

"Sounds great," the producer says. "But what's the catch?"

Bobby?"

Someone pinched my big toe.

"Bobby. Wake up."

"Go 'way," I croaked.

"Somebody's here to see you."

"Who is it?"

"She says she's your wife."

I sat up and reached for my cargo shorts. They were nowhere to be found.

"Did you wash my clothes again, Sara Lee?"

"They were dirty again," she said and shuffled off toward the laundry room.

I wrapped myself in a sheet and walked to the door.

"My God," Natalie said. "It's worse than I thought."

"Jesus, Natalie, you look . . . amazing."

It was true. The extra five to twenty pounds she'd been battling her entire life were gone, her hair was cut short, and the baggage under her eyes had been unpacked and shipped elsewhere.

"How much work did you have done?" I asked.

"Just my eyes. The rest is five mornings a week in the gym." She did a little spin so I could inspect the entire package.

"LA certainly suits you."

"I wish I could say the same about you and Texas."

"It's not that bad, is it?"

"Seen a mirror lately?"

"We try to keep them covered during daylight hours."

Sara Lee appeared with my clothes. "Your shorts are still a little damp," she said.

"Thanks, Sara Lee."

"It was very nice meeting you," Sara Lee said to Natalie. "I understand that relationships are difficult, and I don't know what happened between you and Bobby, but he's a great guy and any woman would be lucky to have him." She walked into her bedroom, and as she closed the door added, "He's shown a lot of faith in me."

"And that was?" Natalie asked.

"Our intern."

"And she does your laundry?"

"Only when I'm too drunk to do it myself."

"Which is?"

"Often."

"Do you have any clothes without grease stains on them?"

"Why?"

"Because I'm taking you to brunch."

As we took our seats in the Café at the Four Seasons Hotel, Natalie said, "This is the only three-star restaurant in town, and their brunch was voted best in the state by *Texas Monthly*."

"Fabulous. How are their Bloody Marys?"

"You'll have to wait until noon to find out. It's Sunday."

I cupped my face in my hands. "I can't wait that long. The pain is too much . . ."

"Don't tell me you've turned into a pathetic drunk now too."

"No way. I'm still the same high-functioning alcoholic you fell in love with all those years ago." I lowered my voice and said, "It's been a tough couple of months."

Natalie stood. "Let me see what I can do."

"Where are you going?"

"To raid the minibar in my room."

"You're staying here too? That must be costing you a fortune."

"Nope. It's part of my deal."

"What deal?"

"I'll tell you when I get back."

I ordered a Virgin Mary as a jazz combo struck up a peppy rendition of "Sweet Georgia Brown." I like jazz and I like brunch. Put the two of them together, and I want to pull my hair out.

"Any chance of the Modern Jazz Quartet turning down the ruckus a couple of decibels?" I asked the waiter when he brought my drink.

"I'll see what I can do," he said, both of us knowing he wouldn't do squat.

Natalie returned and slipped a couple of baby bottles of Absolut under the table.

"They didn't have Ketel One?" I said with a frown.

"I'm saving those for myself."

"Selfish bitch." I eyed the room and dumped the Absolut into my glass. "Now back to my original question. What the hell are you doing here?"

"You're looking at the new producer of *Aquarena Springs.*"

"Is Katherine out?"

"No, but after that disaster with the synchronized swimming scene she might as well be."

"Wasn't that sort of Elias's fault?" And mine for intercepting that e-mail? Did *everything* have to backfire on me?

"It's a director's job to ask for the moon. It's a producer's job to temper it with reality."

"Would you have let Elias shoot the scene live action?"

"Of course not. And I wouldn't have risked everything on a pig recovering from pneumonia either."

I downed half my drink and asked the question that had been on my mind for weeks.

"Did you play me that time Dan Berg showed up on set?"

"Absolutely not."

"I took some heat for that."

"You didn't have to do what I said."

"Yes, I did. I always do."

"Good, because I have a proposition for you."

"I don't like the sound of this."

"No, it's a good thing. I spoke with Greg Allen at the insurance company, and they're going to pay you for Gerti."

"You're kidding me."

"Nope, you just have to pay them back whatever you get from the salvage company. The rest is yours."

I should have been happy, but anger welled up inside me. "So that's what our marriage was worth, huh? A hundred and fifty grand minus tax and tip?"

"You're getting distracted again, Bobby. This can be a new start. Don't blow it."

She was right. Natalie was always right. I ran the numbers in my head. A hundred and fifty grand minus twelve for the insurance company, six for Moose, and six for storage fees. My movie was back in production. I'd quit *Aquarena Springs* and be shooting by the summer. All I needed was a script and a producer.

"There is one more thing," Natalie said, dangling the other shoe over the table and letting it drop.

"Yeah?"

"You have to stay and finish the movie. After the way Andrzej treated Elias, I need you here to help get the crew back on his side. I won't have them thinking he's Andrzej's bitch."

"Want the crew back on Elias's side? Have him pay for two hours of free drinks at the hotel bar. You don't need me."

"That's the deal. Take it or leave it."

"C'mon, Natalie, don't do this. Watching you two canoodling on set all day will kill me."

My cell phone rang, and I checked the number.

"Who's that?" Natalie asked.

"I'm not sure." I said, opening the phone. "Yeah?"

"Bobby, this is Steveo. I'm at Brackenridge Hospital with Sara Lee. She got beat up pretty bad."

"Was it her father?"

"No, it's more complicated than that."

"I'll be there in ten minutes," I said and hung up.

"What's the matter, honey?" Natalie asked. "You're as red as a beet."

"Somebody just fucked with one of my grips."

* * *

Natalie insisted on accompanying me to the hospital. We drove there in her rented Mercedes and found Steveo in the visitors' lounge with his hand wrapped in an ice pack.

"I was out playing golf with the electrics, and when I got back there was this Jeep in the driveway with a couple of kids in the backseat. I went toward the house, and as I get closer I hear all this screaming coming from inside. I opened the door, the first thing I see is this guy punching the shit out of Sara Lee. It was a total having.

"I shout, 'Hey what the fuck's going on?' And the guy starts coming at *me*. I'm sorry, but I had no choice except to throw down. That's when Sara Lee started screaming that he was her husband and to stop. I get the guy in a headlock and say, 'Look, pal, if I let go of you will you calm down?' He said, 'Yes,' but as soon as I let go, he tackled Sara Lee. Her head hit the fireplace, and there was blood everywhere. That was it for me, man. I grabbed that C-stand we keep in the corner, and I fucking waled on him. I said, 'Look, motherfucker, you're out of here right now or I'm going to skewer you with this thing.' Then he took off."

"What did Sara Lee say?" I asked.

"Not much. She was pretty whacked. The best I could do was wrap her head in a towel and bring her here."

I slapped him on the back. "You did good, Steveo."

"Does she want to press charges?" Natalie asked.

"The triage nurse asked the same question, but Sara Lee wasn't thinking very straight. She kept saying that it was all her fault." Steveo shook his head. "I'm sorry, but, husband or not, nobody deserves the pounding she took from that asshole."

"I'll be right back," Natalie said, getting up and walking past the triage desk. She was in take-charge mode, and I was sure she'd find out whatever there was to find out.

"You okay?" I asked Steveo.

He opened and closed his hand a couple of times and said, "Daddy doesn't get in as many fights as he used to, but yeah, I'm fine. I'll drink a couple of Guinnesses when I get back to Grip-haus, and it'll be like it never happened."

"Do you think that guy will come back?"

"I don't know. I hope for his sake Slocum isn't there. Slocum really likes Sara Lee."

"They're not . . ."

"Nah, it's more like a brother/sister thing. She thought Slocum was impressive because he went to Hawaii. That was the word she used, *impressive*."

"That's not the first word that comes to mind when I think of Slocum."

"Me neither. But like I said, she and Slocum really hit it off."

"Do you think she would have made a good grip?"

"Sara Lee *is* a good grip. She has a great attitude, and she doesn't complicate stuff by thinking too much."

"There's nothing worse than when a grip starts thinking."

"First they start thinking, and next they want to eat with a knife and fork."

"It's fucking disgusting."

"Tell me about it."

Natalie returned and said that Sara Lee wanted to see me.

"How'd you find her?" I asked as we walked into the emergency room.

"I stuck my head behind every curtain until I spotted a female grip with a head wound."

"See anything interesting before you found her?"

"Just some old guy getting an enema. It was gross, but strangely compelling."

We slipped behind a curtain and found Sara Lee praying. At least that's what I thought she was doing, because her eyes were closed and her lips were moving. Maybe she was working on her multiplication tables.

"Sara . . ." I said.

Her eyes popped open. "I'm so sorry, Bobby. I let you down."

"You didn't let anybody down, Sara Lee."

"All I ever do is let people down."

"Was that man really your husband?"

She nodded.

"And those were your children?"

She nodded again and began to cry. "I'm not a terrible person, Bobby. I'm really not. I just needed some time to myself, that's all. And Charlie, he never, ever watched those kids. They were one hundred percent my responsibility, and after a while it was like my brain just dried up. I was never a genius or anything, but I graduated with a B average, and I can type almost seventy words a minute. Slocum says there's all kinds of grip work in Austin and that maybe I could work for Richard Linklater or Robert Rodriguez. Or *Austin City Limits*. I don't mind moving either. I could go to Dallas. They shoot *Barney* in Dallas."

"There's some blood on your lip, Sara Lee," Natalie said.

She wiped her mouth with the back of her hand and smiled. "That's not blood. That's chew."

"Chew?"

"You know, Skoal. We all chew it."

Natalie gave me a look of disgust and said, "Oh really?"

"What about your children, Sara Lee?" I asked.

"Once I get established as a grip, I can send for them. They'll understand."

"Do you want to press charges?"

"No. If they put Charlie in jail, we'll lose the house. We've already missed one payment."

"But he beat you up."

Sara Lee shrugged and said, "And I left him high and dry. I guess we're even."

Natalie helped Sara Lee get dressed, and I walked back to the waiting room. I couldn't get the sound of Sara Lee saying "grip" out of my head. Grip, grip, grip, as if it were some kind of lofty goal and the golden ticket out of her shitty life. Didn't she see Steveo and me? Or Slocum and George? We were nothing to look up to. Slocum was broke, Steveo was a stoner, and I was emotional roadkill. It broke my heart that Sara Lee's dreams only went as high as that cinematic booby prize called the grip department. Aspiring to be a grip was like aspiring to be a shoe salesman.

"How's she doing?" Steveo asked when I got back to the waiting room.

"She got seven stitches but nothing's broken."

"What now?"

"Sara Lee's getting dressed."

"She coming back to Griphaus?"

"Where else does she have to go?"

Need I mention that Sara Lee was not covered by health insurance? The bill for her visit was eight hundred bucks, and I paid for it in cash with the per diem I'd saved. Steveo offered to drive her back to Griphaus, but Sara Lee had never ridden in a Mercedes before, and we decided to give her a cheap thrill. She rode in the back with Natalie, and I did my best not to feel like Morgan Freeman in *Driving Miss Daisy*.

"Have you worked with anybody famous?" Sara Lee asked Natalie.

"A few people."

"Like who?"

"Susan Sarandon, Tim Robbins, Steve Martin."

"Ooh, what's Steve Martin like?"

"He's very serious."

"No! He seems so crazy in his movies. Have you ever worked

with Cher? I love Cher." She opened her mouth and sang the opening verse of "If I Could Turn Back Time."

I glanced at Natalie in the rearview mirror, and she winked.

"I've seen all of her movies," Sara Lee said. "*Mermaids, Mask, The Witches of Eastwick.* But *Moonstruck* is my favorite movie ever."

"They shot some of that in our neighborhood," I said.

"No!"

"Yeah, her house was just down the block from us."

"Are there a lot of Italians where you live?" She pronounced it *eye*-talian.

"Not as many as there used to be."

"What about the Mafia? Do you live near the Mafia?"

"The Mafia's everywhere," Natalie said.

"Not in Texas."

"Jack Ruby was in the Mafia. That's why he killed Oswald."

Sara Lee looked at Natalie and burst out laughing. "Ruby killed Oswald 'cause he killed Kennedy. Everybody knows that."

Natalie patted Sara Lee on the knee and said, "Oh, honey, you have *so much* to learn."

After we'd put Sara Lee to bed and stationed Steveo outside her bedroom door with a baseball bat, Natalie turned to me and said, "Pack your stuff. You're moving back to the hotel."

"But I used up my housing allowance to pay for this place."

"I don't care. No husband of mine is living in a frat house. I'll make it part of my deal."

"Did you ever think about beating me up when you found out about Elias?" Natalie asked as we drove to the Omni.

"Of course not," I said. "God, I can't believe you even asked me that."

"I wouldn't have pressed charges either."

"Natalie, stop."

"It's just that—"

"Enough!"

I never would have hit Natalie, but I knew what she meant. That's why I let Katherine kick the crap out of me. It was the easy way out. A few minutes of pain and a bruised kidney, and you were free of the shame. Free of the guilt. It was a punk's choice on either side of the fist. Just thinking about it made me feel dirty.

Natalie must have been looking for a little redemption herself, because she turned to me and said, "I think it's time we put Sara Lee on payroll."

"She deserves it," I said. "And since you're being generous, there's something else I'd like you to do."

"What?"

"Fire Elvira."

"Why?"

"Because she called you a *puta*."

"I *am* a *puta*."

"Maybe, but she didn't have to announce it to the world."

Chapter 32

▖▗▖▗▖▗▖▗

The Battle for
Aquarena Springs

Adiós, muchachos. It's been real.
—From Elvira's final notes on Day 49's call sheet

I T'S EASY TO lose track of your life in this business. There are no sick days, no time off for birthdays, no leaving early to catch your kid in the school play. While the rest of the world measures their lives in days and years, movie people mark their lives by the jobs they've done. Unfortunately, no two people have the same résumés, and it's impossible to triangulate your life with anybody else's. Film sets are limbo lands of temporal confusion where the only thing that matters is the shot you're working on at that moment. It's kind of like Buddhism, only without the enlightenment.

How will I remember *Aquarena Springs*? As the worst job I ever worked on? Purgatory? A three-month rectal exam performed by a team of mallet-wielding pain monkeys? Not even close. Mere words cannot capture the essence of what it felt like trying to keep my shit together when Natalie descended on Video Village and the battle lines were drawn. On one side, I had my wife of ten years and the man she'd been banging like a bunny in springtime, and on the other was the lovely Katherine Bettencourt, whose jiggling belly had become my major *objet d'amour,* and her brand-new boyfriend, Andrzej "The Mad Polack" Koscielny.

That's right, Andrzej and Katherine had become an item. After defending her honor with his patented Warsaw Death Grip, Katherine rewarded him with the pleasure of her company. I didn't love Katherine, but on the morning she and Andrzej slithered onto set in the dewy haze of postcarnal bliss, I felt betrayed. Thank God I'd had the foresight to rescue her crotchless compression garment from their animal lust. (Said garment, by the way, was resting comfortably in room 619 of the Austin Omni, where I was taking *very* good care of it.)

The first skirmish in the war that film scholars would one day call the Battle for Aquarena Springs was over director's chairs. There were only three tall ones, and they had been claimed by Andrzej, Katherine, and Elias. The prop man said he could get a fourth by lunch, but that did not satisfy our new producer, who demanded Katherine's.

"But this is *my* chair," Katherine whined.

"I understand that," Natalie replied. "But I forgot my glasses, and I need to be as close to the monitor as possible."

This was news to me. Last time I checked, Natalie had eyes like a mongoose and could spot the last Yohji Yamamoto mesh cardigan in the Barneys Warehouse Sale at fifty paces.

"Why don't you use Elias's chair?" Katherine replied. "He never sits in it."

"I don't think that sends the right message to the crew. They're called director's chairs, after all, not second producer's chairs."

"I'm not the second producer."

"Call yourself what you want, but according to my deal memo I get the first producer's credit."

"Bullshit. Let me see the memo."

"It's with legal back at the studio. They're still working out the language for my back-end participation."

"You got points?" Katherine screeched.

"Oops," Natalie said, putting a hand to her lips in mock innocence. "I wasn't supposed to mention that."

Katherine reached into her bag and pulled out her cell phone. "I'm calling Hank."

"Here," Natalie said, holding up a cell phone so thin you could see through it. "Use mine. It's newer and gets much better reception than that old thing."

"It does not."

"Does too."

"Ladies," Andrzej cooed. "There's no need to fight on such a lovely morning. Natalie can have my seat." Andrzej got up and carried his chair to where Natalie was standing. "Is this a good spot for it?"

"Yes, Andrzej. Thank you."

"It is my pleasure to make you happy. Oh, Bobby, darling?"

"Yes?"

"Go fetch the F-10 and mount it on the sled dolly so I have a place to sit down."

"Excuse me?"

"Was I not specific enough? Go get your biggest dolly, mount it on twenty feet of track, and place your second biggest dolly on top of it. Is that a less ambiguous request?"

"Yes, Andrzej. But just out of curiosity, is there any way you'd settle for a short director's chair mounted on a couple of apple boxes?"

"I never settle, Bobby, darling. You know that. And please hurry. We don't want to fall behind schedule on Natalie's first day as producer."

Fifteen minutes later, I was laying track for the sled dolly and

Andrzej was dry-humping Katherine against the F-10. Natalie was engrossed in a copy of *Vogue,* and when I looked at her my heart began to tear. I thought I'd made progress in separating myself from her, but now that Natalie was so close, I was right where I was on the day she moved out. To think that I couldn't touch her, or share a snide comment, made me want to walk away and never come back. To hell with money. To hell with movies. To hell with everything.

Elias returned from rehearsing with the actors.

"What's Bobby doing?" he asked. "This isn't a dolly shot."

Natalie closed her magazine. "Andrzej's playing games. You don't want to know about it."

"Yes, I do."

"There weren't enough director's chairs, and I tried to take Katherine's. Andrzej intervened, and this is the result."

"There are plenty of director's chairs."

"Not the tall kind."

"Why didn't you just take mine?"

"Because I wanted hers, okay?"

"What is this? Kindergarten?"

"No. When a new producer shows up, it's important that they announce their presence with authority."

"Is that why you fired Elvira?"

"That was for something else."

"I heard it was because she told Katherine about Bobby sleeping with a prostitute."

"What?" Natalie spun around to face me, but I looked away just in time.

"Look, Natalie," Elias said, "let's just forget about politics for a few minutes and concentrate on my movie, okay?"

"*Your* movie?"

"Yes. *My* movie."

"We'll talk about this later." Natalie turned on the heels of her vintage Dale Evans cowgirl boots and marched toward craft service. So much for Peter and Polly World, Part II.

Elias grabbed his director's chair and dragged it across Video Village. "Here," he said, slamming it down in front of Andrzej. "Have a seat."

Andrzej stopped sucking face with Katherine, wiped the saliva from his lips, and said, "As you wish. Oh, Bobby, darling."

"Yes?"

"You can forget about that dolly for the time being."

"Fine." I pulled out my walkie-talkie and said, "I need all hands on deck for a dolly party."

"I'm gonna need a couple of minutes," Steveo squawked back. "I'm shaking hands with the president right now."

"Get here as soon as you can."

I felt a hand on my shoulder and turned to see Andrzej.

"I warned you not to cross me, Bobby, darling."

"I didn't cross anybody."

"Katherine overheard that you were helping our piece-of-shit director."

Busted. "I'm sorry, but it was that or jail. I had no choice."

"You had a choice. You just made the wrong one. Now be a good little slime and get that dolly out of my site. Now."

George and Slocum had arrived, but Steveo was still in the honey wagon. I pulled out my walkie-talkie and said, "How are things going in the Oval Office, Steveo?"

"I'm still in the receiving line."

"Is there a problem, Bobby, darling?"

To stall for time I said, "No, but now that we're getting things out in the open, I just want to say that I don't think you're right for Katherine."

"And you were?" Andrzej snorted. "Waiting for your divorce papers to arrive and then fucking some hooker? What kind of bullshit was that?"

"Sucking face in front of the entire crew? What kind of bullshit is that?"

"At least I'm better than Dr Pepper. Now are you going to move that dolly, or do I have to shove it up your ass?"

"Cut the crap, Andrzej. You know I need four grips to carry it."

"I count four."

I turned, expecting to see Steveo, and saw Sara Lee instead. She was too busted up to work, but we couldn't leave her in Griphaus in case her husband came back.

"Sara Lee can't carry anything right now," I said. "Just give Steveo another minute."

"No. If Sara Lee can't carry a dolly, then fire her and hire someone who can."

"Sara Lee's an intern."

"I heard she went on payroll this morning."

"I'm not firing Sara Lee."

"Then I will. Sara Lee, darling. Come here for a minute."

"No!" I shouted. "George! Slocum! You guys take the front of the dolly. I'll take the back by myself."

"You sure, boss?" Slocum said through a lip of chew. "That thing weighs a ton."

"Yeah, I'm sure." I grabbed the back of the dolly and said, "On three. One . . . Two . . . Three . . ."

We lifted the dolly and began walking. It was heavy, but I thought I could handle it.

"Nice and easy, guys. Head toward that tree over there and— *FUCK!*"

Lightning shot up my side. It felt like someone was cleaving the muscles from my spine with a garden tool, and my knees started to buckle.

"Put it down!" I cried. "Put it down!"

We set the dolly on the ground, and I collapsed in the dirt. I grabbed my knees and curled into a ball, but that hurt even worse.

Slocum and George hovered over me, telling me to calm down and that everything would be okay. But everything would not be okay, because the only way to stop the pain was with a handful of Vicodin. And I knew that if I took even a single pill, I'd go back to being a full-blown junkie before you could say "Action."

Chapter 33

Agony

THE WORST THING about lower-back injuries—besides the pain part—is the intermittency. One moment, you're kicking back in your hotel room and grooving on Bea Arthur's sweet booty in a old episode of *Golden Girls,* and the next it's like someone's lancing your kidney with a white-hot knitting needle. Even the simplest tasks can cause unbelievable pain. Like checking your e-mail to see if there are any replies from the plastic surgeons you wrote to describing yourself as a five-foot-two-inch, two-hundred-and-fifty-pound woman interested in gastric bypass surgery and requesting before-and-after photos of females with similar body types to make sure you really want to go through with it. You'd think this would be easy, but no. And forget about writing back to the surgeons who replied to your query, calling you a pathetic pervert and that you should be ashamed of yourself.

This ping-pong match between boredom and agony really messes with your mind, and after a while you'll do *anything* to kill the pain. Thus, the popularity of Vicodin and all the other weapons of sweet relief in your doctor's arsenal. Without the benefit of pharmaceuticals I was forced to rely on over-the-counter solutions. The problem was, I had gobbled up so much Advil over the past twenty years that I was practically immune to the stuff, and a dose large enough to stop the pain would have poisoned me. Basically, I was screwed.

There was a knock on my door.

"Who is it?" I called out.

"Elias."

"What do you want?"

"I need to talk to you about something."

"What?"

"I can't discuss it out here," he said in a low voice.

"Hold on."

I tried to sit up and was forced back down by a ridiculous amount of pain. "Shit," I hissed.

"Are you okay in there?"

"Never better." The key was not to lean forward. I dropped my legs off the side of the bed and attempted to push myself into a standing position. Bad idea. I wound up with my legs on the floor and my shoulders on the bed like some kind of limbo dancer in training.

"Do you need me to call someone?" Elias asked.

"No, I'm cool."

It was impossible to return to bed, and my only other option was to drop onto the floor. Sliding across the carpet was easier than I expected, and came with the added benefit of a buttload of electrostatic crackles. I reached the door and tried to turn the knob with my toes. It was useless. I put my mouth near the threshold and whispered, "Hey, Elias, down here."

"Yes?"

"Can we talk like this?"

"Not with so many crew people around. I just said hello to Mark, the boom operator. He's says he hopes you feel better, by the way."

"How nice of him," I said, wanting to kick the door down. "I'm gonna need another minute."

"Are you sure you don't want me to call someone?"

"Yes, I'm sure." Who was this guy? My freaking mother?

My next plan was to fetch my room key and slide it under the door. I static-surfed across the carpet and knocked my cargo shorts off the chair with my feet. The key wasn't there. I looked around and realized it was on top of the dresser with my wallet.

"Shit!" I yelled.

"This is ridiculous. I'm going down to the front desk and getting someone with a master key."

"No!" I yelled, but it was pointless. I wiggled to the bed, knocked the phone off the nightstand, and dialed the operator.

"Thank you for calling the Austin Omni Downtown. This is Stephanie at the front desk, how may I help you?"

"This is Bobby Conlon in room 619. I've fallen and I can't get up."

It was a toss-up what was more embarrassing: Elias and the assistant manager finding me splayed out on the floor in my undies and an old Butthole Surfers T-shirt, or the laptop on the bed showing pictures of sagging women with fresh plastic surgery scars across their bellies. Elias was cool about it, though. He slipped the manager a fiver, closed my laptop, and got down on the floor to talk to me on my level.

"I told you how to handle Andrzej," I said, putting my feet up on a chair to relieve the pressure on my lower back. "Let him deal with the shots and everything will be fine. You never should have given him those storyboards."

"Andrzej isn't the problem."

"Then who is?"

"Natalie. You saw how she was acting. All that nonsense about director's chairs. It's like she's suddenly a different person. I can't work with her."

"You've got to. I mean, after everything she's done . . ."

"I know," Elias said, running a hand through his hair. "She's the one responsible for my being here and everything, but she's turned into this incredible distraction."

"You're just not used to having her on set. Give it a couple of days."

"You don't understand. When she's not fighting with Katherine, she's offering advice on how to shoot the scene—which if I don't take, puts her in a snit. I'm finally getting to a place where I feel comfortable as a director. I can't have her second-guessing everything I do. Especially with Andrzej ready to fuck with me at every opportunity."

"I've worked on a lot of shows. Trust me, the ones that go the smoothest always turn out the worst. A little friction is good for a movie."

"I don't mind input, but Natalie thinks she's the codirector of the movie. I don't have time to fight with her twenty-four hours a day. It's exhausting."

"Please don't send her home, Elias."

"What would you do?"

"It's impossible to say. I wouldn't be in this situation."

"I'll rephrase the question. What would you do if you were me?"

The words left my mouth before I could stop them. "I'd do whatever it took to make my movie."

And that was that. I sighed and neither of us said anything for a while.

"When do you plan on telling her?" I finally asked.

"I'm not sure," Elias said. He picked a piece of lint off the carpet and rolled it between his fingertips. "This is a nice hotel, isn't it?"

"It's not bad, but I'd stay away from the room-service fajitas if I were you."

"I'll remember that." Elias stood and walked toward the door. "Thanks for the advice, Bobby."

"Hold on a second," I said. "I need to ask a favor."

"What is it?"

"This is kind of embarrassing, but I can't go to the bathroom by myself."

Elias took a step back. "What do you mean?"

"I can't lean over the bowl. It's too painful. I need somebody to—you know—hold my thing while I pee."

"I can't do that."

"I know it sounds gross and everything, but I wouldn't ask if I wasn't desperate."

Elias looked down at his feet.

"Please," I begged. "You've got to help me."

Elias sighed and said, "Oh, all right."

I burst out laughing. "You fucking homo! I can't believe you fell for that. There's no way I would let you touch my dick."

His face grew red. "Thanks a lot."

"Sorry, dude. But you should have seen the expression on your face. I thought you were gonna shit."

"See you around, Bobby."

"But seriously, I do need your help."

"With what?"

"Getting off the floor."

"Isn't that going to hurt?"

"Yeah, you better get me a towel to bite down on."

Elias did as I asked.

"On three," I said and held out my arms. "One . . . two . . ." I bit down hard. "Three!"

Elias pulled my arms. Fuck a white-hot knitting needle. This time it was like someone was driving a cement mixer up my spine.

"Jesus Christ!" I screamed.

"Was it bad?"

I spit out the towel. "Like nothing you've ever experienced before."

"Your face is white as an egg."

"Agony will do that to you. Thanks, I'll be okay in a couple of seconds."

"No problem. And thanks for that other thing."

"Sure. And sorry you didn't get to touch my dick."

After paying such a steep price to get up from the floor, I had no desire to go back down there. But where else could I go? It wasn't like I could pull on a pair of chinos and traipse downstairs to knock back a couple of mai tais with Troy and Dusty. Still, I had to do something to help me forget I told Elias to shitcan Natalie. I turned on the TV and leaned against the wall. This was fun for ten minutes, and painful after twenty. I was about to admit defeat when there was a knock on the door. "It's open," I shouted.

It was Moose.

"Butthole Surfers?" he asked, eyeing my T-shirt. "What's that? Some kind of gay beach club?"

"They're a local band. How's it going?"

"Lousy. The Cowboys got lucky on Sunday, and I got cleaned out."

"Sorry to hear that."

"It happens. Hey, I heard a very interesting rumor this afternoon."

"What's that?"

"That we're getting a hundred and fifty grand for your truck."

"We?"

"When do I get my seventy-five Gs?"

"Our deal was for half of what I got from the DeSalvo Brothers."

"Our deal was for half of what you got for your truck. I left it vague in case something like this happened."

"That's not fair."

"Duh."

I ran a hand through my hair. Seventy-five grand, minus twelve for the insurance company, minus the DeSalvo Brothers' storage fee. I was screwed. There was no way I could make a movie with so little money.

"Is there any way we can renegotiate?" I asked.

"Sorry, pal, it doesn't work that way." He took a step closer and lowered his voice. "And don't even think about doing anything stupid. I'd hate to drop a dime on you to those wops in Philly."

"Not my style," I sighed. The pain in my back had gone from bad to unbearable. "I'll let you know when the insurance company comes through with the money."

"I knew you'd do the right thing." Moose opened the door and walked into the hallway. "How's that back of yours doing, by the by?"

"Lousy."

"I thought you'd say that. Here." He tossed me an orange prescription bottle.

"What are these?"

"OxyContin, the filet mignon of painkillers."

"No, thanks, Moose. I don't need—"

It was too late. The door slammed, and Moose was gone.

I shook the bottle. It sounded like the opening notes of a favorite song I hadn't heard since high school. I popped the cap and counted the pills. Twelve. That meant I could take two a day for almost a week. Or one a day for almost two weeks. Or six a day for two days. The possibilities were endless, but only one thing mattered: Where could I get more pills? Moose had a connection, but how reliable was he? Could the guy be counted on to show up when I needed him, or would I have to give myself a buffer? The emergency room quack had given me a scrip for Lortab, which I had almost thrown away. After OxyContin, Lortab would feel like training wheels, but it was a good backup in case I ran dry. Or better yet, maybe I could trade them for more Oxys? I could feel my resolve falling away like a scab.

And why not? After everything I'd gone through, it was obvious that the universe did not want me to direct. It was time to face reality. I could either accept who I was or spend the rest of my life feeling like a failure. When we wrapped in Texas, I'd go crawling back to Dr. Koch, apologize for leaving four hundred and ninety seven messages on his answering machine, and gobble enough Atavan to make sure I never felt like calling "Action" again. It wasn't the life I had dreamed of, but it might not be that bad either. I was a well-respected craftsman in a proud and insane business, and there was some minor glory to be found in that role. Somebody had to drag the stones across the desert to build the pyramids, and somebody had to drag the dolly back to one. I would never be an auteur, but at least I'd be making a contribution to the art form that I loved.

Or at least that's what I tried to make myself believe.

```
Q: What's the difference between a failed
   director and a drug addict?
A: One OxyContin.
```

Chapter 34

Peter and Polly World, Part II

LIKE I SAID, something happens to a guy when he gets to sit in a director's chair. The unyielding pressure, the ten thousand decisions, and the endless hours are suffocating, but if you can rise above the insanity, it's hard not to feel like God. Think about what it must have been like for Peter Bogdanovich on *The Last Picture Show*. The city boy with the encyclopedic knowledge of cinema finds himself in Texas with not just a movie crew, but the entire history of cinema breathing down his neck. Welles, Ford, and Hawks are back in LA, and even though they're rooting for him, they're jealous of his youth and energy and wouldn't shed too many tears if he fell flat on his face. Polly is there too—helping, suggesting, collaborating—but Peter knows that if he fails the blame will be his and he'll spend the rest of his life as a no-talent nobody.

It's the night before the first day of principal photography and Peter can't sleep. Every time he nods off, something else pops into his head: a line of dialogue, a camera angle, a note for an actor. Howard Hawks once told him he used to get so nervous on the first day of shooting he'd have to pull over and vomit on his way to set. Peter can believe it. So much to remember. So many details. So much weighing on him. What if he got sick? What if he died? Who would direct the movie? Who would take care of his daughters? He glances at Polly asleep next to him, and suddenly hates her. How can she sleep at a time like this when their lives, their reputations, their futures are dangling on the edge of oblivion?

Then, *boom*, it's happening. Peter's directing, and it's great. It's wonderful. It's magic. He feels like Gene Kelly in *An American in Paris*, and the entire universe falls in step with his every move. His shots line up, the crew does everything he says, and even the fucking weather cooperates. Yes, it's scary, and sometimes he feels like he's falling down an elevator shaft, but he's really doing it. He's directing a major motion picture. At night he falls into bed exhausted, knowing that he did the best work he was capable of.

The thing with Cybill Shepherd happens almost by accident, like a mosquito bite. He's watching her rehearse the scene with Randy Quaid outside the country club and runs over to give her a bit of direction. He wraps an arm around her the way he would a sister or friend—innocently, platonically, directorially—and she gives him *this smile*. He thinks nothing of it until he's back in his director's chair and then it's all he can think of. Her hair, her smell, her lips. Was she flirting with him? Maybe. But Cybill flirted with everybody. That's who she was. That's why he cast her in the role, for Christ's sake. She wouldn't have anything to do with him. And besides, he's a married man. He glances at Polly, and she's staring at him. Could she possibly know what he was thinking? Was it that obvious? He looks away and sees everyone staring at him. Could the entire crew know what he was thinking? Was his tongue hanging out or something? No, it's just that the rehearsal is over. He was thinking about Cybill and missed it.

"How was that?" the AD asks. "You want another one, or do you want to roll film?"

Peter doesn't know what to do. He has no idea if the rehearsal was good or bad. Panic races through his veins. He's blowing it. This is a pivotal scene in the movie, and he was daydreaming. He looks at Cybill, and there's that smile again. Then it occurs to him. It doesn't matter whether the rehearsal was good or bad. He's in charge, and they'll give him as many rehearsals as he wants. But why rehearse when you can roll film? That's right. Why not shoot when you have the opportunity?

"Let's try one," he says.

After that, it was like a movie. How many centuries had he longed for a starlet to slide off the screen and into his arms? One moment Cybill was in dailies and the next she was in his bed. It was more than a fantasy come true. It was all he had ever wanted. Yes, there were Polly and the girls to deal with, but it was like he couldn't help himself. It was part of the directorial package. Hawks, Huston, Wellman were all lusty men, bedding their actresses like it was part of the job. And maybe it was. The line between life and desire blurred, and Peter woke to realize that his dream had come true. He was A Director. Finally.

But what would have happened if *The Last Picture Show* had turned out to be a disaster? If the shots didn't line up? If Peter couldn't talk to the actors, and directing was like crawling through a forest of razor blades? What would he have done? What if all that desire, all that passion, all that knowledge turned out to be worthless? A waste of time. A hobby. Like building model airplanes or playing checkers. How could he look in the mirror? How could he continue to walk and breathe?

And what would have happened if Peter wasn't a journalist and confidant to the stars, but a humble dolly grip? What would have happened if he sat there alone in Casa de Gaffer's Tape trying to write a script worthy of his idols and had a head-on collision with his own lack of talent and the horrible realization that his life was a lie? What do you do with all that passion? All that desire? It just doesn't go away. You have to do something with it. You have to.

I held twelve OxyContin in one hand and a TV remote in the other. My shirt and underwear were drenched with sweat, and I was flipping channels like a madman. There had to be something on television to distract me from the hot flames of hell that were broiling my lower back. *If I can only find something to wrap my mind around*, I told myself, *I could forget about the pills and the pain for at least a little while.* A face. A shot. A well-written snippet of dialogue. That's all I needed. I whipped past news shows and reality shows, talk shows and nature shows. Everything became a blur. I was going so fast it took a moment to realize I had gone past a face I knew. I flipped back a couple channels, and there he was, the man himself: Peter Bogdanovich.

It was an old episode of *The Sopranos* where Peter played a recurring role as Lorraine Bracco's therapist. An inside joke for film nerds everywhere. He was on-screen for less than three minutes, but I had to smile. Thirty-five years after *The Last Picture Show* and the son-of-a-bitch was still at it. Thirty-five years of hard work, bad breaks, and studio politics. Welles was gone. Hawks was gone. But Peter Bogdanovich was still out there slugging rats. The man was a survivor. A hero. And what did he have to show for it? Never-ending criticism by loudmouth know-nothings like me who claimed his best work was behind him. I had never met the man, but I'm sure he didn't see it that way. Nobody wakes up saying, *Today I'm going to do an okay job, but nothing like what I did thirty-five years ago.* Of course not. You do the best you can with what you've got. Some days you catch your tornado and some days you miss.

But you never quit. Never.

I set the OxyContin on my nightstand and picked up the phone.

"Room service."

"This is Bobby Conlon in room 619. Send me up a bottle of Wild Turkey and a bucket of ice."

"There's bourbon in your minibar, sir. It's more affordable than buying an entire bottle."

"Just send it up."

I didn't care what it cost, a room service bottle of Wild Turkey was a shitload less expensive than twenty years of trips uptown to Dr. Koch's West Side Giggle Emporium. Fuck pharmaceuticals too. I'd numb my pain the old-fashioned way, the way grips had for generations. With booze. And when the pain was gone, I'd make my movie with the money I had left. I didn't care if I had to shoot the damn thing with two sock monkeys and a flashlight. This time, nothing was going to stop me. No one was going to get in my way. Not Moose. Not Natalie. And most of all, not me.

There was a knock on my door. I pulled it open, but the person on the other side was not holding a bottle of Wild Turkey.

"Elias broke up with me," Natalie announced, marching into room 619 for the first time since our conjugal abandonment.

"Nice to see you too, dear."

"He can kick me out of his bed, but there's no way he's kicking me off this movie. If he tries, so help me God, I'll make sure *Ant Eater* goes into turnaround for the rest of his natural-born life."

I leaned against the wall and sighed. "And this has what exactly to do with me?"

"Stop it. You know you're the only one I can talk to about this stuff."

"Why don't you call Becky? You guys used to talk all the time."

"Thanks for the understanding."

Bringing up Natalie's New Best Friend was a cheap shot, but I didn't care. I was one OxyContin away from a life of zombified gripitude, and I didn't need Natalie's problems on top of my own. There was a second knock on my door, and this time it really was room service with my anesthesia.

"It's a lot cheaper if you use your minibar," Natalie said.

"I'll remember that for next time," I replied as I signed the tab. "You want some of this?"

"Sure."

I cracked the seal and took a long pull straight from the bottle.

"Go easy on that stuff. You know how it fucks you up when you mix booze with your meds."

"I'm not taking any medication," I said as I poured two drinks.

"Why not?"

"Because I'm not."

I handed Natalie her glass and she said, "You never told me it was Elvira who ratted you out to Carni about that hooker."

"I didn't think you needed a map."

"I just hate having anything to do with that business-school bitch."

I slammed my glass on the nightstand. "Will you *please* lighten up on Katherine?"

"Why? Are you planning some kind of tearful reconciliation after she's done fucking Andrzej?"

"No, it makes you look mean and petty. Why do you think

Elias doesn't want you on set? All that director's chair bullshit—gimme a break."

Natalie lunged toward me. "Elias talked to you? What did he say?"

"He said you were a distraction."

"A distraction? That dickhead. And what else did he say?"

"Nothing. I told him to give you a couple of days to settle down, but he obviously didn't take my advice."

Natalie sat on the edge of the bed. "Thanks for trying, anyway."

"What are ex-husbands for?"

"You're not my ex-husband yet." She set her drink on the night-stand and knocked my OxyContin to the floor. "What are those?"

"A conciliation prize from Moose. You can have them if you want."

"Conciliation for what?"

"For taking half my money from the insurance company."

"What are you talking about?"

I told her about Moose threatening to rat me out on the De-Salvo Brothers.

"Shit, Bobby. I'm so sorry."

I waved my hand. "I don't care. It's not going to stop me from making my movie."

"What movie?"

"The one I'm making after I'm done here."

"You can't make a movie for seventy-five grand."

"*You* might not be able to make a movie for seventy-five grand, but I can and I will."

"What about equipment? How about editing? There's no way you can do it for that."

I pointed at the door. "Get the fuck out of here. If you're not going to help me, I don't want to hear about it."

Natalie laughed.

"What's so funny?"

"This is how you used to talk when we first got together. I didn't realize how much I missed it."

"This is different. Back then I was full of shit. Now I'm for real."

Natalie picked up her drink. "If I was going to help you in this little endeavor, what would you want me to do?"

"You could start by finding me a screenplay."

"You don't even have a script?"

"Go through that pile in your office, find the one that stinks the least, and get whoever wrote it to give it to us for free. End of story."

"Us?"

"Me, then. I was going to give you a producer's credit, but if you don't want it . . ."

"The hell I don't."

"Then fine. Us."

"Us." Natalie said it like she was unloading an armful of shopping bags. "Look at you," she sighed. "You're a mess."

"Unbearable pain will do that to a guy."

"C'mon, let's get you cleaned up."

"That's okay. I just need some help getting back on the floor."

"Don't be ridiculous, I can smell that T-shirt from across the room." She headed toward my dresser.

"You don't have to do that."

"I know."

She opened the drawer and I began to count. *One . . . two . . .*

"What's this?"

Three. "What's what, darling?"

"This." She pulled Katherine's crotchless compression garment out of the dresser.

"Just something I wore to last month's Halloween party."

"This is *hers,* isn't it?"

I shrugged, and Natalie shook it open to reveal the magical spot where the crotch was supposed to be. "Oh my God!" she screeched. "Is this what she wears to fuck?"

"Don't knock it till you've tried it. Velcro can be quite the turn-on."

"Oh really?" Natalie set the compression garment on the bed. "Then I guess this wouldn't do anything for you?" She lifted her shirt to reveal a flat stomach with a pierced belly button.

"Holy shit, Natalie, you look like something out of *Maxim*."

"You're damn right I do," she said, dropping her shirt. "Too bad you're into recovering fatties or you could have some of it."

"Yeah, too bad."

Neither of us said a word as the lights dimmed, Billie Holiday came on the stereo, and the room was lit by a dozen fig-scented candles. Or at least that's what if felt like.

Natalie tossed the compression garment in the wastebasket. "Do you think we could do it if I stayed on top the whole time?"

"Anything to help the ball club."

Natalie walked toward me. I couldn't tell if it was the bourbon or testosterone, but something made it a lot easier to get down on the floor than it had been getting up. Natalie pulled off my shirt and shorts, and held out her right arm for inspection. "Here," she cooed. "Feel that muscle."

"How long did it take to get like that?"

"Four months. It went a lot faster once I cut sugar and white flour out of my diet."

"What do you eat for fun?"

"There are other ways to have fun besides sugar," she said, pulling off her jeans. The Mohawk was back

It was quite the turn-on to see Natalie in such spectacular shape. Still, it was hard to forget that she had transformed herself for Elias and not me. I concentrated on her supermodel figure and the feel of her hands on my thighs. The urge to merge took over, and blood was rerouted to the appropriate organ. I became Sean Connery in *Dr. No,* Brando in *Last Tango,* Gary Cooper in *The Fountainhead.*

Then Natalie climbed on top of me, and it felt like I was fucking a cinder block. Her tan, her muscles, the laser job under her eyes. It wasn't my wife on top of me, but some desperate middle-aged woman with something to prove. A desperate middle-aged woman without a fleck of fat or a dollop of flab anywhere on her body. Oh, how incredibly fucking cruel! Fifteen years of lusting after those Nautilus queens at the gym, and now that I had one on top of me, all I wanted was the dumpy little woman I married.

Natalie, meanwhile, was treating me to her version of a pole dance. She ran her hands over her breasts, whispered dirty words in my ear, and flexed her "special" muscles. What the hell was she thinking? That the stuff women did on late-night cable was for real? Couldn't we just turn on *Letterman* and cuddle? Her efforts were having a less-than-desired effect on the body part in question, and I could feel myself losing altitude. It was a shitty thing to do, but I closed my eyes and tried to picture Katherine on top of me instead of my Natalie. It didn't help.

"Is it going to take much longer?" she asked a little while later. "I'm starting to get sore."

What could I say? *Sure, honey, I'll be done as soon as you gain twenty pounds?* Instead, I said, "This isn't going to happen for me tonight, honey."

"But I really, really want you to come."

"I appreciate that, but with my back and everything . . ."

Natalie looked me in the eye. "It's very important to me that I make you come, okay?"

"Okay," I sighed.

"Now tell me, big boy, what can I do for you?"

My back was on fire, my wife had lost her mind, and I felt about as sexually aroused as a dead trout. What could she do for me? She could leave me alone and let me get some sleep. But that was not the answer she wanted to hear, and if I was going to resurrect the ghost of Peter and Polly World from the ashes of Miguel-Simm Productions, I had to do something. That was when I noticed the champagne-colored sleeve hanging over the edge of the wastebasket.

"Well," I said. "There is *one thing* you could try . . ."

Chapter 35

The Auteur Theory of Failure

TWO DAYS LATER, I could sit up without feeling like someone was driving a flaming bullet train up my ass, but I was in no condition to work. I continued my convalescence on the floor of room 619, slipped my key card under the door for visiting dignitaries, and assured the cleaning staff that it was perfectly okay to vacuum around me. After our night of awkward passion, Natalie had returned to the Four Seasons to get her head together and enjoy their lavender-scented sheets. I think we were both a little freaked out by how the other had changed in the past year, and Natalie was a firm believer in the restorative powers of a three-star hotel. Me? I just wanted to get back to New York. In addition to being a lousy place to recover from a debilitating back injury, movie sets are a less than optimal setting to reconcile with your wife after a year of cinematic adultery. Still, I was optimistic. Natalie had agreed to produce my movie and that—even more than pulling on Katherine's crotchless compression garment and riding me like a broken-down stallion—was a sign that things might work out.

The phone rang and it was Hank.

"Hey, buddy, how's the back?"

"A little better."

"Natalie says you're getting by without painkillers."

"Natalie has a big mouth."

"Stop that. You should be proud of yourself."

"I'll try to remember your kind words of encouragement while I'm grinding my teeth at four in the morning."

"Don't grind them too much because I need you on set to-morrow."

"There's no way I'll be able to work by then."

"No way is not an option. Julia Roberts is back from Prague for a week, and she's agreed to reshoot the dolly shot that Sir Richard fucked up. We only have her for the afternoon, and I need my best peeps on the scene. Not to mention that Dan Berg is coming to town too."

"You're not listening to me, Hank. My back is wasted. And besides, isn't that shot supposed to take place under the Brooklyn Bridge?"

"Andrzej can fake the angle, and you can wear a back brace."

"And you can suck my dick. I'm not doing it."

"Dan Berg is flying in."

"Have him push dolly."

"C'mon, dude, please don't make me threaten to fire your wife. That's so uncool."

"You wouldn't dare. You'd look like a complete asshole."

"Not when I tell people she went behind my back to get your money from the insurance company."

"Who told you that?"

"This is Hollywood, pal, nobody can keep a secret longer than one round of phone calls. The good news is, I hired a masseuse to come to your room and fix up your back. She should be there any minute."

"Glad to see you've thought of everything."

"My flight gets in around seven. I'll try and swing by your room to see how you're doing. If not, I'll catch you on set tomorrow."

"I'll be the one lying on the ground in unbearable pain."

"Such a kidder."

There was a knock on my door, and I crawled across the carpet to answer it. "Who's there?"

"Deirdre."

"Deirdre? Deirdre."

"The one and only."

I slid my key card under the door and looked up as *Aquarena Springs*'s favorite call girl walked in.

"What are you doing here?" I asked.

"Your buddy Hank hired me."

"He said he was sending up a masseuse."

"He is," she said, dragging a massage table into the room. "Not only am I a licensed massage therapist, but I have an associate's degree in physical therapy from ACC. That's how I supported myself before I figured out that blow jobs paid better than shiatsu."

Deirdre helped me onto the table and pressed her hands against my lower back.

"Ow," I said. "That hurts."

"Your lumbar muscles feel like the bottom of an egg carton."

"Do you think I'll be able to work tomorrow?"

"Nope."

"Could you please tell Hank that?"

"Sorry, but I don't play politics. It's bad for business."

Ultimately, I blame the French for what happened. If Jean-Luc Godard, François Truffaut, and the rest of those movie-loving frogs hadn't invented the auteur theory of filmmaking, nobody would have taken movies seriously enough to start teaching them in college. And without the NYU, USC, and UCLA film programs, Francis Coppola, George Lucas, and Martin Scorsese never would have reinvented movies in the seventies and set the stage for independent film in the eighties and nineties. And without independent film, Natalie never would have fucked Elias.

Yeah, I know there are some holes in my hypothesis, but listen. Before independent film turned our world upside down, people like Natalie and me never would have dreamed of making our own movies. I would have been a fat, drunk, and happy grip and Natalie would have been a successful production manager. We'd have had a bunch of kids, lived on Long Island, and vacationed in Disney World. And we would have been *satisfied*. Instead, we drove ourselves insane with jealousy and desire and spent all our money trying to distract ourselves from how pointless our lives had become.

I remember the day Natalie and I realized we had it all. We were making a list of everything we owned for an insurance policy and the results were impressive: a house in the Hamptons, an apartment in the city, a car, clothes, CDs, computers, wide-screen televisions, and every other doodad required for a comfy middle-class existence. What else was there? We had waited too long to have kids, so the answer was nothing. All we had left to look forward to were forty years of upgrades and death. Okay, maybe we were too quick to blow little Bobby and Baby Natalie's college fund on that month in Tuscany, but we were shattered from the results of our fertility tests, and a deluxe vacation seemed like the right thing to do. We had seen friends go through the drama of reproductive surgery and in vitro fertilization, and neither of us had the stomach for such procedures. And believe me, once you've had Chianti Classico made from 100 percent sangiovese grapes, you'll never look at Italian wine the same way again. The stuff they sell here is bullshit.

"Time to turn over."

Deirdre eased me onto my back and returned to work. I was about to doze off when I noticed she was spending quite a bit of time on my inner thighs.

"What the hell are you doing, Deirdre?"

"Just checking to see if you wanted one of my value-added services."

"What do you suggest?"

"I wouldn't recommend anything too strenuous, but I could give you a happy ending for fifty."

After the disaster with Katherine, I had vowed never to sleep with a prostitute again. Yet here I was with Deirdre's hand on my thigh and my dick at half-mast. I didn't need another black mark on my soul, but as I lay there trying to come up with a nice way of turning her down, my eyes came to rest on the delicious servings of flesh dangling beneath Deirdre's biceps.

"Can I lick the skin under your arms while you do it?"

"That'll cost sixty."

"Sold."

Note to self: Next time you plan on getting your crank yanked while slurping on a hooker's underarm dingle-dangle, it's probably a good idea to chain your door. That way, when your wife decides to pay you a surprise visit using that spare room key you gave her, you have a moment to throw a hand towel over your boner.

"Jesus Christ, Bobby."

I opened my eyes and saw Natalie standing in the doorway with a shopping bag in each hand.

"Shit, Natalie. It's not what you think. Deirdre is a licensed massage therapist. She's even got an associate's degree from Austin Community College."

"What did she major in? Hum jobs?"

"This is probably a good time for me to leave," Deirdre said.

"No, please go back to what you were doing." Natalie dug into one of her shopping bags. "Here," she said, throwing a hot-water bottle at me. "I thought this would make you feel better."

"Not as much as phone sex, but I hear that's only for Elias."

Natalie's eyes grew wide. "He told you about that?"

"Told me? He had you on speakerphone. Half the hotel heard."

"That asshole! I'll fucking kill him." Natalie stomped out and slammed the door.

I glanced down at the place where my erection used to be and said, "That really put a damper on things."

"Did that Elias guy really have her on speakerphone?"

"No, but I figured if she was angry at him, she'd be less pissed off at me."

Deirdre shook her head. "Nice."

Chapter 36

Showdown

I WOULD HAVE BLOWN off work if Natalie had let me apologize, but she refused to answer my calls. I filled the hot-water bottle from the complimentary coffeemaker in the bathroom, packed my lower lip with Skoal, and jammed our divorce papers in my cargo shorts. It was time to have it out. Either Natalie would get back together with me or not. No more bullshit, no more nights in separate hotel rooms, no more value-added hand jobs from comedy club hookers. Natalie and I were man and wife or we were nothing.

We were shooting along the banks of the Colorado River, which, for some silly reason, the locals call Town Lake. It was less than ten minutes from the Omni, and my plan was to convince Natalie of my undying love, tell Hank to go fuck himself, and be back in my room in time to catch *Oprah.* It was a righteous plan, but I forgot to factor in that Video Village had been overtaken by a gaggle of dysfunctional lunatics: Elias wasn't talking to Andrzej, Katherine wasn't talking to Natalie, and Natalie wasn't talking to Elias. Katherine was acting like a baby, Andrzej was acting like an asshole, and Elias was acting like a prima donna. I had to take a number for someone to be pissed off at me.

Julia Roberts was scheduled to arrive at two-thirty, and Natalie wanted to be rolling film by a quarter to five. This would give us half an hour to shoot the scene before things got ugly. Unfortunately, things got ugly as soon as we arrived on set. Andrzej wanted to shoot the scene with a crane. Elias wanted to shoot it with a dolly. And Hank wanted to shoot it with three locked-off cameras surrounded by a team of shotgun-wielding security guards to ensure that nothing went wrong. Katherine teamed up with Andrzej because they were sleeping together, and Natalie teamed up with Elias because she refused to be on the same side as Katherine. Hank tossed a coin and Andrzej's side won.

"Fuck," Natalie shouted and stomped off toward craft service.

"Wait!" I called. I turned to run after her but was stopped short when five fingers of pure Polish sadism attached themselves to my collarbone.

"And where do you think you're going, Bobby, darling?"

"I'll be right back, Andrzej. I just have to—"

"Build the fucking crane," he hissed.

"Okay, I just have to—"

He dug his fingers in deeper.

"All right, all right, all right!" I yelped. He released his grip, and I screamed, "George! Slocum! Grab Steveo and get the crane out here. Now!"

"Fellow filmmakers," Andrzej said, clapping his hands, "we must hurry. We are losing the light."

It was ten minutes after eight in the morning.

The film business is all about overcompensation. If a scene requires an actor to throw a beer bottle across the room, the prop man will have ten standing by. Just in case. The sound department runs a backup recorder. Just in case. Wardrobe carries doubles and triples of every costume. Just in case. On and on it goes. Extra equipment. Extra expendables. Extra crew. There's so much at stake that if something goes wrong, someone *has* to be blamed. Everyone's prepared and everyone's scared. The stories are legend: the effects guy who blew up the bridge before the director called "Action," the PA who left the day's film in the back of a cab, the gun filled with blanks that killed Brandon Lee. The crew tries to act cool about it, but deep down we're shitting bricks on a daily basis.

Andrzej was taking no chances. If something was going to go wrong this time around, it would not be his fault. And if that meant rehearsing the crane shot up and down, up and down, over and over until my back felt like a sizzling slab of brisket, Andrzej was willing to make that sacrifice. It also meant I'd have to postpone my showdown with Natalie until lunch. And I'd miss *Oprah*.

Andrzej was on and off the crane a dozen times, fine-tuning the shot, watching playback, and adjusting the background. This was completely out of character. Andrzej was many things, but he was not insecure.

"What's going on with Señor Polack?" I asked Troy. "I've never seen him so stressed out before."

"Sorry, but I can't tell you."

"Can't tell me? What is this? Summer camp? I'm about to get permanent back damage, and you're keeping secrets. C'mon, dude, what the fuck?"

Troy turned to make sure Andrzej wasn't listening. "Okay, but you have to promise not to tell anyone."

"All right, I promise."

He lowered his voice and said, "Dan Berg signed Choi Park last week."

"Wow! Really? Who the hell is Choi Park?"

"Sssh, not so loud. He's the Korean Jackie Chan, and Andrzej's been trying to make a movie with him for years. Andrzej's already pumped forty grand of his own money into a script and for flying Choi back and forth for meetings in LA. The real reason Dan Berg is coming is to put the full-court press on Hank to do Andrzej's movie instead of Elias's. If Hank says no, Choi's going to do a remake of *The Green Hornet* starring Matt Damon. After that, he'll be one untouchable Korean. This is Andrzej's shot at being a director; if it doesn't pan out he's forty G's in the hole and back to square one. Remember, you can't tell a soul about this."

"Absolutely not," I said, turning to look for Natalie.

The first rule of the film business is that a juicy piece of gossip heals all wounds. The Choi Park rumor was as juicy as it got, and would go a long way toward getting me off Natalie's shit list. Unfortunately, I was chained to the crane and the life span of a hot piece of gossip can be measured in milliseconds. If somebody got to Natalie before I did, my rumor would be worthless.

"Okay, let's try it again," Andrzej said, climbing onto the crane. "This time don't start until Julia is eighteen inches closer."

We rehearsed the move again and again. Andrzej continued to tweak the beginning and end positions, but from where I was standing every variation looked exactly the same. It was over ninety degrees out, and my guys were drenched in sweat. Julia Roberts wasn't due for another three hours, and Andrzej announced that he wanted to work through lunch. Megan fed us water, but the heat and the repetition was too much, and we began to mess up the move.

"What's the matter with you Tootsie Roll fuckwads?" Andrzej screamed. "Do it again!"

We probably would have rehearsed for nine hours straight if I hadn't spotted Georgette and Medea marching toward Video Village. Georgette hated getting sunlight on her face-lift scars and only left the Hair & Makeup trailer for something really important. Something really important like a fat piece of gossip.

Damn, I thought. *She knows about Choi Park.*

"Let's go again," Andrzej belched. "And try not to fuck up so much."

Georgette was twenty yards from Video Village and closing in fast. I looked from Natalie to Andrzej to Elias. It was time to play my trump card

"Okay, guys," I called. "Let's take a fifteen-minute break."

"What? What? What are you doing?" Andrzej screamed. "I didn't say you could take a break!"

"I don't give a shit what you want! I said my guys needed a break a half an hour ago and you ignored me."

"Don't you dare yell at me, you slime! You do what I say or I'll fire your ass right now!"

"Fuck you, you fat piece of shit! We quit! C'mon, guys!"

We left Andrzej floating fifteen feet in the air and headed toward the grip truck.

"Get back here! Get back here right now!"

"That was awesome, chief," Steveo said, coming up beside me. "I've been wanting to do that the whole show."

"We're not really quitting, are we?" Slocum asked. "I need this job."

"Don't sweat it," I said. "There's no way they can put a new crew together before Julia Roberts gets here. By the time I'm done, you'll all get a raise."

"Good," Buzzy said. "Because I'm no quitter."

I climbed into the truck. "If anybody needs me, I'll be lying down on the hardware shelf. Damn, my back is killing me."

"Can I talk to you for a minute?"

I opened my eyes to see Katherine staring down at me. She was wearing tight jeans and her belly flowed over the waistband to form a tasty-looking muffin top. Sigh.

"Sorry," I said. "I'm only talking to the real producer."

"I am the real producer. I—"

"Save it, Katherine. I'm not interested."

"Fine, but Natalie already said she wouldn't talk to you."

"I've got all day."

"Can you at least let Andrzej off of the crane? He's about to have an aneurism."

"Nope."

"Great," she said, turning to go. "Thanks for wrecking my movie."

"Hold on a second." I reached into my cargo shorts and pulled out my divorce papers. "Give these to Natalie," I said, signing them with a red Sharpie. "That ought to speed things up a bit."

"New York State won't accept them like that. They can only be signed in blue or black ballpoint pen."

"Natalie doesn't have to know that."

Katherine smiled. "You're such a dickhead."

"If you really want to piss her off, you could offer to notarize them for her."

Natalie appeared in less than a minute, waving the divorce papers in front of her.

"What the hell is this supposed to mean?"

"Guess why Dan Berg is coming today."

"To get his picture taken with Julia Roberts."

"Nope. To screw over you and Elias." I gave her the short version of the Choi Park story, and Natalie looked as if she were about to have an aneurism herself.

"Fucking Katherine! There's no way Andrzej could have come up with this on his own. It's way too subtle."

"You can't trust anyone nowadays."

"Shut up, you degenerate. I can't believe I wore that bitch's sex garment for you, and less than forty-eight hours later I catch you getting a hand job from some call girl with an associate's degree."

"That never would have happened if you hadn't dashed off to the Four Seasons."

"They have L'Occitane toiletries in the bathroom. What did you expect?"

"You could have invited me along. The soap at the Omni sucks. Look at my skin. It's a disaster."

"I'm sorry," Natalie said.

"I'm sorry too." I held up my hand. "God as my witness, I'll never accept a hand job from anyone with less than a PhD again."

"Fabulous. Now will you please go back to work?"

I whipped out my walkie-talkie. "Break's over. Let the fat man off of the crane."

"Copy," Steveo squawked.

"And everybody gets a fifty-dollar raise."

"Awesome!"

Natalie grabbed for my walkie-talkie. "I never said that."

"Take it out of my pay. Those guys deserve a lot more than fifty bucks for the way Andrzej's been treating them." I hooked a finger into her waistband and pulled her close. "Now how about a little sugar?"

She tried to pull away, but I wouldn't let go.

"Oh, what the hell," she sighed.

All I wanted was a peck on the cheek, but Natalie leaned in and planted a big juicy one on my lips. I tried to stop her before it went further, but she slipped her tongue between my teeth, and I could feel her body go rigid.

"Jesus Christ!" she screamed. "Is that chewing tobacco?"

"It's Skoal, actually."

"Fuck," she said, clutching her stomach. "I think I'm gonna be sick."

Steveo came over my walkie-talkie. "Yo, Bobby, you better get out here."

"Why? Is Andrzej going ballistic?"

"No, it's starting to rain."

We covered the crane with a tarp and tabled a couple of grifflons over Video Village as the sky opened up. Julia Roberts's plane was delayed, but Dan Berg managed to slip in between bolts of lightning. Just another perk for being in league with Satan. In addition to his usual complement of henchmen, he brought along twenty pounds of chili dogs from Pink's on La Brea and five gallons of homemade root beer. He set up court in Ryan Donahue's trailer and invited Andrzej, Katherine, and Hank to join him for "a little nosh."

"Nosh, my ass," Natalie hissed. "They probably laced Hank's hot dog with sleeping pills and are taking pictures of him in bed with an underage schoolgirl and a couple of springer spaniels."

"Easy, princess."

Natalie lit a cigarette. "If we don't get this scene, the studio will cancel *Ant Eater*. Shit! I can't believe we're losing our deal over weather. Script or casting? Sure. But weather? It's like I'm being punished or something."

"You haven't lost anything yet. And look on the bright side: if Elias's movie goes south, we can start shooting my movie that much sooner."

"Except I need the money from *Ant Eater* to pay the credit card bills I've racked up going back and forth to LA. I also planned on hiding most of the development costs for your movie in *Ant Eater*'s budget. Now I'll have to go out and find another job. Who knows when we'll be able to start your project?"

Who knows? Her words did not leave a warm and fuzzy feeling in my tummy, and I could feel my movie—and Natalie—slipping away. Fucking Andrzej.

Natalie's cell phone rang. She listened for a moment and said, "Fine, thank you."

"Who was that?" I asked.

"That was my connection at the airport. They just cleared Julia Roberts's plane for landing. Let me see that walkie-talkie."

I switched my walkie-talkie to the production channel and handed it over.

"Reg, the eagle is about to land. I want to see everyone in Video Village in two minutes."

"Copy."

Natalie looked up at the sky. "We can still shoot if it's sprinkling. We only have an hour of daylight left, but as long as it doesn't pour we can shoot." She turned to me and said, "You know something? We might just pull this off."

Despite all our work and preparation, we were right back where we started on the day Sir Richard blew the dolly shot—flying by the seats of our pants. I pulled the tarp off the crane, threaded the video cable through the armature, and wiped down the seats. Slocum tossed a can of Skoal back and forth, and Steveo munched on a cuticle.

"Don't worry, guys," I said. "You're gonna do great."

"Man," Steveo said, "I so wish I was back at Griphaus right now watching a ball game and sucking on a fatty."

"You'll be there before you know it."

"Rehearsal with stand-ins," Reg called through his bullhorn. "Everybody to one."

"Calm your pits, Reg. We still have to balance the crane for Andrzej."

"Oh right," he said with an embarrassed smile. "Andrzej, can we have you on the crane, please?"

Andrzej barreled toward camera. You could tell from the bounce in his step that his meeting with Dan Berg had gone well. He placed one foot on the crane, stopped for a moment, and let out a loud fart.

"Jesus Christ, Andrzej."

"Sorry, Bobby, darling. Hot dogs make me gassy." He sat down, turned to George and Slocum, and screamed, "Hurry up, you fucking ballerinas."

"Chill, Andrzej," I said. "They're going as fast as they can."

"That's not fast enough, now, is it?"

"Eat shit."

Andrzej smiled. "It's a shame I won't be shooting any more movies, Bobby, darling, because I so enjoy torturing you."

The crane rose into the air, and I said, "Slocum, swap out that last ten-pounder for a five, and we're good to go."

"Stand by for a rehearsal with stand-ins," Reg called.

"Hold it!"

We turned to see Elias jogging toward us.

"I'd like to ride one."

"Things will go much faster if you watch from the monitor, Elias, darling."

"That's okay," he said. "I've always wanted to get my picture taken on one of these things."

Andrzej's face grew red, but there was nothing he could do. "Just make sure you buckle in good."

"I'll take care of that." I walked around to the other side of the crane and secured Elias's safety belt. "Listen very carefully. *Never* get off the crane until I tell you to, okay?"

"Sure."

"And nobody touches that belt but me."

"How come Andrzej doesn't have to wear a safety belt?"

"Because Andrzej's an idiot."

"I'm aware of that," Elias said with a grin. "But how come he doesn't have to wear a safety belt?"

"Good one," I said, slapping Elias on the back. "Good one."

"I'm glad you find that amusing, Elias, darling. You know what I find funny?"

"What?" he asked.

"The puny size of Bobby's penis."

"That didn't bother you last time it was in your mouth," I replied.

"Oh, so very funny. When I was banging Katherine last night, she said your dick was so small that you had to fuck her like a little doggy just to stay inside. Tell me, Elias, did Natalie complain about that too?"

Elias smiled, and I wanted to kill him. I wanted to kill them both.

"All set, boss," Steveo called, and the camera platform rose off the ground.

I walked back to Andrzej's side of the crane. "I hope your meeting with Dan Berg went well, you fat fuck, because you're gonna need a lot of money to pay for your divorce."

"What are you talking about?"

I turned toward Video Village, where Natalie was talking on her cell phone. I waved, and she waved back.

"Did you really think Natalie would do nothing while you queered her deal with Hank? She's on the phone with your wife right now telling her all about you and Katherine. She even took some pictures with her camera phone. You are soooo screwed."

And then I spit in his face.

"You fucking shit!" Andrzej screamed.

"No!" I yelled, but it was too late.

Andrzej landed on top of me and the crane shot into the air. As I hit the ground, I caught a glimpse of Elias Simm, the man

who had fucked my wife and made the last year of my life unbearable. His expression was identical to the one I saw through
that taxicab window on the day I found out about him and Natalie.

Merry Christmas to all, and to all a good night.

Chapter 37

What I Really Want to Do . . .

Mother Teresa dies and goes to Heaven. She arrives at the pearly gates, and Saint Peter sends her straight to see God.

"My child," God tells her, "you are the most blessed creature to ever walk the face of the earth. Say the word, and anything you desire shall be yours."

"Anything?" Mother Teresa asks.

"Anything."

"Well," Mother Teresa says, her eyes growing wide. "What I really want to do is direct."

GOOD THING ELIAS was wearing his safety belt. My view was blocked by Andrzej's sweaty body, but those watching said that when the weight bucket hit the ground, Elias was catapulted across set with his seat still strapped to his ass. He landed in a pile of grip equipment, and that seat was all that saved him from being impaled by a grip stand. I guess you can't have everything. He was knocked unconscious and his shoulder was shattered in a dozen places. Not bad for an afternoon's work.

Andrzej, of course, was fucked. Everyone knew he never wore a safety belt, and after the fiasco with Sir Richard, he had no excuse. The moment he dove off that crane, his career was over. It also didn't hurt that Dan Berg could make ten times more money with Choi Park in *The Green Hornet.*

"Get off of me," I screamed, but Andrzej didn't move. He was shaking and doing everything he could to fight back the tears. Why are the biggest bullies always the biggest crybabies?

"Steveo? Slocum? You guys okay?"

"We're cool, boss."

"Then get this fat piece of slime off me. I can barely breathe."

Steveo and Slocum grabbed Andrzej by the elbows, and Troy and Dusty escorted him off set. Meg called for an ambulance, and announced no one could touch Elias until the paramedics isolated his neck. This gave me the opportunity to enjoy the tableaux of my wife's former lover cradled in a pile of grip stands and apple boxes. It was quite touching.

"You did that on purpose, didn't you?"

I turned, and Natalie was standing next to me.

"Did what on purpose?"

"Uh-huh . . ."

"Who were you on the phone with, anyway?"

"My landlord in LA. I was trying to break my lease."

"Did you?"

"Almost, then you sent Elias to the moon."

"Andrzej did that, not me. You calling the cops?"

"As a formality, but I doubt Elias will press charges."

"Where's Katherine?"

"Hiding."

"And Hank?"

"He's on his way to release Julia Roberts. Poor guy. He can forget about that third movie."

"Why?" I asked, looking up at the sky. "We still have twenty minutes of daylight left."

"A lot of good that'll do us without a director."

"We have a director," I said. "George! Slocum! Get over here!"

I ran to the riverbank and drew a line in the mud with my sneaker.

"I want eight pieces of track starting here. Steveo, find Troy and tell him to put a fifty-millimeter lens on B camera. I'll be right back."

I spun around and almost crashed into Natalie.

"What the hell are you doing?" she asked.

"Directing."

"You can't do that. You're not even in the guild."

I grabbed her by the shoulders. "Do you want a new life or not?"

Her face cracked into the most beautiful smile imaginable. "What do you want me to do?"

"Rally the troops. We're losing daylight."

I raced toward Julia Roberts's trailer. Hank's knuckles were a half inch from the door when I reached him.

"Thank God I got to you," I said.

"I don't even want to be seen talking to you, you crazy fuck. I'm sending Julia Roberts home, and then I'm drinking myself into a coma."

I wrapped an arm around Hank's shoulder and led him toward the grip truck. "You don't have to do that. I'm here to save you."

"What are you talking about?"

"*I'm* going to direct the scene."

"No, you're not."

"Listen to me. My guys are laying track for the dolly shot as we speak. The camera department is prepping B camera, and there's still fifteen minutes of daylight. We can do this."

"Julia Roberts is not going to let some grip direct her."

"She doesn't have to know I'm a grip. And Ryan's cool. He'll let me slide because we're both Irish guys from New York."

"Then why don't we have Moose direct the scene?"

I pulled out my walkie-talkie. "Steveo, grab a short arm and meet me by the side of the truck."

"Copy."

"C'mon, buddy," I said to Hank. "I know it sounds crazy, but this is the stuff legends are made of. We could be heroes. Give me a shot, dude. I *deserve* this."

Hank looked me in the eye and shook his head. "I'm sorry, Bobby. I can't."

Steveo appeared and handed me the short arm. "The dolly's good to go," he said. "What next?"

"Hang out by the lift gate and don't let anybody back here."

Steveo ran off, and I faced my former friend.

"Listen very carefully," I said, raising the short arm in the air. "Either you let me direct this scene, or I'll crack your skull open."

Hank laughed. "Bobby, Bobby, Bobby. You're confusing the Killer Instinct with actually killing somebody. It doesn't work that way."

"Oh yeah?" I swung the short arm in a wide arc and smashed his left leg.

"Motherfucker!" Hank screamed and fell to the ground.

"Is everything okay, boss?" Steveo asked, coming around the side of the truck.

"Go to the back of the lift gate!"

"Jesus, Bobby. Maybe you should—"

"Get the fuck out of here!"

Steveo disappeared, and I placed a knee on Hank's chest.

"That was a warning shot. Now, are you going to let me direct this scene, or do I have to beat you senseless?"

"Okay, okay, you fucking psycho, you can do it!"

I reached down and pumped his hand. "Thanks, pal, you won't regret it."

"I'm already regretting it."

"Don't be negative. Now take off your clothes."

"What?"

"You heard me. Take off your clothes. I'm not going to direct the most famous actress in the world dressed in cargo shorts."

Hank's pants were baggy in the seat, but otherwise I looked okay. Back on set, the paramedics were isolating Elias's neck with a brace. He was conscious but groggy and in a ton of pain.

"He gonna be okay?" I asked one of the paramedics.

"Probably," he replied in a thick New York accent. "But he'll never pitch for the Yankees again."

"Don't sweat it. He's a Boston fan."

"Fuck him, then."

"My attitude completely. Do you mind if I talk to him for a second? It's kind of important."

"Be my guest."

I knelt down and said, "Elias, what did you tell Ryan and Julia about the scene?"

"What?"

"The scene. What direction did you give them?"

"Why?"

"Because I'm going to direct it."

He snapped out of his daze. "*You're* going to direct?"

"Pretty cool, huh?"

"You bastard."

"Don't be that way. C'mon, what did you tell them?"

"I told them not to take direction from any grips."

"Talent on set!" Reg called through his bullhorn.

"I'm not a grip anymore, pal."

"Yes, you are," he hissed. "You'll always be a grip."

I climbed to my feet and reached for my wallet. "Do me a favor," I said to the paramedic as I pulled out a twenty. "Take the long way to the hospital and hit every bump you can."

I ran to the camera where Troy and Dusty were standing by. "Okay, guys, same drill as back in New York. We open wide, start the move when the actors get to a medium shot, and end in a tight two."

"Who's pushing dolly?" Troy asked.

"I am."

"Who's the DP?" Dusty asked.

"I am. Take a light reading and open up a quarter stop for the background."

"You sure you know what you're doing?" Troy asked.

"Are you kidding?" I said, unable to contain my joy. "I've been waiting for this my entire life."

Reg tapped me on the shoulder. "The talent is here."

I turned and saw Ryan Donahue and Julia Roberts.

"Good luck, buddy," Troy said.

I took a deep breath and went to meet my actors.

"Hi," I said with my most award-winning smile. "I'm Bobby Conlon."

"Julia Roberts."

"It's a pleasure to meet you," I said. "Sorry for all this insanity, but if you bear with us, I think we can get through it alive." I turned to Ryan Donahue and said, "Hi, I'm Bobby Conlon."

Ryan stared at me and the world froze. He glanced toward Video Village, where Dan Berg and the Bryant/Berg Dancers sat spring-loaded and ready to destroy my career before it began. Dan

Berg gave Ryan a shrug, indicating that the decision was up to him. It took forever for Ryan to turn back to me, and it felt like I was teetering on the edge of everything I had ever dreamed about.

"It's a pleasure to meet you," he said.

"It's a pleasure meeting you, Ryan." I leaned in close to the actors and said, "I don't know what Elias told you, but I saw the footage Sir Richard shot and your performances were excellent. Try to get yourselves back to that place. The only thing I can add is that when something like this happened to me, I never stopped thinking about how much I loved my wife. The anger, the sadness, the loss. It all came from that." I turned to Reg and said, "Let's go."

"Last looks!"

The vanity crafts descended on Ryan and Julia, and I went to camera.

"You guys set?"

"Like a jelly," Troy said. "Keep an eye on my right hand. I'll signal you if the actors get too close or too far away."

"Lock it up!" Reg called through his bullhorn. "This is for picture."

I went back to the actors. "You guys set?"

Ryan nodded and Julia said, "You know, you look familiar. Have we ever met before?"

"Ever see Alfred Hitchcock's *Spellbound*?"

"A few weeks ago, but— Wait a minute! You're that grip!"

"Sssh," I said, putting a finger to my lips. "Don't tell anyone."

I took my place behind the dolly.

"Roll sound!"

"Hold it!" Dusty called out. "The clouds are breaking up."

I looked up and saw a patch of blue in the middle of a cloud-filled sky. "What do you think, Dusty? Is there enough blue for an entire take?"

He held a contrast viewer to his eye and stared at the sun. "It'll be close."

"Roll it, Reg," I said. "Dusty, take a reading the moment the sun comes out, and I'll call action."

"Roll sound!"

"Sound speed."

"Rolling!" production assistants shouted.

"Camera."

"Speed."

The sun popped out, and Dusty held his meter in the air. "A hair under five six."

"Action!" I yelled, and for the first time in twenty years the world belonged to me.

"Action!" Reg called through his bullhorn.

And it was even better than I could have hoped for. Two months of playing Robert Marcus had improved Ryan's performance a hundred times over. The first time around, he'd played the scene like a guy with twenty pounds of sadness in his shoes. Each step dragged him deeper into despair. But this time, instead of wading through a river of pain, he really listened to what Julia said. His face expressed every emotion, every nuance of what a man goes through when he is forced to ask himself if there was something, anything, he could have done to prevent his life from falling apart. It was riveting.

And Julia? She was spectacular. Each syllable, each gesture seemed more authentic than the one before it. I felt like I was eavesdropping on a pair of lovers and had to force myself not to turn away and give them their privacy. It was magnificent and heartbreaking all at the same time.

And the sad part was we were going to blow it. Without all that sludge in his shoes, Ryan was moving faster than he had in New York, and we did not lay enough track. I reached the end of the rails and eased the dolly to a stop. Troy panned the camera to keep the actors in frame, and when they stopped, Ryan was blocking Julia's face from the camera. It was a disaster, and I could feel everything slipping away—the scene, the movie, my life. Our patch of blue was gone, and there was not enough light to do it again. My career as a director was over.

"I can't go on like this," Julia said. "I need someone who'll treat me like a person, not like a character in a story. I'm Anne O'Hara, damn it. Not Anna Karenina."

Except I couldn't just stand there and let everything fall to pieces. I set the brake on the dolly and moved next to the camera.

"Liverwurst," I whispered.

Julia Roberts smiled.

"Liverwurst, liverwurst, liverwurst."

She fought back laughter, and tears welled in her eyes.

"Baloney, salami, Camembert cheese."

Julia Roberts buried her face in Ryan's shoulder and burst out laughing. Her face filled the frame, and from the camera's perspective, it looked like she'd burst into tears. I glanced up at the sky and watched as the patch of blue disappeared.

"Cut."

"That's a cut!" Reg called.

I ran to the actors.

"Did you get it?" Julia asked, wiping the tears from her eyes.

"I think so."

"Liverwurst?" Ryan asked. "What the hell does liverwurst have to do with anything?"

"Do you want to tell him or should I?"

"I'll tell him," Julia said.

"Are we going again?" Reg asked.

"No," I said. "Either we got it or we didn't."

We huddled around the monitor to watch playback. You could feel the entire state of Texas tense up when Ryan blocked Julia's face, but when she leaned forward and smiled it was like heaven.

"What do you think?" I asked, unable to turn away from the monitor.

"You did it, honey," Natalie said. "You really did it."

I looked up, and everyone was staring at me: sixty nervous people with families, mortgages, and assorted substance abuse problems whose jobs I had just saved.

"Call it, Reg," I said.

"Ladies and gentlemen, that's a wrap."

And the entire crew applauded. For me.

I took a deep bow and rose from my director's chair to find Julia Roberts standing beside me with a big smile on her face.

"So," she said. "What other Hitchcock films do you like?"

Chapter 38

Location Scout

SIX MONTHS LATER I was standing in Harvard Square with a viewfinder held to my eye.

"How about if Elias walks out of Harvard Yard, cuts across Mass Ave, and meets his dealer on the corner of Dunster?"

"In one shot?" Bev, the location manager, asked.

"Sure," I said. "It'll establish the entire geography of Harvard Square."

"We'll never be able to shut down that many streets and businesses."

"How about if we just show him coming out of Harvard Yard and cutting across Mass Ave?"

"We can shut down Mass Ave for five-minute intervals, but the university won't let us show him coming out of the Yard to buy drugs."

"It's just pot."

"Last time I checked, pot was illegal."

"Believe me," I said, "I know."

"Can I see that for a second?" Natalie asked, reaching for the viewfinder. "We can get everything you want by having him come out of the subway instead of Harvard Yard." She held the view-finder to her eye and panned across the square. "Yeah, it'll work perfectly."

"We still won't be able to shut down that many streets and businesses," Bev said.

"I have an idea," Troy said, taking the viewfinder from Natalie. "How about if we steal the shot of Elias coming out of the subway and crossing the square? Then we can just pick him up on Dunster Street. That way we only have to control one block, and it'll look more like a drug deal."

"Works for me," I said. "Just make sure he's wearing something bright so we don't lose track of him in the crowd."

"No problem," Reg said. "I'll tell wardrobe."

It was our third day of location scouting for *The Ant Eater Goes Down*. Despite my negative feelings toward its author, *Ant Eater* was the best script in Natalie's pile of putrid screenplays. The studio had already spent a boatload developing the project, so it wasn't hard to talk them into letting me direct it as the third picture in Hank's deal.

With a few changes, of course. The main character always struck me as a little too self-important and humorless. We hired a couple of comedy writers to punch up the dialogue and add some funny material to the first act. My two favorite scenes were now a circle jerk at summer camp, and Elias's first day of prep school, where the older boys spray-paint his ass in the school colors and hang him out a second-story window. America would never look at Elias Simm the same way again.

Natalie and I were back living in Brooklyn and getting along better than we had in years. We saw a couples counselor twice a week, and that was the only time we allowed ourselves to talk about what had happened. This wasn't as hard as it sounds. Having one movie in preproduction and another in postproduction took every bit of our time. The editing of *Aquarena Springs* was going well, but the studio was growing less enthusiastic about the movie with each passing day. We had previewed it twice with an audience, and the general consensus was that it had been miscast. The girls who had lined up to see *Trail of Broken Hearts* didn't like seeing Ryan Donahue as a sad-sack college professor, and fans of the book didn't buy such a young guy playing Robert Marcus. I could have told them that six months ago, but back then nobody listened to a word I said.

That was no longer the case.

"You have three more locations to look at before we fly back to New York," Reg said. "Do you want to break for lunch here, or after the next location?"

"Let's break now. There are a lot more restaurants in this neighborhood."

Reg checked his watch. "Okay, folks, let's meet in the hotel lobby at two. I'll have Sara Lee meet us with the fifteen-passenger van, and we'll try to knock out the remaining locations by four o'clock."

"Sounds good. Anybody want to join us for lunch?" I asked.

"I'm going back to the hotel for a nap," Reg said.

"How about you, Troy?"

"Bev and I are going to check out that museum on Quincy Street."

I turned to Natalie. "I guess it's just you and me, kid."

"I need to call the production office," she said, pulling out her cell phone. "Oh, and you'll never guess who Dan Berg wants us to cast as the history professor."

"Ryan Donahue."

"No, Choi Park."

"What happened to *The Green Hornet*?"

"Matt Damon is doing another *Bourne Identity*, and *The Green Hornet* got pushed back a year."

"Can Choi Park even speak English?"

"Dan Berg says Bryant/Berg will pay for the dubbing if there's a problem."

"Choi Park must really need a job."

"The guy moved his entire family to LA, including his in-laws. He's going out of his mind."

"Bring him in for a reading."

"You can't be serious."

"I owe Dan Berg a favor. And who knows? Maybe Choi Park can act."

"You're doing it just to piss off Andrzej, aren't you?"

"I have no idea what you're talking about," I said with a grin. I stepped off the curb and said, "I'll be right back. I need to get some money from that bank machine over there."

I walked across the street, slipped my bank card into the ATM, and entered my secret code.

"Spare some change?"

I turned and saw a panhandler hovering over my shoulder. He was at least six inches taller than me and easily could have seen my PIN. My New York Radar kicked in, and I glanced around to make sure there were plenty of people around.

"Spare some change?"

"Sure." I reached into my pocket and handed him some coins.

"Thanks, man."

"No problem."

I watched him walk away and slipped my bank card and money into my wallet. I turned to cross the street and stopped.

Wait a second, I thought. *Something isn't right.* I reached for my wallet and pulled out the receipt from the cash machine. There were supposed to be fifty-eight thousand dollars in my account, but the receipt said there were only eight.

Fifty thousand dollars were missing.

I tried to remember all of the places I had used my bank card, but my mind was a blur. I ran across the street and found Natalie talking on the phone.

"Hang up!" I screamed. "We have to call the bank right away. Somebody's hacked our account."

"I'll call you right back," Natalie said, closing her phone. "Now what's the matter?"

I handed her the receipt. "We had like fifty-eight grand in there last time I checked and now there's only eight. That was all the money from my truck."

"Nobody ripped us off. I withdrew the money."

"Why? What for?"

"I gave it to Hank. It was part of our deal."

"What deal?"

"This deal."

I stared at her. "Let me get this straight. You *paid* Hank to let me direct this movie?"

"You practically broke the guy's leg. He was going to have you arrested."

"I can't fucking believe this. That was the money from my truck. Do you know how hard I worked for that?"

Natalie grabbed my shoulders. "Look at me. You wanted a new life, right?"

"Yeah."

"Then fifty grand is a bargain. Chalk it up to career development and let it go."

"I guess . . . But it just doesn't feel right having to pay for it."

"It didn't stop you with that hooker in Austin."

"That's not what I'm talking about."

"That's what I'm talking about."

"Save it for couples therapy."

I reached out and adjusted Natalie's blouse to hide the champagne-colored compression garment beneath it.

"You know what I really want for lunch?" I asked.

"What?"

"Ice cream. Let's try that place on Brattle Street that Bev was raving about."

"Ice cream's the last thing I need. I've already put on ten pounds since we started this job."

"C'mon, just one scoop." I wrapped an arm around her waist. The ten pounds were an improvement, but there were still stomach muscles lurking beneath the fat.

"What the hell," she said. "One scoop won't kill me."

"That's my girl."

Ten pounds down, twenty to go.

Acknowledgments

THIS BOOK WOULD not have happened without the friendship, advice, and support of David Liss.

Leigh Feldman came up with the title as well as many other great ideas that are far too numerous and profane to mention here.

Peter Borland, my editor at Atria Books, gave me everything a novelist could ask for—including the help of Nick Simonds, who did much of the heavy lifting. Dave Cole did a terrific job copyediting, and Sybil Pincus answered all my production questions with speed and wit.

Dean Bell laughed in all the right places; Travis Preston, Matthew Reiss, and Karen Eisenstadt never lost faith in me; and Mom, Dad, Colleen, Margaret, and Lisa have put up with me no matter what.

Tammar Stein, Kate Hayward, Elizabeth Wymer, Paul Kastel, Marjorie Brody, Stewart Smith, Beaty Spear, Diane La Combe, and Jacqueline Parmenter read early drafts, and this book is a hundred times better because of their suggestions.

Everything I know about the real Peter and Polly World I learned from Peter Biskind's *Easy Riders, Raging Bulls* and Roger

Corman's *How I Made a Hundred Movies in Hollywood and Never Lost a Dime.*

Rich Ludwig, Billy McDevitt, Jerry Lee, John Minardi, and the late and terribly missed Richard Audino kept my dolly running smoothly on countless low-budget movies.

Liam Taylor showed me the delights of being a full-time dad and kept his second nap until I finished the last draft.

Kate Taylor came late to the party, but was thoughtful enough to do so between rounds of editing when I could give full attention to her joyous arrival.

And finally, Anne Kastel provided all the love, faith, and encouragement a husband could ever want. Thank you, my darling.

About the Author

BILLY TAYLOR worked as a dolly grip on dozens of movies and TV shows, including *My Cousin Vinny* and *Pee-wee's Playhouse*. He lives in San Antonio, Texas, and can be contacted at www.billytaylor.com.